HERO
INES

HERO INES

Powerful Indian Women of Myth & History

IRA MUKHOTY

ALEPH

ALEPH

ALEPH BOOK COMPANY
An independent publishing firm
promoted by *Rupa Publications India*

First published in India in 2017
by Aleph Book Company
7/16 Ansari Road, Daryaganj
New Delhi 110 002

ISBN: 978-93-84067-49-6

3 5 7 9 10 8 6 4

Printed by Parksons Graphics Pvt. Ltd. Mumbai

For Yashoda and Devaki,
the genesis of this book

Whenever someone who knows you disappears, you lose one version of yourself. Yourself as you were seen, as you were judged to be. Lover or enemy, mother or friend, those who know us construct us, and their several knowings slant the different facets of our character like a diamond-cutter's tools. Each such loss is a step leading to the grave, where all versions blend and end.

Salman Rushdie, *The Ground Beneath Her Feet*

CONTENTS

INTRODUCTION

In the middle of the Bay of Bengal there lies an archipelago of serene islands, somnolent in the sun. On a recent visit, I discovered that all is not what it seems, for the Andaman Islands are home to man-eating saltwater crocodiles, a handful of aboriginal tribal hunter-gatherers, and a pervasive and baffling nostalgia for the crumbling ruins of the Raj. In the late-nineteenth century, the British built the infamous Cellular Jail in the Andaman Islands, a penal settlement where the heroes of the Indian Uprising of 1857 were incarcerated in chain gangs and often tortured and worked to their death. Despite this, these islands, which were named after British soldiers who put down the very same Uprising, still retain the old names. While Havelock Island is named after a Baptist evangelical soldier, Neill Island, also in the Andamans, is named after Colonel James George Smith Neill who called himself the instrument of divine wrath. Amongst other atrocities, he spread terror in 1857 with his infamous 'hanging parties' in which countless villagers were hanged from mango trees by teams of British volunteers.

I have picked the instance of the naming of the Andaman Islands because it was the most recent example I have noted in our country of a puzzling phenomenon. Look anywhere and you will see a similar disregard for its heroes and heroines from every historical period. Further, given the patriarchal culture of the country, it is women who have suffered the most neglect.

A few years ago, I decided I would try to do something about this erasure of India's great women from the country's history. I was a woman living in post-colonial India, raising two daughters, and it seemed that this was a necessary mission for me to undertake. I began to search for the stories of great Indian women.

Women with heroic destinies and rare courage. Indian stories, to counter the blight of our colonial past that contrived to linger on—in our educational system, our cultural discourse, our collective memory. Stories of women to provide ballast against the overwhelming patriarchy of Indian culture. This book, then, is a result of that search.

In searching for these stories I ran into two major obstacles. In the first instance, myth and history in India are not the clearly separate entities one might expect. Myth slides into history and truth sometimes fragments out of apparently mythological constructs. Laxmibai of Jhansi was a historical figure, certainly, but over time she has attained quasi-divine status akin to the most powerful figures from our pantheon of gods. Draupadi belongs to the Mahabharat, an allegorical song dreamed into being by a cohort of seers, but she is as real to modern-day Indians as any historical figure, if not more so. The heroines in this book include two women from mythology—Draupadi and Radha—alongside six historical ones. For if mythological women are held up as examples to the daughters of today then it is worth exploring the truth of their legacy. By understanding their essence, it is my hope that they will once again become relevant, as they were in their glory, for the young women of India.

If Indian history, especially ancient history, is difficult to set down accurately—given that it is shrouded in myth—then writing the history of India's women presents even greater challenges, because of the neglect they were subjected to. Occasionally, though, they make an appearance, and it is from these scant offerings that one has to begin. One such representation of women in ancient times comes from Mohenjodaro. These female terracotta figurines have been described as mother-goddesses. According to historian John Keay, they are 'pop-eyed, bat-eared, belted and sometimes mini-skirted', and of 'grotesque mien.' The finest specimens discovered are tiny, only a few centimetres high, and very few in number. They include the precious 'Dancing Girl', perhaps the first real heroine of India, mute yet eloquent, enigmatic yet challenging.

Closer to us in time but still one of our oldest treasures is Draupadi, tentatively located in 950 BCE. I chose this most flawed and human of the mythological heroines as the fulcrum to this collection because though she fails, and makes mistakes, and is shockingly volatile, she will remain, all her life, true to the call of her heart. She maintains her claim for vengeance and justice though it casts her, alone, against all the forces of the ruling patriarchy. She claims justice, moreover, in the name of all women, when they are maligned. Sita, the heroine of the austere and even more ancient Ramayan, on the other hand, uses acquiescence and obedience as her virtue and self-annihilation as her final retort. While her story is more nuanced than it would appear, it has been used by a patriarchal culture as an example of the ideal, submissive wife. Too many generations of Indian women have been urged to follow Sita's example of wifely submission. Draupadi, however, will have none of it and rails against a culture that values a king's duty and a brother's loyalty above a wife's honour. Her battle, moreover, is for that most ethereal of things, a woman's sacred inviolability. No self-effacing denial of life and suicide for Draupadi. She wrests from fate and from an intimidating array of men her right to be restored as the dharma queen. Her heroism is her fearlessness in demanding justice even though this means challenging the status quo and, more pertinently, challenging every male figure in her life; her husbands, her father-in-law and king, and her gurus.

Draupadi is the flamboyantly dark-skinned heroine of Indian mythology par excellence. Indeed, the Mahabharat itself is replete with heroic figures who are also resplendent in their dark complexions. There is Krishna, mesmerizing to men and women alike; Arjuna, the beguiling archer who could never belong to only one woman; Satyavati, the matriarch, irresistible to a king even in her tattered fisherwoman's garb; and Draupadi—who is so beautiful that men forget their sense of propriety in their desire to possess her, whose dusky beauty is celebrated in endless verses comparing her to the night sky, the blue lotus, and the warm and sombre glow of gold.

Draupadi's scandalous example has caused consternation over the centuries and she has never been held up as a role model for daughters and sisters and wives. Over time, her portrayal has been sanitized and disempowered and Draupadi has become the doe-eyed, weeping, fair damsel of Raja Ravi Varma's kitsch poster art. It is only right, in this age of obsession with light complexion and uniform blandness, to restore this truly remarkable Indian heroine to her rightful place in our collective psyche.

◆

The idea of heroism in women is not easily defined. In men, the notion is often associated with physical valour and extravagant bravery. Men have had, historically, a much wider tapestry against which to play out their feats. Stormy rivers to navigate and savage continents to discover and subjugate. Women's heroism has tended to be of a very different nature, less easily contained and categorized. However, all the women in this book share with Draupadi an unassailable belief in a cause for which they are willing to fight, in one form or another, unto death. In every case this belief, whether it has to do with a divine love, a mystic truth, or a denied kingship, leads them to confrontation with a horrified patriarchy. And every woman described in this book refuses to borrow a man's prerogative, whether a father's, a husband's or a son's.

To be able to convey a sense of the antiquity of India, this book covers the lives of eight women, real or imagined, across three thousand years of India's stories. There is a Mughal princess, a Turkish Mamluk warrior, and a Brahmin widow. There is a courtesan, a princess of Chittor and a begum who was of part-African descent. Yet in time, all these differences are scuffed or overlooked and the women become representative of a universal, north-Indian ideal of beauty—fair skinned and buxom. The fire goes out of their eyes as does the strength in their limbs which once wielded talwars and scimitars. More corrupting still is the effacing of their personalities, the sublimation of their faults and their unacceptable transgressions. Revered or admired in their own day, some are now altogether forgotten. Their lives have been reordered, and their glory dimmed. This is, more often than not, the case where men have taken over the narrative. When the men controlling the narrative are colonial masters, as is the case in Laxmibai, for instance, the distortion is immense; she is transformed into a 'jezebel', an object of libidinous curiosity, whereas to her own armies she was that most holy of Indian women—a mother and a widow.

Later, the Indian nationalists appropriate Laxmibai's story and integrate her in the lore of freedom fighters, quite ignoring her earlier career—as that of an intelligent and shrewd diplomat and ruler.

These are all women who transgressed in some way. Theirs was an indelible transgression, whether it was the casting off of purdah, the relinquishing of the safety of the marital home or the challenging of ancient, ossified practices. The nature of the transgression differs through the ages, but all of them are a challenge to the accepted status quo of that fragile and illusory creature: the honourable woman living in Indian society.

Some transgressions are seemingly minor, as in the case of Jahanara Begum. This princess lived her life as the dutiful daughter, in the shadow of the 'King of the World', the great Mughal, Shah Jahan, and followed him into banishment until his death. Though her revolt was more nuanced, her ambition was blistering. She claimed the blessings of both Allah and the Prophet Muhammad and wished 'never to be forgotten'. The epitaph on her humble grave, open to the sky, which lies next to that of the Sufi saint Nizamuddin Auliya in Delhi, points to the enduring enigma that Jahanara was:

Let nothing cover my grave except
The green grass
For the green turf is covering enough
For the poor

Her parents' mausoleum, the Taj Mahal, that 'gateway through which all dreams must pass' is of an altogether grander scale. And yet, despite the poverty she claims, Jahanara was one of the richest women of her time, one of only three women to own trading ships through which she increased her already immense personal fortune, inherited from her mother, Mumtaz Mahal. But her struggle and her triumph were in the intensely private, passionate sphere of Sufi mysticism, which can be glimpsed in her verse:

> The Beloved has placed a noose on my neck.
> He pulls me wherever He wishes.
> If I had any control over these things,
> I would always choose to be around Him.

As for the other women discussed in this book, they all discard either purdah, or their assigned roles in their homes, or both. Though the two mythological heroines, Draupadi and Radha, return to their homes eventually, the most significant period is the years they spend in the wildering space outside their homes. Very little is known of Radha's life when she returns to her marital home after Krishna leaves Gokul for Mathura, forever. And for Draupadi there is little consolation to be had as lonely dharma queen after the carnage of the Kurukshetra War. For the historical women, on the other hand, the sacrifice of home is ruinous and complete and they never return to their earlier lives. For them there is either death on the battlefield, as for Raziya Sultan and Laxmibai, or exile, as was the fate of Hazrat Mahal, or disappearance into legend, in the case of Meerabai and Ambapali.

The women in this book all come from the north of India. From the long-ago cities of Hastinapur and Vaishali, through Mathura and Delhi, Jhansi and Awadh, and back again to Delhi—a crosshatch of territory that covers the geography of the north (especially the Gangetic plain), its fertile plains and hungry fields, its vast rivers and bleached white skies. There are no women from the Deccan, Bengal or the Himalayan region. This is partly due to the need to contain the scope of this book and also to reflect a certain historical continuity. Beginning with Draupadi, all eight heroines reflect the changing pattern of human movement and settlement in north India. As settlers came in through the northwestern frontier, great cities were formed along the life-giving rivers of the Ganga and the Yamuna. Along the centuries, always under pressure from further incursions through the Khyber Pass, these settlements moved further east, to Varanasi and Pataliputra. And always, through two thousand years of history, Delhi, or a version of it, is the epicentre of all this movement. This blood-soaked city of cities, created and destroyed seven times, is intrinsic to the lives and fortunes of two of our heroines—Raziya Sultan and Jahanara Begum. Only Meerabai, in her extraordinary peripatetic wandering, went beyond this landlocked swathe of Indo-Gangetic scrub plains to the western coastal city of Dwarka. All the others dreamed their impossible longing into being within this geography of the north.

Of the eight women discussed here, all but one stepped out onto the great north Indian road—dusty, shifting, endless, and full of dangers for the unaccompanied woman—where even in modern-day India, women are often forbidden from venturing. They set out barefoot, like Radha and Ambapali, searching for a different kind of truth, or on horseback like Laxmibai, Raziya Sultan and Hazrat Mahal, at the head of armies of men, demanding a justice that had been denied. They made the journey alone, unaccompanied by husband or father or adult son. Raziya proudly claimed the title of Sultan, refusing its 'delicate' feminine corollary, Sultana. Only Draupadi was accompanied by her husbands, but, paradoxically, she is all the more alone for the surfeit of husbands she has as more often than not they fail to protect her. In the heroic context, it may not appear to be very momentous to leave one's home and the security of society in search of a personal goal, but even today, women in India face society's opprobrium or worse for being seen to 'transgress' or even when they are just going about their lives. Women are mutilated and murdered on cold December evenings in Delhi outside movie theatres, and they are raped on balmy Mumbai afternoons in abandoned textile mills. They are killed, and brutalized and tortured in Haryana, Punjab, Rajasthan, Uttar Pradesh and beyond, for leaving their homes with men of the wrong religion, or caste or colour. This is why the obduracy of that first step, which took these eight women outside the safety of their known universe, was truly remarkable, because every woman in India understands why such a decision was momentous.

Once out of the confines of their homes and settled society, the women had to deal with the realities of the open road, forests and grasslands. Radha and Meerabai had an organic, nurturing relationship with the forest. For them, the forest was a place of safety. The natural world, the animals, the birds and the flowers, were complicit in the women's desires. Both Radha and Meerabai substitute elements from nature for the visible, man-made symbols of suhaag that they have both abandoned: the flower necklace for the gold, clinking seed pods for pearls. For Draupadi, however, and also for Laxmibai, the forest and the countryside were places of violence. Especially for Draupadi, each day spent in the forest is an assault on her former life as a queen. For Laxmibai, too, life outside her beloved Jhansi was full of physical hardship and emotional pain. The last verifiable sighting of Laxmibai is by the Brahmin traveller Vishnu Bhatt Godshe—he describes her as mud-streaked and exhausted, scouring the parched countryside for some scummy water at the bottom of a well. This is not the story that the burnished metal of the statues, which have immortalized Laxmibai, tell us.

Most of the women discussed in this book have been similarly glossed so that all their individuality is diluted. Even the physical differences of these women, who were all so very different from one another, have been forgotten. Draupadi's beauty dazzled all who saw her. As I have mentioned, her dark complexion was her most alluring feature (she is described as being the colour of the blue lotus and is given the names Shyama, dark as night, and Krishnaa, the dark one) but that has been brushed out of the way. Raziya Sultan, whose father was the Turk Iltutmish, would have had classically Central Asian features, high cheekbones and almond eyes. Laxmibai was 'not very pretty', according to Governor General Canning 'but had beautiful eyes and figure'. John Lang, her lawyer, is more enthusiastic and candid in his praise and claimed 'her expression is very good and very intelligent. Eyes particularly fine and nose very delicately shaped. Not fair, but far from black'. Begum Hazrat Mahal, who was a courtesan before becoming one of Nawab Wajid Ali Shah's mu'tah wives, had African slave ancestry through her father and had a dark complexion and fine, strong features. Some of these women were very beautiful, like Ambapali, but some were not. Of Jahanara Begum and Meerabai we are told almost nothing about their physical appearance. Modern iconography, however, has transformed these women and Meerabai is now almost always depicted as a pale-skinned woman in sparkling white robes, a mystifying rendition of a woman who spent the bulk of her years wandering the monsoon forests and arid fields of north India.

It is not only the physical appearance of these women that has been reconfigured and sanitized for the modern age. Their personal idiosyncrasies and fallibilities have been obscured, if not forgotten. In the light of modern history, there is no allowance for frailty. And yet the loss is always ours, when we smooth out the jagged edges. These women are sometimes scheming, often manipulative, but always brave and very human in their ecstasies, doubts and triumphs. Across two and a half millennia, Draupadi's despair comes across to us when we hear her lament to Krishna:

I have no husband, no sons and no brother
Even you, Krishna, are not really mine at all.

How intensely moving is the knowledge that Laxmibai lived a night of fear and uncertainty as the British cannons pounded the walls of Jhansi. That her courage vacillated briefly, before she tied on her pearl necklace and anklets, strapped her sword onto her belt and rode into immortality and legend on her silver horse in the lustrous light of a full moon.

That Jahanara Begum, devout Sufi though she was, had a ruinous love of expensive paan and wine, and the company of young people, does not make her less admirable, only more human. And Radha's married status makes her love for Krishna more intense, her sacrifice more complete and her surrender to a divine love more absolute.

India, along with China, has the oldest continuous cultural traditions in the world. And while our ancient legends, scripture and literature live on, our historical records are almost non-existent. There are many plausible explanations for this gap in written records—the notoriously destructive climate for a start. There is also, it has been suggested, a lamentable disregard for the things of antiquity, a notion that the past has had its day and does not require tedious archiving. There have been wars, and savage retribution and endless destruction of cities, of libraries and of the guardians of the past. After the Great Uprising of 1857, for example, many historical records were destroyed by the British in the vindictive carnage that followed the re-taking of Delhi, Meerut, Agra, Lucknow and other centres of the revolt. Many manuscripts and eyewitness accounts were destroyed or remained hidden within families for generations for fear of reprisals from the British.

If such is the fate of written history as a whole, then the neglect of women in history should come as no surprise. Take Ambapali, for example. She is known only due to the fortuitous overlapping of her life with that of the great men of her age—the Buddha and King Bimbisara of Magadha. Ambapali's story is recorded in the Buddhist canon as an example of the saving of a wretched life. Ambapali speaks of her journey from courtesan to nun in verses such as the following:

> Glossy and black as the down of the bee
> My curls once clustered.
> They, with the waste of the years,

Liken to hempen or bark cloth.
Such, and not otherwise, runneth the rune,
The word of the Soothsayer.

For other women, memory is further complicated by Muslim lives lived in the zenana, forbidden to the gaze of biographers and visitors. Much published material of the sixteenth and seventeenth century Mughal courts comes to us via the writings of European travellers to India. And yet these European chroniclers, as pointed out by historian Faraz Anjum, were limited in their writings about women in two ways: 'as foreigners they possessed limited resources to understand the language and culture of the locals'; and, moreover, 'they were all male and thus the private domain of the women was nearly completely inaccessible to them'. Inaccessible, yet clearly not out of bounds, for the fantasy of the harem with its supposedly limitless supply of nubile females excited the libidinous imagination of the European travellers. Niccolao Manucci, the seventeenth-century Italian adventurer and traveller, speculated about the imagined debauchery of the Muslims who 'were very fond of women, who are their principal relaxation and almost their only pleasure.' These travellers soaked up bazaar gossip and lascivious rumours—even the royal princesses, Jahanara Begum and her sister Roshanara Begum, were not spared. They did not hesitate to spread rumours about drunken orgies and even incest to a European audience that found such prurient details 'fascinating and loathsome'. Even the battle-scarred warrior princess Raziya Sultan was not spared the breathless, horrified interest of Persian and British writers. Her supposed liaison with an African slave, it was believed, was what brought about her downfall, rather than the carefully calibrated and easily disrupted game of diplomacy and brinkmanship she played with the Turks of the court.

Rani Laxmibai, that most faultless of modern heroines, a Hindu widow, a martyr and a patriot, has been called an 'Indian Joan of Arc'. And yet, as Joyce Chapman Lebra has pointed out, 'Joan of Arc has inspired over twelve thousand volumes in French alone, not to mention a long list in English, and is said to be the most written-about individual of the fifteenth century', whereas for Laxmibai there are only 'a few novels, plays and biographies'. It is through the oral tradition primarily that her memory is venerated—through the folktales, ballads and stories of the poets of Bundelkhand that pay tribute to their most beloved heroine.

The most successful narratives are when women tell the stories of other women, using song and verse. It is through the oral medium that the censorship, deliberate or inadvertent, by men in the written medium can be sidestepped. It is the women who have the largest corpus of oral literature who best survive historical negligence and erasure. This is how the lives of Meerabai, Laxmibai and Radha are most accessible to us even today. Their stories have been sung and bartered by women and by the disempowered through the centuries and have thus avoided the censure of the powerful. But if the oral medium has helped keep vigil over the fragile legacy of women, it is also sometimes suspect, and impossible to verify. Some historians and scholars argue that many of the poems attributed to Meerabai were actually written much later, in the eighteenth and nineteenth centuries, by unknown authors. A few, like John Stratton Hawley, have even questioned the authenticity of Meerabai's entire corpus and the historicity of much of her life. This questioning undermines the fabric of Meerabai's life, her courage in repudiating her patriarchal destiny as a cloistered bahu of a Rajput clan.

The history of India's women, indeed of India itself, is further complicated by the polyphony of voices that records their story. Through three thousand years of history, India's stories have been told in the language of the elite, which has changed each time a new force has appeared. Thus India's history is written in Sanskrit, Turkish, Persian, Brajbhasha, Hindi, and English, besides many other vernacular languages. It is skewed, moreover, by the gaze of each subjective writer. So the Persian chronicler is aghast by Raziya Sultan's abandoning of purdah, the Pali texts prefer to omit Ambapali's relationship with their patron king Bimbisara, and the British accounts of Mughal India and the rajas of Awadh are irrevocably tainted by their 'Orientalist' view of the harem and Muslim women. History, where it is written, is naturally that of the victor—the Mughals, the foreign travellers, the British colonists. It is suspect and filled with prejudice. 'Truth hides somewhere at the bottom of the deepest well,' Jawaharlal Nehru wrote, talking about British Indian history. 'Falsehood, naked and unashamed, reigns almost supreme.'

◆

'People do not throw their geniuses away,' the African-American writer Alice Walker wrote, referring to the corpus of writing by women writers of colour in America. 'And if they are thrown away, it is our duty as artists and as witnesses for the future to collect them again for the sake of our children, and, if necessary, bone by bone.' And so bone by bone, verse by verse, we need to assemble the fragmented lives, the silenced voices, because these women are stepping stones going back all the way to our origins, when we first conjured up myths in an ancient and sombre language. These women form a cartography, a faint and shimmering image, of who we are and where we come from. And for each woman annotated in language, there are countless more who will never be known. But we need to make a start somewhere. This book is one of those beginnings.

Draupadi
Dharma Queen

The heroes are dead. The evil is done. Our kingdom has
been laid waste.
We killed them and our rage is gone. Now this grief holds
me in check.

These bleak and terrible words are spoken by Yudhishthira, one of
the conquering heroes of the Mahabharat. He says them, moreover,
at the end of the battle at Kurukshetra in which he and his brothers,
the Pandavas, are victorious. It is a mighty war and will deliver to
the Pandavas what they have been hankering for all their lives, their
birthright and the kingdom of the Kurus. This battle was meant
to be a dharma-yuddha, a just and righteous war. But at the end
of the eighteen days of relentless brutality, when their enemies are
lying dead on the scorched and trampled battlefield, theirs is not
an exultant victory. These are ambiguous and unusual heroes, who
doubt the very meaning of their Kshatriya dharma. Unlike the
other great epic, the Ramayan, in which Ravana is the confirmed
villain and Ram the hero, the Mahabharat is nuanced and full of
shadows. The heroes do not die on the battlefield, in the full glory
of their Kshatriya destiny. Instead there is old age, melancholy and
enduring disappointment. Arjuna, one of the Pandava brothers and
the greatest warrior of his age, loses his heroic powers towards the
end of his long life and is unable to protect the Yadava women of
Krishna's tribe from ordinary robbers. Krishna himself, their splendid
Yadava clansman, dies a lonely death when a hunter accidentally
shoots him in a forest.

'It is rich irony,' writes Gurcharan Das, 'that the Pandavas waged
a war reluctantly in support of a dubious claim and then employed
deceit to gain a victory for which they were rightly censured.' In
this tale of heroic chivalry, then, dharma itself is uncertain. Duty,
justice, and moral certitude are fluid notions depending on the

individual player. The authors of the Mahabharat admit the subtlety of righteousness when they write:

Heroes [are] of many kinds.
Heroes of sacrifice, heroes of self-control
Others who are heroes of truth
Heroes of battle are also proclaimed
And men who are heroes of giving
Others are heroes of intellect, and heroes of patience are others
And also heroes of honesty and men who lie in tranquillity

If the men of the Mahabharat are grave and unsettled by doubt, oblique in the path they choose, then the women glow with the conviction of their beliefs. They are appalled by the men's indecision; Draupadi, the co-wife of the five Pandava brothers, even asks a scathing question about the duty of kings and justice for the dispossessed.

'What is left of the dharma of kings?' Draupadi asks before an assembly of men and elders when she is being humiliated publicly by one of them. 'This ancient eternal dharma is lost among the Kauravas... For this foul man, disgrace of the Kauravas, is molesting me, and I cannot bear it.'

If Andrea Custodi has described Draupadi as being, on the one hand, 'extolled as the perfect wife—chaste, demure, and devoted to her husbands', when she appears in the assembly hall, in one of the defining scenes of the Mahabharat, she is a vision of hell. She has been gambled and lost by her husband Yudhishthira, with the complicity of the other Pandavas, during a game of dice. Yudhishthira first lost his kingdom and his worldly goods to his cousins, the Kauravas. Goaded by the Kauravas, Yudhishthira then stakes and loses Draupadi. In his attempt to show the Kauravas that Draupadi is indeed a worthwhile stake, Yudhishthira describes his wife and gives the listeners a clearer image of Draupadi than almost any other heroine of the Mahabharat:

She is not too short, nor is she too large, nor is she too dark, nor is her complexion red. She has eyes reddened from passion. I will stake her—whose eyes and fragrance are like autumnal lotuses. Attached to modesty, she is, in beauty, equal to *sri*, the goddess of beauty. ...Like the jasmine flower, the *mallika*, is she: with her perspiring face she appears similar to a lotus. She has red eyes, long hair, a waist as slender as the sacrificial altar and a body with no excessive hair.

When Draupadi is dragged into the assembly hall by Dusshasana, the Kaurava prince, her hair is dishevelled and she is wearing only a single piece of cloth stained with blood as she is in her monthly cycle. A menstruating woman was considered deeply polluting and was confined to separate quarters. Her unbound hair is also a disquieting symbol—a woman with groomed hair was a sign of domestication, of a potentially dangerous force sequestered and restrained. For a woman and a queen to be dragged by the hair, as Draupadi was, and displayed in her inauspicious avatar in front of men, kin, and elders, was an outrage which would become the spinning heart of the Mahabharat.

The Pandavas, when they staked and lost their kingdom, Indraprastha, dissipated the prestige and the wealth they had finally wrested from fate. Watched over by their mother Kunti after they were made vulnerable orphans upon the death of their father Pandu, they were able to reclaim their birthright only after their marriage to Draupadi. The great wealth of her clan, the Panchalas, supplies the necessary heft to their ambitions; with Draupadi by their side, they are finally able to leave the ignominy of forest life and march into the capital, Hastinapur, as true claimants to the throne of the Kurus.

Now Yudhishthira has lost this kingdom, so hard won, and his freedom, and that of his brothers as well. When Draupadi is brought to the assembly hall, the Pandavas are slaves, their jewels and silk shawls removed, their turbans on the ground. The sight of her husbands in this shameful condition would have been a terrifying revelation for Draupadi. This is the moment at which Draupadi is abandoned for the first time and she begins to inhabit her lonely destiny, which will earn her the terrible descriptor 'nathavati anathavat'—husbanded, yet unprotected.

And yet Draupadi, in these dreadful circumstances, does not behave as one unprotected or repudiated. Instead, she poses a question to the gathering of Kshatriya warriors and elders. A question so unexpected it momentarily stuns the gathering of men.

'Whom did you lose first, yourself or me?' Draupadi asks the mortified Yudhishthira. She then poses a further challenge to 'these Kurus stand[ing] here in the hall, lords of their daughters and daughters-in-law'. Besides her husbands, she then specifically asks her assembled kinsmen, her father-in-law, and her elders, 'What is the dharma of a king?'

Despite the humiliating circumstances, Draupadi has the courage and intelligence to question the all-male assembly about the legality and morality of her situation. She wants to know, initially, whether Yudhishthira could have legally staked her after he had lost his own freedom, and that of his brothers. The men prevaricate and stumble over their words, circling uneasily around the issue of the ownership of women. The bleak truth is that at the time that the Mahabharat was written the ownership of women, as defined by control over their reproductive potential, resided with their fathers and upon marriage with their husbands. Manu was soon to write in his *Manusmriti* that in childhood a girl was subject to her father, in youth to her husband, and if her husband died, to her sons.

The Mahabharat has many instances of women who are treated as wombs on rent, as submissive, procreating beings owned by their husbands. Princesses and women of high birth were even more likely to be viewed in terms of the value of their reproductive potential. The princesses Ambika and Ambalika must produce heirs for the Kuru clan through niyoga (surrogacy) with the sadhu

Vyasa because their own husband is dead. Pandu, believed to be impotent, commands Kunti in a similar manner, despite her reluctance, to have sons through niyoga. But Draupadi retains her unshakeable belief in the power of justice and dharma. She radiates rage, claiming for herself the outrage her husbands hesitate to feel on her behalf. She confuses and undermines them and questions the honour they arrogate to themselves as Kshatriyas and protectors of women. Finally, Bhishma, the wise and impartial Kuru statesmen, professes that dharma is subtle, and he is unable to give Draupadi a clear answer to her question.

Yudhishthira is shackled by the many conflicting dharmas he feels he owes allegiance to. He is a king, and must obey the dharma of kings but he is also now a slave, having lost his freedom. He is a husband and an elder brother, and has the dharma of a protector but he is also a gambler who has lost and must honour the code of the game. The silence of the men is shameful both for Draupadi, who is doubly bereft, and the Kshatriya warriors, who are unable to fulfil the most basic Kshatriya dharma of protecting a woman's honour. Before the inevitable war at Kurukshetra, Kunti will tell Krishna that 'what irked the most was not losing the kingdom or the exile of my sons, but the humiliation of that great dark woman weeping in the assembly hall as they mocked her. Nothing was more painful than that insult'. It is only the empathy of a woman that redeems Draupadi's lost honour and shameful humiliation.

Draupadi alone has the fierce and true conviction of the righteousness of her demand. In the face of humiliation and degradation from Dusshasana, Duryodhana and Karna, when there is no male authority willing to speak up for her, she refuses to use the 'womanly' way and beg and plead for her freedom. Instead she uses rage, and the threat of violence, to chastise the gathered men about their bewilderingly friable dharma. The justice Draupadi seeks is simply the duty towards the honour of a queen, a wife and a Kshatriya woman. Two thousand years later, as we will see subsequently in the book, a very different queen, Laxmibai of Jhansi, would ask the same question of the English colonists and pay a price in blood for that honour.

Draupadi also summons the spectre of blood, always an unsettling thing when used by a woman. After Karna has called her a whore for marrying five men, Dusshasana has tried to disrobe her and Duryodhana has lasciviously bared his left thigh to her, inviting her to sit on his lap like a common prostitute, Draupadi makes a declaration which is part malediction and part promise:

> I shall never forgive the Kauravas for doing what they have done to me. I shall not tie my hair until I wash it in Dusshasana's blood.

The violence of this imagery is provocative and indelible. Draupadi uses two powerful symbols, unbound hair and blood, to flaunt her disgrace for the remainder of the Mahabharat. When the Pandavas and Draupadi are finally exiled for thirteen years, she will keep her hair loose, a constant reminder to her husbands that she is defiled and that blood will need to be spilt to redeem her honour. Her unbound hair also questions her husbands' masculinity and therefore their virility since they are not able to protect her.

Despite the inability of any of the men present to answer Draupadi's question categorically, they are unsettled by the outrage done to her and her repeated questioning of the righteousness of their dharma. There are deadly and ominous signs; jackals are heard howling outside the assembly hall and Dhritarashtra, the blind father of the Kauravas, is thoroughly perturbed. He goes up to Draupadi and offers her three wishes. Draupadi asks for the freedom of her husbands and the restoration of their worldly goods and nothing else for herself.

The skill and courage with which Draupadi has saved herself and her husbands is summed up by Karna. He says it to further taunt the Pandavas at their lack of 'manliness', but it is true nevertheless.

Up till now we have heard of many beautiful women in the world, but no woman has done anything equal to what Draupadi has done here today. The Pandavas and Kauravas were burning with anger, and in that conflagration no one can say what might have happened, but Draupadi has re-established peace. Like a boat she has saved the Pandavas when they were about to drown in a sea of disgrace.

Even Krishna will later acknowledge the enormity of Draupadi's achievement in the assembly hall when he says:

That day Krishnaa [Draupadi] did a deed exceedingly pure and difficult.
Herself and the Pandavas she lifted up
As in a ship from the swell of the terrible sea.

In both these descriptions, Draupadi is the redemptory boat, saving the battered and silent Pandavas from drowning in disgrace through her moral courage, the force of her dharma and her unexpected eloquence. This is a momentous admission, for the Mahabharat is an epic that is replete with references to women as helpless and dependent on their husbands. Her question remains unanswered till the end of the epic, when she will learn of the scandalous price required of her for the restoration of her womanly honour. For now, destiny must follow its unalterable course. Yudhishthira is challenged to yet another game of dice, he accepts and loses once again, and the Pandavas and Draupadi are exiled from the kingdom for thirteen years.

When Draupadi leaves Hastinapur for exile in the forest with the Pandavas, she is dressed in skins and bark, her hair is unkempt and she has removed all her jewellery. She has repudiated her auspicious avatar as Lakshmi, goddess of the home and the plenitude of the domesticated woman. Sita, on the other hand, when she accompanies Ram into the forest, is dressed like a bride, in all her finery. She embraces her auspicious nature and takes her queenly attributes with her into the forest. But Sita, unlike Draupadi, follows her husband Ram into the forest out of choice because she cannot bear to be separated from him. Draupadi accompanies her husbands into the forest for two reasons. On the one hand, she is needed to keep the Pandavas united in their ultimate dharma of reclaiming the throne of the Kurus. These five brothers will always need the alchemy of a woman's will added to theirs to keep them focused despite their burning ambition. First, it will be Kunti, their mother, and then Draupadi. On the other hand, Draupadi is determined not to be thwarted in the trajectory that will lead her to justice for her besmirched honour. The visible symbols of her dishevelled hair and unadorned body will be a constant rebuke to her husbands during their years in exile.

That Draupadi is no ordinary woman is made abundantly clear in the epic from the moment of her birth. Like the Greek heroines, who are all demigods born of an immortal parent, Draupadi also has a supernatural birth. She is born fully formed from the sacrificial fire that Drupad, king of the Panchala tribe, is conducting to create an heir who will avenge an ancient humiliation. Drupad's yagna will produce a prince, Dhrishtadyumna, to kill the sadhu Drona, but it also yields his beautiful twin sister:

> And also a Pancali girl arose from the middle of the sacrificial altar, well-apportioned with limbs one ought to see, a waist like a vedi, a delight to the mind. Dark, her eyes like lotus petals, hair dark-bluish and curling, having taken human form clearly possessing the hue of an immortal, her fragrance, like that of the blue lotus, wafted for a league.

Athena is born out of the skull of Zeus, Durga is born of the combined energy and fury of the gods, and Draupadi is born of the great Vedic sacrificial fire—the first of many sacrificial fires which will shape her life.

The Mahabharat is ordered and anchored by sacrifice and yagnas and Draupadi, from the moment of her birth, is the great yagna queen. When Yudhishthira becomes king of Indraprastha, Draupadi is consecrated queen in the great Rajasuya sacrifice and at the end of the devastation of the Kurukshetra War, Draupadi participates in the carnage and massacre of the Ashvamedha yagna, the horse sacrifice, in which, as queen, she must lie in obscene mimicry next to the slaughtered sacrificial horse.

A heroic woman, then, with a great and supernatural destiny but there is a splinter of corruption lodged within it from the very beginning. The yagna during which Draupadi and Drishtadyumna are born has been performed by King Drupad to bring about the death of an enemy and one who is, moreover, a Brahmin and this 'is an abominable crime in itself.' This is an abhichara sacrifice, a black magic rite which deals with death and Drupad has to search for a year for a Brahmin willing to conduct this inauspicious yagna. Drishtadyumna's role is to kill Drona, as per his father's wishes, but Draupadi is born for a greater and deadlier purpose altogether. She is born of the gods' combined desire for the destruction of the entire Kshatriya race and the renewal of the earth's depleted energy. Her birth is accompanied by a prophecy, a heavenly voice which announces to the participants of the yagna:

> Best among all women, Krsna will lead the Ksatra to destruction. The fair-waisted one will in time accomplish the work of the gods. Because of her, a great fear will arise for the Ksatriyas.

Born of the controlled chaos of fire, Draupadi is an agent of destruction, and one that will bring an end to a yuga itself. The Kurukshetra War marks the end of the Dvaparayuga, the third age of mankind and the beginning of Kali Yuga, the fourth and final age. She is an instrument of the gods, designed to bring about the end of an effete age in which the moral order is crumbling and dharma is uncertain. It is unsurprising, therefore, that Draupadi is imperious in her demand for justice and scathing when her husbands equivocate.

The cause of a great deal of the vicissitudes in the Mahabharat is the uncertainty and obscurity surrounding the lineage of the various clans and heroes. Bhishma, the son of Shantanu and Ganga, is the true heir of the Kuru clan. However, he is made to relinquish his claim to the throne when his father remarries the fisherwoman Satyavati. Satyavati marries the king on the condition that *her* sons will inherit the throne of the Kurus. Even though Satyavati's sons, Chitrangada and Vichitravirya, die before they can have any children, she is determined to not be denied her inheritance. She coerces her daughters-in-law Ambika and Ambalika to have children through niyoga with Vyasa, the son she had before she married Shantanu. Ambika's son, Dhritarashtra, though he is the eldest, is born blind and therefore deemed unfit for kingship. Ambalika's son Pandu, who is shackled by a mysterious illness, is crowned the yuvraj. In time, Dhritarashtra becomes the father of a hundred Kaurava princes. Duryodhana, despite being the eldest of Dhritarashtra's sons, is plagued with bitterness over the doubts regarding the legitimacy of his claim to the throne. Because his father is blind, Duryodhana's cousins, who are Pandu's sons, the Pandavas, are considered the rightful heirs. The Pandavas, moreover, are not the biological children of their father, Pandu. Owing to a complicated curse, Pandu is effectively impotent and his wives Kunti and Madri can only have children by invoking a holy mantra Kunti has earned by serving a sadhu.

The Mahabharat repeatedly throws up the issue of the ownership of the fertility of women. Kunti's sons are appropriated by Pandu despite his lack of virility and given the patronym Pandavas although biologically they all have different fathers, none of whom is Pandu. Draupadi is married to the five Pandava brothers and there is concern and dismay at the thought that no one will know who the real father of her children is. It is then decided, after her marriage, that Draupadi will live exclusively with one brother for one year so that the issue of the paternity of her sons is less complicated.

In a folk narrative, Duryodhana's wife, Bhanumati, sneers at

Draupadi asking her how she manages five husbands. Draupadi's cutting reply is that among her in-laws the number of husbands has always been rather excessive, referring to both Satyavati, who has a son out of wedlock before she marries Shantanu, and Kunti who has three sons from three men, divine though they may be, as well as a son before marriage, the magnificent warrior Karna.

Though this anecdote reflects Draupadi's quick wit and confidence, her polyandrous marriage to five brothers is something she will repeatedly face humiliation for. Though she is won by Arjuna during her swayamvar, Kunti complicates matters by insisting that all five Pandava brothers jointly marry Draupadi as if she were an evening's gleaning to be 'shared' amongst them. Despite this, she makes the best of what might have placed a lesser woman at a considerable disadvantage, and becomes the anchor of the Pandavas during the years of their forest exile. Even though the Pandavas have lost much, for Draupadi the sacrifice is immeasurably greater. She must give up any hope of an exclusive love for Arjuna, as she has been parcelled out between the brothers. She must also constantly guard against all accusations of immorality as people are quick to judge a woman with so many husbands. In the assembly hall, Karna claims that this marriage to five men automatically makes a whore of her, since according to tradition any woman who lies with more than three men becomes a common prostitute.

◆

The archery task set out for the would-be suitors at the swayamvar that King Drupad had arranged for his daughter was deliberately made difficult and almost impossibe to achieve, as befitted a bride as superior as Draupadi. After a whole day of failed attempts by a legion of Kshatriyas and princes, Arjuna is able to hit the target and win the hand of Draupadi. In the commotion that follows the swayamvar and then Kunti's ruinous insistence on the sharing of Arjuna's prize, we do not hear Draupadi's voice at all. Although her father and her twin brother argue gallantly to change Kunti's mind about this polyandrous marriage, the poets do not tell us what Draupadi is thinking. Whether Draupadi's reaction was later redacted by vigilant authors or whether as a young bride Draupadi was, in fact, unable to voice her misgivings, we will never really know. By the time Draupadi reappears for the second time in the epic at the scene of the craven gambling match, she is an altogether different woman from the shy, demure bride of her swayamvar. Never again, for the duration of the Mahabharat, will Draupadi remain mute and submissive. She will argue, chastise and rebuke, she will implore and demand, and she will rage, passionately and eloquently, against the injustice done to her and her husbands. Draupadi walks the path to redemption with none of the hesitancy and doubt her husbands show.

Heroic though she undoubtedly was, Draupadi is paradoxically quite unlike the classic Hindu model for the perfect dharmic wife, the pativrata. An ideal wife or pativrata must be 'obedient and completely servile, putting her husband's needs and existence above her own.' Tryambaka, the eighteenth-century minister in the court of Thanjavur, wrote a treatise on 'The Perfect Wife' in which he writes that a wife 'seems to be no more than her husband's shadow.' The pativrata wife par excellence in Hindu mythology is Sita, who 'gave up palace life for accompanying her husband to the forest. Her loyalty and steadfast devotion to Rama, her complete confidence in him and dependence on his omnipotence, are at times touching, especially when compared with his occasional unjust treatment of her.' Scholarship regarding the character of Sita has shown her to be not entirely the subservient wife of popular memory but in many ways she is celebrated as being the exemplary pativrata. So restricted became the notion of pativrata in the epics that Sita, unswerving in her devotion to Ram, was banished by him only for aspersions cast on her chastity by the people of Ayodhya following her kidnapping by Ravana. The demure Subhadra, Krishna's sister and one of the numerous women Arjuna marries after Draupadi, is the placid counterfoil to Draupadi's excess and rage. Subhadra is fair where Draupadi is dark-complexioned. She is 'auspicious', untroubled and quiet. At the end of the Kurukshetra War, it is perhaps telling that of all the princes and warriors only Subhadra's grandson survives, last heir to the Kuru legacy. All Draupadi's sons are slaughtered, without glory and almost beyond cultural memory, murdered in their sleep after the war is over.

After the episode of the gambling hall, in which Draupadi shows such a shocking lack of restraint in arguing legality and morality with her elders and her in-laws, the Pandavas and Draupadi leave for exile for a period of thirteen years. During this time, no more children are born to Draupadi (after Indraprastha) and her focus is on maintaining her husbands' resolve to reclaim their kingdom from the Kauravas.

In a famous conversation, a year into their exile, Draupadi even accuses Yudhishthira of lacking manly resolve and determination. She taunts Yudhishthira with comparisons between Duryodhana's situation and their own. Whereas Duryodhana is living the life of a king, surrounded by luxury and all the marks of a glorious Kshatriya prestige, Yudhishthira is clad in rags and smeared with dust and mud. This proud daughter of a great king finds it intolerable that the natural order of her place in the world has been dissolved. This, she argues, should provoke manyu, or kingly assertiveness, in Yudhishthira to rail against this injustice done to him and his brothers and to take up arms to restore the equilibrium of the social world.

'There is no Kshatriya without manyu,' Draupadi further tells Yudhishthira. 'This saying is well known in the world. In you, however, I now see a Kshatriya who is like the opposite.'

In response to Draupadi's declaration, Yudhishthira makes a philosophical case for the need to control anger and the use of ksama, or forgiveness, in their current situation. At this point a true pativrata should submit to the superiority of her husband's reasoning but Draupadi does no such thing. She calls into question Yudhishithira's abstract notion of dharma that makes him indifferent to his brothers' and his wife's suffering. She refuses to indulge his metaphysical leanings and brings back the argument to a more immediate, visceral plane in which she and the Pandavas suffer ceaselessly because of their lost honour. She even accuses Yudhishthira of being deluded in his beliefs and argues that he should instead be using every possible resource available to him to regain his stolen kingdom and his lost glory.

The debate between Yudhishthira and Draupadi continues for a long time, with Draupadi even questioning the righteousness of the 'arranger' of things who rewards the dharmic Yudhishthira with suffering and loss. Draupadi compares the force that moves the universe to a puppet-master:

> This blessed God, the self-existent great-grandfather, hurts creatures with creatures, hiding behind a guise, Yudhisthira. Joining and unjoining them, the capricious blessed Lord plays with the creatures like a child with its toys. The arranger does not act towards his creatures like a father or mother, he seems to act out of fury, like every other person.

Yudhishthira is clearly shocked by Draupadi's views and tells her it is heresy to doubt the ways of the gods and a transgression to doubt the reliability of dharma. He says Draupadi is in danger of being an atheist, a nastika. Eventually Vyasa must intervene, so both Yudhishthira and Draupadi can save face.

If absolute acceptance of a husband's opinion and beliefs was what constituted an ideal pativrata, then Draupadi was an altogether unusual one. Throughout the remainder of the epic, she follows the dictates of her own sense of justice, even if it repeatedly brings her in clear opposition to Yudhishthira's thinking.

A few years into their exile when Krishna, along with an entourage of clansmen and Kshatriyas, comes to the forest to meet the Pandavas, Draupadi will once again remind him of the great offence done to her:

Krishna, why was a woman like me, wife of the Parthas, your friend, O Lord! And sister of Drishtadyumna, dragged into the assembly? Menstruating, tormented and trembling, with blood flowing and wearing but one garment, I was dragged into the assembly of the Kurus.

Draupadi then goes on to berate her husbands:

I blame only these strong Pandavas, men held to be the best in battle, who watched their lawful and illustrious wife being tormented. A curse on Bhimasena's strength, a curse on the archer Partha's: both of them stood by while vile men insulted me, Janaradana.

Not only does she not abide by the pativrata ideal of accepting her husbands' every action, she actively reviles them in front of their peers. She questions the very scaffolding of Hindu dharma, where 'strong' and famous warriors have been emasculated, unable to protect their virtuous wife. Her bitterness and sorrow at the collective incapacity of her husbands, who are meant to protect and honour her, thrums clearly through the centuries. Finally, in a moment of bleak premonition, Draupadi says to Krishna:

I have no husbands, no sons, no brothers, no father, no relatives, not even you, Madhusudana. As if free from all grief, you all stood by while vile men insulted me.

This is a devastating declaration by Draupadi. If a woman and a queen are defined by their place in society and their relationship to the men in their lives, then she is equating her own status with that of an orphan, a widow, and a bereaved mother. Finally, it is Krishna who swears to avenge Draupadi's honour, but she will be forsaken before the end of the epic.

Before the end, before loss, and before a sparkling death, Draupadi has further humiliations to face. Twice she will be assaulted by men who are captivated by her great beauty.

Jayadratha, the king of the Sindhus, who sees her during her time in exile when she is alone at a sadhu's hermitage, says that 'having seen her, all other women look like female monkeys!' Clearly Draupadi has a seductive beauty that sets her apart from other women. This beauty, paradoxically, endangers her because it provokes a violent lust in the men who try and possess her. Her chastity is constantly at risk and her husbands must repeatedly intercede to assert their masculinity in their ability to defend their wife's honour and safeguard her sexual purity. Sita is also described as being very beautiful but her beauty does not cause outrage. Even when Ravana kidnaps her, he does so to avenge his sister Surpanakha who has been grievously insulted by Ram and Lakshman.

Jayadratha, despite knowing that Draupadi is married to the five Pandavas, propositions her and Draupadi curses him. When he forcibly grabs her, Draupadi defends herself vigorously and pushes him to the ground. Jayadratha finally carries her away and the Pandavas must chase him and then fight to get her back.

During their thirteenth year in exile, when Draupadi is living as a maid at the court of King Virata of Matsya, she is attacked by the queen's brother, Kicaka. Once more, Draupadi defends herself and pushes Kicaka to the ground. Kicaka follows her to the court of King Virata to which Draupadi has fled. Yudhishthira is also present at the court, disguised as a priest, and though he witnesses Draupadi's humiliation, he does not intervene to save her, we are told, because he does not want to give away his alibi. Kicaka drags Draupadi by the hair and kicks her and though Draupadi is able to get away, she is incensed at the uselessness of her husbands' valour. 'How do [my] strong and illustrious husbands, like eunuchs, endure me—their dear and faithful wife—being assaulted by the son of a suta?' she rages. 'Where is the anger, virility and courage of those who do not wish to defend a wife being assaulted by a wicked man?'

Unlike Sita, Draupadi physically defends herself each time she is assaulted. In Sita's case, when she is abducted by Ravana, the overwhelming feeling is that of terror and horror. In Draupadi's case, it is always rage, and a scouring bitterness directed at her husbands who are at fault for allowing her to be so vulnerable. Sita, more in keeping with her pativrata image, never blames Ram for her abduction. Her anger, when her sexual chastity is repeatedly questioned by Ram, is directed inward and there is an unassailable though self-destructive logic when Sita asks the earth to swallow her up at the end of the Ramayan rather than face any more humiliation.

In the court of Virata, meanwhile, Draupadi is preoccupied with the need to contain Kicaka's lust. She decides to approach Bhima, most impulsive and fiery of her husbands and complains to him at length about the degradation of her condition and Yudhishthira's inability to protect her. 'How can you, Partha,' Draupadi asks Bhima, 'slayer of enemies, think me happy, overcome by hundreds of troubles on account of Yudhishthira?' Always easily goaded to action, Bhima now vows revenge and, as per Draupadi's plan, lures Kicaka to a meeting where he beats him to death with his bare fists. Draupadi exults in this death, just retribution for her tainted honour and thinks 'my enemy is dead, now let me feast my eyes on his corpse'.

In all these instances, we are shown a Draupadi who is a 'troubling' heroine. Veering constantly off the path of ideal pativrata, Draupadi is not an easily contained example of womanhood. Her outspokenness and fury are in stark contrast to Yudhishthira's description of her:

> Were a man to desire a woman, she would be like this one, on account of her kindness: she would be like this one, on account of her beautiful figure: she would be like this one, on account of her perfect character. She is the last to sleep and first to awaken. She knows everything, down to the jobs both completed and not yet done by the cowherds and shepherds.

Later, during her years in exile, Draupadi has a conversation with Krishna's wife Satyabhama. Satyabhama is curious to know how Draupadi manages to keep five husbands happy in their married life. In her response to Satyabhama, Draupadi again adopts for herself an idealized role and assures Satyabhama that she shows an impossible degree of wifely perfection. She serves her husbands, and her husbands' other wives, she is careful never to speak ill of her mother-in-law Kunti to whom she is entirely subservient. She 'serves her husbands without regard for her own likes and dislikes...never bathes nor eats nor sleeps until her husband has: she renounces what he renounces, eats and drinks what he does and so on.' Even more suspect is Draupadi's description of her own temperament:

> I avoid excessive mirth (arrogance) or excessive vexation and anger and am always, Satya, engaged in serving my husbands.

Astonishing declarations from a woman who, though she is certainly virtuous in many ways, always struggled to maintain a wifely equanimity in the face of her endless trials. Instead, these words seem designed to create a distraction from Draupadi's aberrant nature. A later interpolation by doubtful authors, possibly, to obscure the extent of Draupadi's aggressive and 'transgressive' nature. The reference to Draupadi laughing only demurely and never excessively is particularly galling because it is her inappropriate and arrogant laughter that earns Draupadi one of her most powerful enemies.

When the Pandavas and Draupadi initially return to Hastinapur after their wedding, the kingdom is split between the Kauravas and the Pandavas and, for a decade, the two clans coexist in relative peace. The Pandavas build a magnificent new capital city at Indraprastha, with a glittering white palace filled with mirages, mosaic tiles and trompe-l'œils. Pleased with their new palace, and anxious to finally show the Kauravas their newly acquired opulence, the Pandavas invite their cousins to Indraprastha. While Duryodhana and his friend Karna visit the new palace, seething silently at its splendour, Karna stumbles into a reflective still pool, mistaking it for a smooth floor. Watching from behind a latticed balcony, Draupadi laughs at Karna's discomfiture, going against the rules of hospitality and embarrassing a guest in her house. Karna is furious, and will have his terrible revenge later in the gambling hall.

◆

Despite her many human frailties, Draupadi remains one of the greatest and most enthralling of the epic heroines. She is beautiful, articulate and intelligent. She is a pativrata in the most demanding sense of the word. She shares the destiny of her husbands, wherever it takes them, and theirs is a peculiarly peripatetic fate. Daughter of a king and sister of a prince, Draupadi shares her husbands' destitution and their fate. She even sheds her name and her noble Kshatrani status to live in disguise along with the Pandavas for a year. She has an impeccable sense of justice and will be indefatigable in her quest for her lost honour. Unique amongst all the women of the epics, she has a god as a special friend—the complicated and beloved Lord Krishna—who is her sakha. When her husbands fail her, it is Krishna who will swear bloody and all-consuming revenge on her behalf. And yet, for all her sacrifice, Draupadi's fate is always tinged with sadness. Draupadi's is a crumbling happiness, dissipated before she can ever fully grasp it.

We have witnessed the various humiliations she had to endure, but even after the Pandavas have won the war and her honour is redeemed, when Bhima smears her hair with Dusshasana's blood, Draupadi is still the one who has lost in more ways than one. She has fulfilled her destiny as an instrument of the gods, destroyer of the Kshatriya race. But this has been achieved at great cost. Her father Drupad and her beloved twin brother Dhrishtadyumna are killed, as are all her other siblings and her five sons. Indeed, the mighty clan of the Panchalas is completely decimated, as are the Matsyas, the Kurus and the Gandharas. The only true heir, apart from the Pandavas themselves, to have survived the carnage is, as we have seen, Arjuna and Subhadra's yet to be born grandson, Parikshit.

Parikshit is also Krishna's nephew, and Draupadi has a sobering realization that this great kingmaker, clansman of the Pandavas, has watched over the survival of his own tribesmen rather than hers.

In the stark palace of Hastinapur, which is now haunted by the Kuru widows, Draupadi finds herself increasingly alone. In a few years time Kunti and Gandhari, along with Dhritarashtra, will retire to a forest life and Draupadi will be deprived of their consoling presence. The Pandavas have other wives apart from Draupadi and other families they can escape to. Draupadi is now dharma queen as Yudhishthira is crowned dharma-raj at an elaborate and bloody Ashvamedha yagna sacrifice, but this is hardly any consolation. She has no further children, and there are no grandchildren, only the icy comfort of justice served and her honour avenged.

◆

If Draupadi is admired, beloved and respected even today, she is never emulated. She is not considered a role model for young women to aspire to. Our daughters are never named in her honour. She remains, essentially, an untamed woman. She was never domesticated by motherhood, and we hardly hear anything about her children, who were sent away to her parents' home when she leaves for exile. Her unbound hair, her association with blood and uncensored speech is shocking even today. It is Sita, obedient wife and daughter with her less violent transgressions, who is revered. (Although even Sita, with her steadfast heart and quiet ways, is doubted time and again by Ram.) An ideal pativrata, Sita realizes that her chastity is ultimately no protection against the society of men, a bitter truth after her years of penance and sacrifice. It was Draupadi who was to have the satisfaction, however austere, of having her vows fulfilled and her honour restored.

There has been a resurgence of interest in Draupadi in recent times. Writers have increasingly tried to understand this seductive, fiery and occasionally infuriating character. All too often, though, the fascination is with Draupadi's polyandrous marriage or her imagined love interest. But to reduce Draupadi to the facile iconography of a woman scorned, a woman in love or a woman obsessed by a doomed love, is to do her a grave injustice. Nor is she a woman in need of rescuing, helpless and weeping, which is another familiar representation of Draupadi. For Draupadi famously and shockingly relinquishes the protection of all men; husbands, fathers and sons. Repeatedly betrayed by her men's inability or reluctance to fight for her honour, Draupadi uses every weapon available to her to keep that fight alive herself. She is heroic in claiming revenge when the great weight of the patriarchy is against her. She does this knowing the terrible price that will be asked of her, the abiding loneliness at the centre of the chaotic vortex that is her life. And in the end, justice is hers. If Sita is the proud mother of sons, she is still repudiated and must end her life, dispossessed and abandoned. Draupadi loses all her sons, but her honour is restored and she is the last great dharma queen of her era. At the end of Yudhishthira and Draupadi's reign, the world slides into the Kali Yuga.

When Draupadi was first imagined, millennia ago, her association with violence and retribution was explained by equating her with Prithvi, the burdened earth, ridding herself of her noxious, warring humans. But goddess though she became, she is a flawed and paradoxically human one. Unusual in the pantheon of irreproachable goddesses, Draupadi remains accessible and poignant. Where Sita is immaculate in her various womanly avatars—daughter, wife, mother—Draupadi stumbles and affronts. While Sita's rebellion is muted and internalized, Draupadi's is raucous and will not be ignored.

Though her story is three thousand years old, Draupadi is a heroine for our times. We can empathize with her impossible longings and the small betrayals that shackle her. We understand her need for justice above everything else. And if a goddess can rage so eloquently for one woman's honour, then, we are assured, so can we.

Radha

Illicit Goddess

Across five thousand years of myth and legend in India, countless goddesses have walked the land. There are rustic forest goddesses and solicitous village goddesses. There is the virginal Kanyakumari and there are the divine consorts Lakshmi and Saraswati; the terrifying Kali, destroyer of illusion; Prakriti, the Earth herself, and also the great goddess, Mahadevi. In this swirling excess of female forms there is one figure who stands out. She is, variously, the Nayika (woman in love), Parakiya (belonging to another), Rasika (the passionate one), Padmini (lotus woman), Kamini (a desirable woman) and even, paradoxically, Dulhan (the bride). Despite her many names, there is much about her that is unknown—we don't know for certain who her parents were or if she had children. We don't know whether she lived to be an old woman or how and when she died. All the stories about her describe only a short span of her life. And yet, she has been the beloved of countless generations of devotees—if she has not often been enshrined in the temples of India, she is always to be found in the tender care of household shrines. In Vraj, the land of her mythology, her name even today is a salutation: *Radhe Radhe!*

By the fifteenth or sixteenth century, after a millennium or so of storytelling, Radha had been transformed into the mother of the cosmos itself. In the *Brahmavaivarta Purana*, the creation of the universe is described in these words:

> In the beginning, Krishna, the Supreme Reality, was filled with the desire to create.
> By his own will he assumed a two-fold form.
> From the left half arose the form of a woman, the right half became a man.
> The male figure was none other than Krishna himself: the

female was the Goddess' Primordial Nature: otherwise known as Radha.

And so, from the sublime coupling of Radha and Krishna, the universe was created. In the course of their aeons-long union, Radha's sighs gave rise to the winds of the earth and the sweat from her exhausted limbs created the oceans. Into this ocean she gave birth to a golden egg from which, in time, the entire universe was created. By the late medieval period, we have a Radha who is the eternal feminine, the supreme mother—beyond form and attribute, impeccable and untouchable.

The very first allusions to Radha, though not by name, are much less exalted and appear to be in the songs of the Ahirs, a cattle-herding community of northern India. In Puranic literature she is first mentioned in the second-century text, the *Harivamsha*, a supplementary text to the Mahabharat. The *Harivamsha* describes the early life of Krishna in the idyllic, rural setting of Vraj, in central north India. According to Diana L. Eck, 'it is a fine country of many pasturelands, with well-nurtured people and cattle, the soil ever moist with the froth of milk. It is a land flowing with buttermilk, filled with cowherds and milkmaids, the air resonant with the sound of the sputtering churn.'

In the *Harivamsha*, the gopis or milkmaids are always mentioned as a group—no gopi is singled out by Krishna. The feelings of the gopis are changing from the maternal affection they had for the child Krishna to the sudden desire they now feel for the charismatic adolescent he has become. It is also clear from the *Harivamsha* that this attraction is illicit when they are unmarried, and adulterous when they are. When the gopis go to meet Krishna, they must, therefore, 'elude the restraints of their mothers, fathers and brothers and they are prohibited in vain by their husbands, brothers and fathers'.

The text is frank in its depiction of the sexual allure of the young Krishna playing his flute on the warm autumn nights of the forests of Vrindavan. Hearing this music the women of the village rush to Krishna, hurriedly setting aside their housewifely chores and responsibilities—food is left to burn on the stoves, families are abandoned at mealtime and clothes are in disarray. Krishna is not just an enticement, he is a conjuring from the deep unspoken desires of their hearts. With him they dance the Raas Leela, the joyous and unrestrained dance of love.

In the sixth century, Radha is first mentioned by name in popular folklore and poetry, but it is only in the twelfth century that she becomes immortalized in Sanskrit in Jayadeva's *Gita Govinda*. Over the next couple of centuries, this text will make her a pan-Indian phenomenon. Jayadeva was a court poet in Bengal, an ascetic in his early life who met and fell in love with Padmavati, a dancing girl in the temple of Lord Jagannath. Perhaps in an unconscious mirroring of his own transition from austerity to passion, Jayadeva 'personalizes' the Raas Leela, breathing new life into the persona of Radha.

The *Gita Govinda* begins with Krishna's father, Nandalal, asking Radha to take Krishna home, as night is approaching and rain threatens. On the way home, Radha and Krishna disappear into the forest and make love.

> Clouds thicken the sky
> Tamala trees darken the forest
> The night frightens him
> Radha, you take him home
> They leave at Nanda's order
> Passing trees in thickets on the way
> Until secret passions of Radha and Madhava
> Triumph on the Jumna riverbank.

From the very first stanzas of the *Gita Govinda*, there is a hint of the forbidden. It is clear that Radha is older than Krishna, since she is entrusted with his care and it is Krishna's father Nanda who seems to be complicit in this arrangement. The reader is left wondering who Radha could be. Is she just another gopi or is she a seductress? By naming her, and giving her agency in the opening lines, Jayadeva shifts the listener's attention to Radha and it is apparent that this is going to be her story. And Radha, who will become an irredeemable part of the sacred geography of India, is unlike any other gopi who has been described thus far.

In the *Gita Govinda*, Radha is the daughter of Vrishbhanu, a cowherd and a clan chief from the village of Barsana. The people of Barsana migrated to Vrindavan before those of Gokul, Krishna's native village, and it is on the way to Vrindavan that an adolescent Radha first sees the toddler Krishna. This is Krishna, the butter thief, the endearing and incorrigible child who was already bewitching the women of Gokul. As Radha walked by, dressed in her favourite blue skirt, and gauged him with a steady glance, might she have faltered, ever so slightly, in an intimation of the destiny she was to inhabit? She may already have been married, already parakiya; even if she were not, Krishna was forbidden to her anyway, hiding his princely Kshatriya birth behind a rustic guise till the time came for him to claim his inheritance.

As Jayadeva develops this theme of illicit love, Radha—and her capricious, essentially human, nature—becomes the fulcrum of his story. As writer David Kinsley has noted, from the physical manifestation of love in various women, such as trembling, frantic haste, shuddering when hearing the flute and other such external signs which are mentioned in the older texts, the focus in the *Gita Govinda* shifts to the internal, cascading moods of one specific woman. In the early stages of her love, Radha is unsure and vulnerable, hesitating to mention her feelings even to her close friends. She is tentative and respectful in her interactions with Krishna, and horrified when her friends suggest playing a prank on him to pique his interest.

Their story is also inextricably associated with the forest and the poetry of gathering monsoon clouds. For the other heroines of Indian mythology the forest will be an area of lurking uncertainty. While Draupadi will spend her years in exile in the forest shoring up her husbands' courage and bitterly regretting her lost honour, for Sita the same forest will be transformed into a place of shadows and nightmares where she is tricked and abducted by Ravana. For Radha, on the other hand, the forest will always be a place of shelter and complicit love.

As the story progresses, Radha's love for Krishna deepens, their meetings begin to take place furtively at night. It soon becomes clear that she belongs to another man and their relationship is not sanctioned by society. This is the theme of love in separation, or viraha, which runs through the *Gita Govinda*. Though it is never explicitly stated that Radha is married in the text, it is evident that she is parakiya and Krishna, moreover, is unfaithful in his love. As a result, Radha's feelings are complex and stumble between passion and uncertainty. These very human traits are developed in the later plays by Rupa Gosvami, a leading theologian of the Vaishnava movement, in which Krishna himself comments on his lover's many moods:

Now assuming a steadfast pose
Now showing signs of wavering
One moment uttering scornful sounds
The next, words of eagerness
Now with a look of innocence
Now with a glance bewitching
Radhika is split in two
Swayed now by anger, now by love.

At other times, she is the charming and confident lover who, after the *Gita Govinda*'s explicit sexual encounters, demonstrates her power over Krishna:

Adorn my breasts with leaf designs of musk
Put colour on my cheeks
Fasten the girdle around my hips
Twine my heavy braid with flowers

And jeweled anklets on my feet
And thus requested by Radha
Krishna who wears the yellow garment
Did as she asked him to, with pleasure.

Increasingly, however, Radha is unmoored in the monsoon forests
of Vrindavan. Her jealousy and her longing for a lover who is every
gopi's friend is delicately described by Jayadeva:

When spring came, tender-limbed Radha wandered
Like a flowering creeper in the forest wilderness
Seeking Krishna in his many haunts
The God of love increased her ordeal
Tormenting her with fevered thoughts
And her friend sang to heighten the mood.

True enough, Radha's jealousy is stinging and she rebukes Krishna
when she realizes he has spent an evening with another woman:

Your drowsy red eyes
From being awake through the night
Betray the intensity of passion
That you cherish for that other woman.

Alas! Alas! Go Madhava! Go Kesava! Leave me
Do not try to deceive me with your artful words
Go after her, you lotus-eyed one
She who soothes your grief.

At other times Radha is reflective and painfully honest, admitting
her helplessness despite Krishna's indiscretions:

My heart values his vulgar ways
Refuses to admit my rage,
Feels strangely elated,
And keeps denying his guilt
When he steals away without me

To indulge his craving
For more young women,
My perverse heart
Only wants Krishna back.
What can I do?

But Krishna is always full of remorse and tries to charm or pacify
Radha out of her jealous sulks. This Krishna is no longer the
indifferent lover of the Bhagavad Gita but one who is equally
tormented by his love for Radha. That she had a unique place
in Krishna's heart had already been demonstrated in some of the
earliest references to her as, for example, in this passage from Hala's
Gaha Sattasai where he is tenderly blowing away a speck of dust
from her eyes:

Krishna, removing cow-dust from Radhika
With the breath of your mouth
You sweep away the high esteem
These other cowherdesses have for you.

This intimate and at the same time commonplace affection also
helps to explain the immense popularity of these texts across India.
As Pavan K. Varma says in *The Book of Krishna*, the woman in
medieval Indian society lived a circumscribed life hedged in on all
sides by her 'stri dharma' or womanly duties to her husband, in-laws
and children. As per Manu's infamous treatise, the *Manusmriti*, a
woman was mandated to go from the proprietary possession of her
father to that of her husband, living out her days in endless chores
and obligations. In the polygamous society of the time, moreover,
wifely chastity was an undisputed expectation whereas the men
had other distractions. With husbands away from their homes for
long periods of time, the notion of viraha was an aching reality.
So endemic was this pain of the absent husband that an entire
genre of poetry, Barmasa—the twelve-month period—was created
to channel the anguish of these women.

Saavan clouds are pouring down, fields are flooding but I
burn with viraha
Punarvasu's constellation has appeared, my husband has
not. I'm going mad, where can he be?
My tears of blood fall on the earth and scatter like scarlet
rain-insects.
My friends have hung swings with their lovers, green is the
land and saffron their clothes.
My heart swings, too, to and fro, tossed by viraha with
violent blows.

In Radha's incandescent passion, women through the ages found
the perfect vehicle for their suppressed desires. Her uninhibited
desire and the erotic fulfilment of her love channeled their endlessly
constricted and unspoken emotions. In Krishna they found a
particularly personal god who strayed and digressed but always
returned. He submitted to Radha's jealous moods and showed
remorse and longing himself. He was never disinterested or remote
and the unlovely years of their tired domesticity faded away in the
telling of these tales of love beyond separation.

The parakiya nature of Radha's love for Krishna is essential in
understanding the appeal of the *Gita Govinda* and other associated
texts. Married life in India presupposed a husband's implicit
authority over his wife and the woman's obligation to revere her
husband. Radha's love is untainted by duty and the expectation of
reward. Through her desire and love for Krishna a solitary, proud
and passionate Radha stands apart from society and all its strictures
on women. In time, popular folk culture and later theological works
will transform Radha's desire into devotion and she will become
synonymous with the human soul's desire for a divine union.

From the fourteenth to sixteenth centuries, a host of poets
carried forward the legacy of Jayadeva. These poets wrote in the
language of the common people. Candidasa wrote in Bengali,
Vidyapati in Maithili, Surdas in Bihari and Brajbhasha and

Govindadasa in Brajabuli. As Pavan K. Varma has expressed it, through the works of these poets, 'their erotic love play made a transition from the refined, if passionate milieu of Sanskrit poetics to the earthy and seductive medium of the language of the masses.'

Both Vidyapati and Candidasa are clear in stating the illicit nature of Radha's love. Rather audaciously, they describe Radha as being a married woman, who has much to lose in pursuing her love for Krishna:

Casting away
All ethics of caste
My heart dotes on Krishna
Day and night
The custom of the clan
Is a faraway cry
And now I know
That love adheres wholly
To its own laws.

The language now is more robust than in the *Gita Govinda*, a reflection of the more prosaic and direct diction of the people. Radha's independence in the face of society's sanction is unequivocal in Candidasa's powerful verses:

I throw ashes at all laws
Made by man or God
I am born alone
With no companion
What is the worth
Of your vile laws
That failed me
In love
And left me with a fool
A dumbskull?
My wretched fate

Is so designed
That he is absent
For whom I long
I will set fire to this house
And go away.

In these ferocious lines, Radha is savage in the description of the wasteland of her life. The poet uses the transgressive imagery of ashes, which can be either sacred in the Hindu context (vibhuti) or the unholy relics of the cremation ground. Radha throws these ashes at the laws of the world which keep her bound to a 'fool' for a husband; the poet then extends the metaphor of fire by having her threaten to burn down her house. If the home is indeed the ultimate sanctum of a woman's existence then these desolate lines are unambiguous about the extent of Radha's repudiation of worldly honour.

That the illicit nature of Radha's love potentially called for the sacrifice of society's benevolence preoccupied many poets:

If I go to Krishna I lose my home
If I stay I lose my love.

And Radha chose love, always, willing to sacrifice her respectable status as a married woman and all the fetters this binds a woman with. Over the centuries, the capacious love she was capable of became the definition of bhakti itself, a love divine.

In the sixteenth century, a devotional movement arose in Bengal based on the worship of Krishna. This Bengal Vaishnava movement, as well as other similar movements centered on Krishna devotion, celebrated the passionate working of Krishna. Radha became the devotee par excellence and even the illicit nature of her love was subsumed within this movement. Adulterous love was projected as a superior love since it is given freely, with no obligations or duties imposed upon it. Even Radha's jealousy is condoned since Krishna, as the saviour of all humanity, cannot limit himself to only one woman:

He promised he'd return tomorrow
And I wrote everywhere on my floor:
'Tomorrow'

The morning broke, when they all asked:
Now tell us, when will your 'Tomorrow' come?
Tomorrow, Tomorrow, where are you?
I cried and cried, but my Tomorrow never returned

Vidyapati says: O listen, dear
Your Tomorrow became a today
With other women.

In the plays of Rupa Gosvami, Radha has made the transition to
the perfect bhakt or devotee. Her mind is unwaveringly focused
on Krishna and her obsession becomes unassailable. The feeling is
reciprocated by Krishna who loses his sleep and his peace of mind:

Radha appears before me on every side
How is it that for me the three worlds have become
Radha?

Though Krishna still dallies with the other gopis, he ingratiates
himself with Radha, bending before her so that the peacock feathers
in his hair brush the dust at her feet. The message in this imagery
is clear: Radha herself is becoming worthy of worship. Indeed, she
is now Krishna's Hladini Shakti, the Shakti of Bliss, most refined
of the essences of Krishna. As Radha is deified and made worthy
of adoration, her human qualities disappear: 'She reddens her lips
with the betel leaf of intense attachment and the guile of love is
her mascara. She reclines on a couch of conceit in the chamber
of charm.'

It is in the short, staccato padas of the blind poet Surdas that
we hear the crackling flirtation between Radha and Krishna:

'So pretty! Who are you? he asks
And where is your family? Your house?

You've never been seen around here'
'Never you mind—I stay in my place:
right here in my yard where I play
For Nanda's boy is out to steal
our curd and butter, they say'
'Now what would I possibly steal that you've got?
Come on, let's both of us play'
The charm of Sur's lord, his facile words
Disarm poor Radha, simple girl.

The narrative of Krishna and Radha's fugitive love lasts only for a season. Krishna must step into his destiny, slay the evil Kamsa, and walk into legend as King of Mathura. When he leaves Vrindavan and all the gopis, he will never return. His life will reverberate with adventures and battles, but for Radha there will only ever be Krishna. In time, the heft of this love proves equal to the pain of loss.

◆

With time, the legend of Radha bifurcated; for one school of thought she became the embodiment of the Earth while Krishna was the Spirit. She now became an immaculate object of veneration. Radha and Krishna became two bodies with a single soul. In the later poems of the *Sur Sagar*, they are even called, for the first time, bride (dulahini) and groom (dulah). In the second school of thought, Krishna and Radha became the embodiment of a more purely erotic emotion.

In the eighteenth century, as poetic interest shifted to the patronage of the princely courts of north India, a secular tradition of poetry in the Braj dialect known as the Riti School emerged. This genre of poetry was defined by the Sringara Rasa or erotic mood, and the nayika or woman in love became a favourite subject of these poets. Descriptions of the nayika became very popular, even spawning a subgenre that described all possible categories of nayikas. The poets relied on ancient erotic texts such as the Kama

Shastras and the *Natya Shastra* and Radha and Krishna came to symbolize the ideal courtly lovers of the erotic mood.

The kind of women eulogized in this form of poetry were one-dimensional and similar in their charms:

> The embodiment of beauty
> Young, intelligent
> Graceful, lovely, brilliant
> Thus is the nayika described by all.

The Riti poets began to focus increasingly on descriptions of the physical perfection of the nayika. Specific body parts, such as the woman's breasts, would be described at length and compared, in one instance, bewilderingly, to 'two whirlwinds colliding' or in another impressive geographical allusion as 'shattering the pride of haystack, dome, mountains and even Himalaya.' In fact, so detailed did these physical descriptions become that a separate subgenre of Riti poetry, the Nakh-Sikh or toe to the top of the head, became the most popular category of this form of poetry. In this genre, Radha was used to describe all facets of the perfect woman in love, from Padmini or the lotus woman of the *Kama Shastra* to the Citrini or woman of the arts—fond of dance, song and poetry. As writer Karine Schomer has pointed out in 'Where Have all the Radhas Gone?', Radha became depersonalized, an abstract symbol rather than a woman haunted by love.

Thus, by the end of the second millennium, Radha had drifted in two opposite directions. From the earthly world of Vrindavan where 'the cows are well fed and rich in milk and the fields are awash with the pastel shades of ripening rice', to the eternal celestial paradise of Goloka where she is the queen of the universe, the heavenly Radharani. According to the *Brahamavraita Purana*, Krishna's very reason for coming to earth from Goloka is to accompany Radha. Unhinged by her jealousy towards the other gopis, Radha quarrels with Sridama, Krishna's attendant. Sridama then curses Radha, she is expelled from Goloka and born on earth to a human mother.

Radha is now that most despised of women, the screeching nag, and has fallen so low that even a servant has power over her. Even the delicious ambiguity of the episode when Nanda tells Radha to take Krishna home is hopelessly altered. In this version, Krishna is a handsome youth living in an improbable house of gems and he reminds Radha pedantically of their former existence in Goloka. Brahma himself appears to sanctify their union. Radha and Krishna's Raas Leela is preordained and sanctified, so the issue of Radha's legitimacy and parakiya status becomes unimportant. Her defiance of all worldly sanctions is now unnecessary and Radha is disempowered. Her love in separation is merely symbolic, since she is now the eternal consort.

On the other hand, the excessive erotic obsession of the Riti poets had transformed her into a Ramani (a sexually enjoyable woman) and a Kamini (a desirable woman). Moreover, the descriptions of Radha's beauty and erotic love were for the purpose of creating the Sringara mood and were almost voyeuristic in their tone. Radha had become a woman for men to lust over, rather than someone women identify with. In the twentieth century, as Karine Schomer has shown, this depiction of Radha slowly disappeared from contemporary Indian literature. In the landscape of emerging nationalism, there was no place for the imagery of the Riti poets. Not only were the poets now distancing themselves from the theme of Sringara Rasa, but the very language of the Riti poets, Brajbhasha, fell into disrepute. This lyrical dialect, born in the mythical context of the Mahabharat and forever associated with the Bhakti poems, was no longer considered appropriate for the age of nationalism. The modern poets now wrote in Hindi and embraced nationalism, turning their attention to martial women like Rani Laxmibai and Rani Padmini. Languid and erotic depictions of women fell out of favour.

As Ratna Kapur has pointed out, the idea of women's purity, safeguarded within the home and representing the purity of Indian culture, was fiercely guarded. This instinct was, of course, shaped by the rules of Victorian sexuality imposed by the British Raj. Women's sexual purity became synonymous with Indian culture, and separate and apart from a 'corrupting' western model.

In the last decades of the twentieth century, the revival of interest in mythology in mainstream culture—via popular television serials and bestselling books on the Indian epics—brought Radha back into people's homes, usually sanitized, deified or infantilized. In Ekta Kapoor's 2008 TV series *Kahaani Hamaaray Mahaabhaarat Ki*, the initial meeting of Radha and Krishna takes place in an altogether different environment than what is described in the ancient texts—the two meet in front of a Lakshmi-Vishnu temple where Radha has come to pray, thereby setting her firmly within the Stri Dharma tradition of the pious Hindu woman. This Radha is a composed woman, leery of Krishna's intentions. When Krishna asks her who she is, she tells him that she doesn't speak to strange men. This Radha is weighed down by jewellery and make-up and covered in layers of clothes—gone is the Radha dressed in garlands of flowers who dances with great abandon.

Heidi Pauwels has pointed out that in Ramanand Sagar's hugely popular 1993 TV series *Shri Krishna*, even the gopis are careful not to transgress the bounds of maryada, or wifely duties, during the Raas Leela. In one scene, their 'physical bodies' are depicted dutifully at home, serving food to their husbands and looking after the children while their spectral bodies rush in the direction of the sound of Krishna's flute.

◆

India is a land teeming with gods and goddesses. There is the bewilderingly large number of Hindu deities to which may be added the borrowed avatars from other religions. This vast tribe of gods is both a benediction and a constraint. Our cultural memories are wrought by the grace of magnificent goddesses and powerful devis. This can very often be a source of comfort and strength to many women but, paradoxically, it can also be suffocating and restricting. Very often, the stories of the goddesses are used to convey a subtle message reinforcing accepted patriarchal values. In addition, so poweful and formidable are these goddesses that it is often impossible for everyday women to identify with them. They are objects of veneration and awe, certainly, but not of tender empathy.

In choosing the second woman from mythology to include in this collection of portraits I wanted to find a character who had not only done something extraordinary, but whose actions resonated with ordinary women through the ages. Radha is unique in that, her popularity has not only increased over time, but that she is a truly pan-Indian goddess, beloved in every region in this land. There have been young Radhas as daughters in every caste, community and corner of India. Rather unusually, Radha is adored equally by both male bhakts and women devotees and by people from non-Vaishnava sects, for whom she remains a comforting presence in household shrines or in subliminal memory.

Radha's enduring appeal has to do with the fact that she channels an emotion that is at the very heart of the human condition— anguished longing in the face of impossible odds. Radha pursues this forbidden love in the face of every possible obstacle. Krishna has other lovers, society is disapproving and she even acts against her own better judgement. Yet what Radha is ultimately able to achieve is a reciprocal love on her own terms, on an equal footing with the object of her adoration. That is a triumph not only for the simple village girl that she is but for any Indian woman. The Hindu epics have not generally been kind to sexually assertive and confident women. Ravana's sister Surpanakha, seduced by Ram's virile beauty, wishes to marry Ram (believing him to be umarried). In return she is mocked, humiliated and then tortured and disfigured by having her nose sliced off by Lakshman, a shocking act for a warrior and a prince. Savitri marries a man of her choice, Satyavan, but to do so she must become an exemplary woman in every way, an impeccable wife and daughter-in-law. Radha, on the other hand, remains flagrantly human. She rails and chides and sulks.

She is tormented by jealousy and is assailed by foreboding and the imminence of loss. And yet her own society and the earlier writers of her story are complicit in her illicit love. They understand that a transgression is needed to forge this sublime love.

For so many women in India, the partner they choose or are assigned will determine the future trajectory of their lives. And yet, even a cursory examination of Indian society today shows us how little control most women exercise in this most vital decision. Women, and men, are tortured and murdered for the crime of loving people of the wrong caste, religion or background. So alarming has this practice become that there is even a call for specific legislation to deal with the perpetrators, either individuals or khap panchayats, of the shameful atrocity that is 'honour killing' in the subcontinent today. At the core of this violence is that ancient and noxious idea of shame, and the linking of women's chastity to male honour. The particular ferocity of these attacks on women is an eloquent testimony to the deep malaise in some sections of Indian society. Fathers have beheaded daughters, brothers have scalded sisters with acid and entire villages have stood by silently while young girls have been burnt to death.

Radha, on the other hand, is never shackled by notions of shame or retribution. She is superbly free in all her actions and her society, though it may mutter disapprovingly sometimes, never punishes her for her transgressions. Radha's obsessive love resonates with us even today because we empathize with that longing and yearn for a similar, incorruptible love.

Ambapali
The Glory of Vaishali

480 BCE. Vaishali, in eastern India, on the northern frontier of modern day Bihar, is a gana-sangha or large town fortified on three sides with thick mud walls and guarded with gates and watchtowers. A wide and busy arterial street—thronged with townsfolk, labourers, bullock carts and travelling mendicants—runs through the town. A century later, one of Alexander the Great's admirals, Nearchus, will describe the clothes worn by the people of Vaishali as mostly cotton, 'of a brighter white colour than found anywhere else' which 'the darkness of the Indian complexion makes so much whiter'. Nearchus's description is admiringly detailed, he talks of 'the parasols used as a screen for the heat and the shoes of white leather, whose soles are made of great thickness, to make the wearer seem so much taller'. The houses of Vaishali are of mud and brick and well built, and the larger ones, which are numerous, have a central courtyard and sometimes an enclosed garden with lotus flowers, hibiscus shrubs and fragrant mango trees. Outside the town is a coronation tank and several sacred enclosures and groves. These are the kuhala-shalas, the spaces where audiences gather to hear the different truths spoken by passing holy men. Beyond the groves lie a number of villages dotting the emerald rice fields and, finally, there is the thick forest, spreading its way right up to the foothills of the Himalayas.

There is a large crowd at one of the kuhala-shalas this monsoon evening. The man they are impatiently waiting for, and who arrives at last in a swirl of ochre robes, is one of the greatest sons of India. In this age of the wanderers, he is the greatest parivrajaka of all. He is Siddhartha—the Awakened and Enlightened One—the Buddha.

A woman stands on the balcony of one of the largest houses in Vaishali, watching people streaming towards the kuhala-shala. She wears a diaphanous white and gold skirt and jewellery that shines with precious stones. From the courtyard behind her come the strains of musicians tuning their instruments for the evening's entertainment. As dusk fills the sky, the wealthy men of the town, merchants and noblemen, enter the courtyard and seat themselves on the clean white diwans. This is the salon of the most famous courtesan of Vaishali, Ambapali, who got her name from the mango orchard where she was deserted as a baby. Now Ambapali is the glory of Vaishali and her accomplishments, grace and beauty, are the pride of all the townsfolk. According to the Buddha's biographies, she is 'beautiful, good to look upon, charming, possessed of the utmost beauty of complexion, clever at dancing and singing and lute-playing and much visited by desirous people.' In a more prosaic aside we are told that 'she went for a night for fifty kahapanas' (at a time when a slave could be bought outright for one hundred kahapanas).

The countless spies in her employment have informed Ambapali of the arrival of the Buddha. She has heard of his gentle smile and kind eyes, and the message he carries:

To cease from evil,
To do what is good.
To cleanse one's mind:
This is the advice of all the Buddhas.

Ambapali turns away reluctantly from the veranda to attend to her guests. She resolves to meet the Buddha the next day, perhaps even invite him to her own home for a meal. He is a holy man and she is a courtesan, but she has heard it said that the Buddha does not differentiate between anyone, rich or poor, man or woman. Ambapali doesn't know it yet, but as a result of her encounter with the Buddha, she will destroy all the trappings of her current life and will walk into a whole new reality.

◆

It is from the sixth century BCE onwards that we have a firmer grip on our history as written records of kings—their existence and their achievements—begin to surface. From this period onwards in north India there is a gradual movement towards the Gangetic plains in the east, away from the Punjab and the sacred lands of the Kurus in the Doab. Permanent settlement in towns gives a distinct geographical identity to a clan for the first time. As these towns coalesce into territories that need to be governed, two systems of governance emerge: kingdoms, and republics or gana-sanghas.

The kingdoms spread along the vital river, the Ganga, and control commerce and trade. They rule through hereditary power that slowly acquires legitimation through Kshatriya status and association with Brahminical ritual. Three great kingdoms will emerge by the mid-fourth century BCE—Kashi, Kosala and Magadha. But it is the tribal republics or gana-sanghas which, for a short while, will dominate the Gangetic plains. Within a span of twenty years, the republics of Sakya and Vaishali will witness the births of two of the greatest thinkers of India, and indeed the world: Gautama Buddha and Mahavira. A gathering of republics, including Vaishali, will be locked in bitter battle with the rising kingdom of Magadha and its visionary leader, Bimbisara. It is the biographies of these two extraordinary men, the Buddha and Bimbisara, whose lives would be intertwined with Ambapali's—and the fortuitous foray of the Greek armies to India around the same time—that give us a glimpse of the woman she was.

That the organization of the republics tolerated, and even fostered, various belief systems is highly probable. These republics, which kept something of their tribal origins, were moving away from the strict ritualism of Vedic Brahmanism. Instead of the four caste varnas, the clans only had two. The ruling clan heads were the Kshatriya families and all the other people were dasa-karmakara—slaves and labourers. Not surprisingly, the Brahmin orthodoxy did not think much of these clanships and referred to them as degenerate Kshatriyas, and even Shudras, as they did not observe Vedic ritual. Moreover, instead of the clear stratification of power in a monarchy, the clans governed their territories through an assembly of the heads of the families belonging to the clan. These positions were not hereditary. When discussions could not be resolved, matters were put to the vote.

One of the defining characteristics of the age of the gana-sanghas and early kingdoms was that it was a time of great intellectual and spiritual ferment. There was resistance to the increasingly ossified Brahmin orthodoxy and holy men strode across the lands, holding forth on philosophical topics in order to gain followers.

Ambapali, at the time when the Buddha was visiting Vaishali, would already have been familiar with some of the teachings of these esoteric holy men. Indeed, the great Mahavira, who had died only a few years before, had been a prince of the city. Mahavira's mother belonged to the Licchavi tribe, the leading clan of the Vrishni confederacy of Vaishali. Everyone knew the stories of his asceticism, his rigorous penance, of his wandering naked and reviled until he attained peace. Like Mahavira had done, the Buddha had created an order of female monastics, and called it the Bhikkuni Sangha. His own aunt and foster mother, Mahaprajapati Gotami, shaved her head and took the sacred robes and followed him, beseeching to be allowed to join the sangha. The Buddha was initially reluctant, mindful of the opinion of the patriarchal society they lived in but also of the practical difficulties in ordaining a sisterhood that would function independently. But eventually, the Bhikkuni Sangha was created and hundreds of women would join to live a life of renunciation and meditation.

There had already been women donors and patrons of the Buddha's sangha—and this in itself was extraordinary—but to have ordained women and accorded them the same spiritual potential as men was truly revolutionary. This was at a time when in Brahminical Hinduism, women were prevented from performing religious rites, and even the knowledge of the Vedas was kept away from them. The Vedic-Upanishadic philosophy exalting the male-principle (purusha) held sway and was used to justify the exclusion of women from all relevant social and spiritual activity. These attitudes would become more entrenched in the centuries to follow. When he was compiling his laws at around the same time, Manu seemed to acknowledge the fallibility of men when he warns that they 'be uncouth and prone to pleasure...and have no good points at all'. Even so, we are piously informed, a good wife 'should do nothing independently even in her own house and should ever worship her lord as a god.' Nevertheless, for a time at least—in the republics especially—there was freewheeling enquiry and discourse.

The following day, Ambapali rides to the sacred grove in her horse-drawn chariot, accompanied by the chariots of her maids and female companions. The Buddha greets them with the ease and complicity of an old friend and directs the women to sit in front of him. With their rich clothes and smooth, perfumed skin, the group of women are an incongruous sight amongst the monks.

'Do not go upon what has been acquired by repeated hearing; nor upon tradition; nor upon rumour; nor upon what is in a scripture,' the Buddha begins. These opening lines are rather subversive—in a world of elaborate Vedic rituals they are being asked to put aside all hearsay. 'You yourself must know,' the Buddha adds, 'these things are good; these things are not blamable; undertaken and observed, these things lead to benefit and happiness, enter on and abide in them.' Ambapali is mesmerized by this man who tells her to rely on her own instinct, who looks at her with eyes full of compassion, she who is used to seeing only lust and desire in the eyes of men.

When the Buddha says, 'Subject to birth, old age, and disease, extinction will I seek to find, where no decay is ever known, nor death, but all security,' it is as if he is speaking about Ambapali's deepest fears. His words have a profound effect on her, as she begins to realize that her beauty is an illusion and youth only fleeting. She gets up to bow low before the Buddha and invites him for a meal to her house, along with his coterie of monks. The Buddha smiles and agrees to visit Ambapali the following day.

On the way back to town, she encounters the magnificent chariots of the Licchavis. The clansmen expect Ambapali to make way for them but she, emboldened by the Buddha's acceptance of her invitation, refuses and they must edge past her chariots impatiently. They too are on their way to see the great master and invite him to their homes and are upset to learn they have been pre-empted by this upstart courtesan, this 'mango woman'.

When the Buddha and his followers go to Ambapali's house the next day, it is an act that breaks age-old taboos against caste, food and pollution. Taboos so deep-seated that a mere glance at a menstruating woman, for instance, was considered sacrilege. Given this environment, Ambapali must have been aware of the true extent of the Buddha's generosity when he crosses the threshold of her mansion. He is entering the home of a woman who is neither a child in the care of her father, nor a married woman in the care of her husband, nor a widow virtuously living with her son. He seats himself along with his monks on the floor of the courtyard and Ambapali joins her women in serving the monks.

After the meal is over the Buddha speaks to the women once more about the impermanence of the world of the living and the Eightfold Path of the Dhamma. Craving and the desire for the things of this world causes suffering, he tells them. Give up these cravings now and stop your suffering. Ambapali bows before the Buddha and takes off her ivory bangles, her earrings and heavy gold necklace. Within a few short years of her meeting with the Buddha, she will give away her considerable fortune—her talking parrots, ivory-handled vanity mirrors, carved wooden spice boxes and trunks full of silk—which she has spent a lifetime accumulating, and beg to be ordained into the Bhikkuni Sangha. She will shave her long braid and exchange her fine linen clothes for the coarse ochre ones of the sisterhood.

◆

The Ambapali who steps barefoot onto the forest path is

indistinguishable from the other Bhikkunis—she has completely shed the regalia of the courtesan she once was. This is, however, not the first time that she has reinvented herself. The respectability and fortune she has renounced were hard won, for Ambapali's birth was far from auspicious. She was a child of unknown parentage, discovered abandoned in a mango grove. The gardener who found her brought her up and she grew into a beautiful young girl. We are told that the adolescent Ambapali attracted the attention of a great number of men, and tensions arose over this matter. Probably influenced by the possibility of the wealth to be made from her beauty—her adoptive parents allowed her to be seen, and gauged, by men of influence and power. With prurient men lavishing their attention on her, prostitution could easily have become Ambapali's natural fate. But instead, we learn from one account, so keen was the interest in Ambapali that the clansmen of Vaishali decided to make her a ganika—a courtesan of the city.

The courtesan in ancient India was much more than an exalted prostitute. She was a woman of 'pleasant disposition, beautiful and otherwise attractive, who has mastered the arts... [She] has the right to a seat of honour among men. She will be honoured by the king and praised by the learned, and they will seek her favours and treat her with consideration.' Some of the arts a courtesan or ganika needed to be skilled at, according to the *Kamasutra*, included singing, dancing, drawing, adorning the body, word play, and poetry writing, as well as more esoteric arts such as a knowledge of chemistry and mineralogy, gardening, sorcery and the peculiar art of mimicry. While some of these skills were probably superfluous to most courtesans, it is clear that a ganika was meant to provide witty, entertaining and stimulating company for the discerning and educated men of the city, much in the tradition, in years to come, of the Japanese geisha or the Mughal tawai'f.

The clansmen clearly saw something in the foundling child of the mango grove for them to invest in her education. They would have employed a veshyacharya—a male instructor—to educate her and train her in the arts of seduction. It would have taken years to transform a gauche, illiterate young girl into one of the most admired women of her age. One who could, as a high-ranking, respected courtesan, 'have temples and reservoirs built, arrange pujas and offerings to the gods'. Through fierce intelligence, determination and skill, Ambapali transformed herself from a powerless little girl to the pride of the city and found a place of safety in society without being either a daughter or a wife or a mother.

The Buddha's biographers, writing a few centuries later, use the example of Ambapali as a very useful tool in teachings on sexuality, the nature of women and the impermanence of the body. When a courtesan like Ambapali converted to Buddhism, it demonstrated the Buddhist teaching that all people can be saved, even the greatest of sinners, not only women, but even the worst of women.

While Ambapali was thus transforming herself, Vaishali was living its last decades as an independent state. In the tussle between chiefs and kings, the kingdom of Magadha was gaining ground. The ruler of Magadha, King Bimbisara, used the policy of matrimonial alliances, arguably for the first time in India, by marrying princesses from the ruling families of Koshala and Vaishali to strengthen the position of Magadha. He established an administrative system with officers appointed to various categories of work. He was ruthless in dismissing inefficient officers and involved village headmen in discussions about the best way to govern. He used military means to expand his kingdom, conquering Anga to the southeast. He travelled extensively, exchanging courtesies with all his powerful contemporaries. Bimbisara, and later his son Ajatashatru, were possibly the first Indian kings to dream of an empire far beyond the scope of their ancestral lands. Bimbisara was also an enthusiastic supporter of the Buddha.

The very first canon of Buddhism, the Pali canon, speaks glowingly of Bimbisara's rule. He is believed to have met the Buddha before the latter's enlightenment, when he was still Prince Siddhartha. Bimbisara's initial, rather fatherly, advice to the Buddha was to reclaim his Kshatriya role, to abandon the idea of asceticism and to reclaim his destiny as prince of the Shakya clan. In time, however, Bimbisara became a disciple of the Buddha and an influential donor to the sangha. The Pali canon mentions Bimbisara's generosity but is conspicuously silent about one aspect of his life: his patronage of courtesans, in particular, Ambapali. The later Mahayana version of the canon, however, is more explicit about Bimbisara's liaison with Ambapali. This story appears to have survived in the oral tradition, popular memory and a later Tibetan text. According to these sources, Bimbisara visited Vaishali at some point while Ambapali was still a courtesan. He was in disguise, given his ongoing skirmishing with the Licchavis. It is said that he spent a week in Ambapali's company. That Bimbisara, the most powerful man in the Gangetic plain if not north India, would have heard of Ambapali's beauty and refinement is entirely plausible. Certainly for the pragmatic Ambapali, her alliance with such a man would only have increased her prestige. Though the veracity of this story is not entirely known, what is interesting is that after Bimbisara's liaison with Ambapali the attacks of the Licchavis on Maghada intensified. The war lasted for over a decade. It is quite possible that this liaison was responsible for this upswing in hostilities in the way that the abduction of Helen of Troy sparked off a war. In the end Bimbisara was killed, however, not by the Licchavis but his son Ajatashatru.

In 493 BCE, Ajatashatru, impatient to become the king of Magadha, murdered his father in what is believed to be the first historically documented act of regicide and parricide in India. Tradition has it that Ajatashatru set a bizarre and abominable precedent—he was succeeded by five patricidal kings.

When Ajatashatru became king of Magadha in the early years of the fifth century BCE, it marked the end of the gana-sanghas. He strengthened his capital city of Rajagriha, the famed Pataliputra of the later Mauryan empire, and set about annexing the kingdoms of Kashi and Koshala. During his military campaigns, formidable new weapons were used for the first time including a 'large-sized catapult used for hurling rocks and a chariot fitted with a mace for driving through the enemy's ranks to mow them down.' The clan of the Vrijjis of Vaishali proved the most resilient. In the end, when military might could not succeed, Ajatashatru used deception to sow discord among the various tribes of the Vrijji confederacy and Magadha won the war for supremacy over the Gangetic plains.

At the time when Ambapali asked to be ordained into the sisterhood, Bimbisara had been dead a few years and Ajatashatru had begun his remorseless attacks on the Vrijjis. It is not inconceivable that the death of Bimbisara also led to her decision to renounce all her worldly success. Perhaps the loss of her powerful patron at a time when she was beginning to question the permanence of her beauty and success contributed to the appeal of the Buddha's sermons. What is certain is that when Ambapali stepped barefoot onto that forest path, she was walking into a life of privation and austerity, a world completely removed from the one she had known till then.

As a Buddhist nun, the only possessions Ambapali would have been allowed were a set of clothes: undergarments, an outer garment, a cloak, a waistcloth and a belt with a buckle. These would have been provided by the charity of the lay people, or made by monks from rags, naturally dyed to give them an ochre colour. The only other possessions allowed were practical ones, such as a begging bowl, a razor, a piece of gauze for filtering water to drink, a needle, a walking stick and a bag of medicines. Also permitted were an umbrella made of leaf fronds for walking in the sun and a simple hand fan.

Her days would have been anchored by meditation. After the morning meditation the Bhikkunis would have walked to town, careful never to cross over the threshold of houses, to beg for alms. The sole meal of the day, eaten at midday, would have included rice, chapatti and water. Only the sick were allowed ghee, oil, honey or sugar.

There would also have been certain humiliating restrictions on the nuns. As we have seen, when the Buddha reluctantly established this order of nuns, he was wary of going against the social fabric of the time. He needed to continue functioning amicably within the laity who were the patrons of the Sangha. And so the nuns of the Sangha were always to defer to male monks no matter how junior they be. They were always to be accompanied by monks during pilgrimages and retreats and, most galling of all, a Bhikkhu, or male monk, could admonish a nun, no matter how venerable or old she be, but never vice versa.

In the Pali canon there is a subsection called the *Theratherigatha* (Verses of the Elders) which contains the Psalms of the Sisters. Though these nuns were contemporaries of the Buddha, and would have composed their verses in the sixth century, the poems were only committed to writing in about 80 BCE. These verses are said to be the work of some seventy-three Sisters of the Sangha. Though it is impossible to ascertain how many of these women actually lived or how much of the writing is apocryphal, these verses do give us some insight into the lives of actual women 2,500 years ago. One of these psalms is the Song of Ambapali:

Black and glossy as a bee and curled was my hair:
Now in old age it is just like hemp or bark-cloth.

My hair clustered with flowers was like a box of sweet perfume:
Now in old age it stinks like a rabbit's pelt.

Once my eyebrows were lovely, as though drawn by an artist:
Now in old age they are overhung with wrinkles.

Dark and long-lidded, my eyes were bright and flashing as jewels:
Now in old age they are dulled and dim.

My voice was as sweet as a cuckoo's, who flies in the woodland thickets:

Now in old age it is broken and stammering.

Once my hands were smooth and soft, and bright with
jewels and gold:
Now in old age they twist like roots.

Once my body was lovely as polished gold:
Now in old age it is covered all over with tiny wrinkles.

Such was my body once. Now it is weary and tottering,
The home of many ills, an old house with flaking plaster.
Not otherwise is the word of the truthful.

It may not be a stretch to imagine that these stark and meditative
lines on the impermanence of physical beauty betray a kind of
relief Ambapali would have felt, a laying down of arms, after a life
spent bartering her beauty and her charm for a variety of favours.

That many other women found a form of freedom in the
sisterhood is clear from almost a quarter of the Sisters' Psalms
that describe emancipation—from harassments and burdens in the
physical world—as the reason for joining the Sangha. Some of
the realities the nuns wanted freedom from included intolerable
domestic and social conditions, mental suffering, and the drudgery
of extreme poverty:

O free indeed, O gloriously free am I,

free from three crooked things;
from quern,
    from mortar,
    and my crooked lord

Equally unequivocal is the nun known as Sumangala's mother when
she says:

So thoroughly free am I—

    From my pestle,

My shameless husband
And his sun-shade making,
My moldy old pot
With its water-snake smell.

The monks, on the other hand, were more likely to talk in more noble and abstract terms of the impermanence of the human condition and the rotting of human flesh.

Once Ambapali entered the Sangha, she disappeared into the anonymity and comfort of the sisterhood. Over the next few centuries, the Pali, Chinese and Tibetan canons would recount her story as an anecdote on the conquering of desire and the redemption of sinners, each version slightly altered depending on changing societal conditions. In the Buddha's time, the stories showed no opprobrium for a respected courtesan of independent means, but, as noted earlier, the early Pali texts omit the connection with Bimbisara because he is a valued royal patron while later texts are more ambivalent about the social standing of a ganika.

For the next two thousand years, Ambapali is absent from Indian literature although her story, especially her liaison with a Magadhan king, survives in the oral tradition. It is only in 1948 that she is resurrected in the Hindi novel *Vaishali ki Nagarvadhu* (The Bride of the City) by Acharya Chatursen. Ambapali is altered from the gracious courtesan to a haranguing woman who constantly bemoans the act of injustice perpetrated by the Vaishali clansmen in making her a ganika. When Bimbisara comes to see her, she demands that he punish the Licchavis and conquer Vaishali. It is not hard to see that the author is influenced by nineteenth century Indian and Victorian ideas of morality and sexuality. For instance, there is no description of her dancing and entertaining a group of men as courtesans were required to do; instead, in the novel, Ambapali only dances for individual, worthy men in private, while they, rather chastely, accompany her on the veena.

That Ambapali, in her twentieth century avatar, should be a

woman so bereft of agency is a particuarly galling sacrilege. Ambapali invented and reinvented herself twice in her life. In both instances, she used her intelligence and talent to shape an incandescent destiny far removed from the vulnerable and uncertain beginnings she had. Ambapali lived in a rigid, patriarchal milieu, when a woman's purpose was to be an ideal pativrata who was expected to serve her husband in every way possible, even unto death. This was an age when the only life available for women was to get married and have children, and when they could be repudiated for not giving birth to male children. Despite such male tyranny, she was able to transform herself into an ornament that graced the city she lived in. And then, when she grew tired of that life, Ambapali renounced the security of her wealth to follow an ascetic who, for one of the first times in history, granted the same spiritual potential to women that men were believed to have. While many women joined the Bhikkuni Sangha to escape a life of drudgery, or sorrow, Ambapali left behind a resplendent life seeking a greater glory than the one she had. She had the courage to gamble everything she had fought so hard to achieve for the uncertain but alluring possibility of a life eternal. Ambapali became not only one of the first female followers of the Buddha and then a member of the Bhikkuni Sangha, but also a revered 'Theri', a senior nun. She wrote a haunting poem on the impermanence of life that was recorded in one of the first collections of writing by women in India and possibly anywhere in the world. Through this poem, and her biography in the canon, we can imagine the splendid heroism of this extraordinary woman who, disregarding all male strictures, claimed for herself the ultimate freedom—freedom from rebirth.

Ambapali confronted her fate and chose the only two options available to women outside the sanctity of marriage. In one instance she used her sexuality to gain wealth and respect, and in the other, she renounced it in her quest for immortal life.

Raziya bint Iltutmish

Slave to Sultan

In 1205 CE, when the army of the unified tribes of Mongolia, the Khamag Mongol Ulus or the All Mongol State, rode across grasslands of the central steppes, they kicked up a gigantic column of dust that swirled about them. Along with the rumbling of thousands of hooves and the guttural war cries of the approaching horde their hapless victims would have heard the howling of Tibetan mastiffs, brought from their icy homes, adding to the nightmare. The leader of the horde was the Great Mongol Genghis Khan, the 'Scourge of God'. Within a few decades, the Mongols would have established the largest contiguous empire in the history of the world comprising all the lands between the Caspian Sea and Zhongdu or modern-day Beijing.

That same year, a girl was born to Iltutmish, the first ruler of the Delhi Sultanate, who would grow up to be Raziya bint Iltutmish, the Great Sultan, the first and only Muslim woman monarch in India. Remarkable as it might seem, the rise of the Turkish slave dynasty in Delhi and the enthronement of one of the first women in Islam, was a consequence of the rise of the Golden Horde of Genghis Khan.

From the tenth to the twelfth centuries in India, the development of urban centres slowly shifted westwards from Pataliputra towards the city of Kanauj, in the ancient Indian heartland of Madhya Desha. Kanauj was the great Hindu city of the early medieval period, consecrated by a monumental stone temple and governed by Brahminical orthodoxy and the heirarchy of caste. At this time, Muslim raiders and adventurers conquered the area of Sindh in the northwest, thereby securing the passage of goods to and from the Middle East. This created a porous frontier between the Islamic world—Dar al-Islam—and the 'pagan territory' or Dar al-Harb. As the authority of the Abbasid Caliphate slowly dwindled in

Arabia, semi-independent amirs or governors grew in power; a faction controlled the Sindh province, plundering the riches of India including slaves, cattle, camels, goats, slaves, arms and other valuables. Among these opportunist plunderers was Mahmud of Ghazni whose India campaigns, it was said, 'were like bandit raids—he fought several quick battles, slaughtered enemy soldiers and people in multitudes, destroyed temples and smashed idols and sped back to Ghazni'. A century later, Muhammad Ghori crossed the Hindu Kush and challenged the Hindu kings of the north including, famously, Prithviraj Chauhan. These raids—like the earlier campaigns of Mahmud of Ghazni—left a trail of death and destruction in their wake. As soon as the short north-Indian winter spiked into the heat of spring, the raiders returned to the temperate climate of their homelands. For the Indian heat, as the sixteenth century scholar and historian Muhammad Khwandamir rather glumly stated, 'consumed the body as easily as flame melts a candle.'

At the same time, the formation of the Mongol empire was beginning to have devastating consequences for the people of Central Asia. The nomadic tribesmen of Genghis Khan spread through China and Central Asia razing cities to the ground and assimilating various nomadic tribes. Upon reaching the magnificent city of Bukhara, it is said, Genghis Khan ascended the pulpit at the Friday mosque and announced: 'O people, know that you have committed great sins, and that the great ones among you have committed these sins. If you ask me what proof I have for these words, I say it is because I am the punishment of God.' Ravaged and plundered, the Middle East returned to a nomadic lifestyle, its great cities reduced to dust and rubble.

China suffered too. It had thought itself invincible, guarded by its Great Wall to which six dynasties had contributed—it was twelve metres high and more than 10,000 kilometres long by the thirteenth century. But the Chinese underestimated the Mongol forces, who burst through gaps in the Great Wall and captured

Zhongdu (later Peking and now Beijing). Fortunately, the natural barrier to the northwest of India—the Himalayas—from where the Mongols could have entered the country, was not so easy to penetrate, which was one of the reasons India was spared a similar fate. There was another reason India escaped a large-scale invasion by the Mongols and that was the sturdy Central Asian horse. The great strength of the Mongol horde was also its greatest weakness. Indispensable to the success of the Mongolian tribesmen was their cavalry. Six out of every ten Mongol troopers were mounted archers. Trained from childhood in horsemanship and archery, the Mongols were redoubtable fighters. Clad in light armour, unlike their contemporaries the crusader knights, they were extremely manoeuvrable, quick and mobile. Each Mongol soldier typically maintained three or four horses, changing mounts as they tired. This enabled them to cover huge distances at disconcerting speed. The drawback of this system was that it required a steady and continuous supply of grasslands as pasture for the horses. In India there were no grasslands, only the Hindu Kush, the Thar Desert, and then dense forests and marshy lands further east. In addition to these topographical factors, the presence of the Delhi Sultanate in northern India during the entire period of Mongol supremacy ensured that the nomad armies were kept at bay.

Instead of a Mongol invasion, a corridor opened up between the eastern Islamic world and India. In addition to the regular intrusion by a Muslim elite through the frontier lands, the arrival of people fleeing the Mongol hordes in Central Asia now added to the influx of peoples into India. In the early decades of the thirteenth century, the occasional trickle became a swarm as Delhi became a land of safety and refuge for armies, princes, scholars and artisans from all over Turkestan, Khorasan and Afghanistan. This led to a great mingling of cultures—Persian, Iranian, Turkish and Hindustani—and the exchange of habits, languages, food, music and architecture that would lead, in time, to the magnificent Indo-Islamic composite culture. In the immediate future, however, this converging of people led to the formation of the Delhi Sultanate: a Turkish tribe of slaves who became kings and enthroned the first and only female Sultan of India.

Turks had been recruited as military slaves since the ninth century, when the Abbasid caliphs used them as an elite guard corps in their capital cities. As the power of the caliphs disintegrated, the rising independent amirs used them to shore up their own reigns. By the ninth century, Turkish slaves formed a part of most armies in the Middle East including on Islam's Indian frontier but it was Muhammad Ghori who was most enthusiastic in acquiring them. When he died, in 1206, the rule of his Indian territories fell to his senior slaves and one of them, Qutb-ud-Din, made himself ruler of Lahore from where he controlled much of Pakistan and north India. But Qutb-ud-Din died, falling from his horse, only four years later and in 1210 it was his own slave, Shams-al-Din Iltutmish, who seized the throne and made Delhi the capital of his empire, becoming the first ruler of the Delhi Sultanate—the leading, and sometimes the only, Muslim-ruled state in India for the next two hundred years.

Shams al-Din Iltutmish died of natural causes in 1236 after a reign of twenty-five years. By then, his first-born son and heir apparent, Malik Nasir al-Din, was also dead. Clamouring for the throne of Iltutmish were his oldest surviving son, Rukn al-Din, a dilettante with a concupiscent interest in adolescent boys who was being supported by his mother, a vicious woman by all accounts; his third son, Ghiyas al-Din, commander of Awadh; and unconventionally, for the time, his twenty-nine-year-old unmarried daughter, Raziya. However, the most powerful and volatile player in the mix at this time was not an individual, but a group of men called the Chalisa (the Forty)—the experienced senior slaves among Iltultmish's retinue, also known as the Shamsi Bandagan, military slaves, or Bandagan-i-Khas, the elite slaves.

The rise of the Shamsi Bandagan, essentially a political coalition of slave soldiers, was a phenomenon unique to the Delhi Sultanate.

Through the early decades of the thirteenth century, as the ghulams or satraps were given military command of annexed urban centres, they established slave retinues of their own to help them in their campaigns. As the elite ghulams distinguished themselves through acts of valour or loyalty, or through a personal kinship with the sultan, they rapidly advanced through the Bandagan hierarchy. Unlike in all the other regions of the world in which slavery existed, in the Delhi Sultanate a past as a slave was never a barrier to promotion. The historian Sunil Kumar has pointed out that by the end of Iltutmish's reign in 1236, the influence of the Turkish Bandagan on the political structure of the Sultanate was quite disproportionate to their number and social status.

When Muhammad Ghori formed his Bandagan, they were led by a corps of military slaves of largely Turkish ethnic background, assigned to protect the life of the sultan during military campaigns. Kumar writes that by 'reputation at least, during moments of military crisis, they stood by their master and were the last to retreat.' These slaves, usually procured at a very young age, would have been trained so that they could gradually be given military responsibilities. Removed from the land of their birth and their ethnic origins, they were made to undergo a process of 'natal alienation and social death' that would ideally lead to the creation of strong new ties to each other and to the service of their master, the sultan. Along with their military training, the slaves were given religious instruction in Islam, and tutored in etiquette so they could interact with the sultan and his family without causing too much distress to their royal masters. Some of these slaves were new recruits and trained by the sultans or previously trained by slavers in which case they were much more valuable. Iltutmish, for instance, was highly valued because of 'his comeliness, his fairness, and agreeable manners'. The slavers felt that 'the further (the Turk slaves) are taken from their hearth, their kin and their dwellings, the more valued, precious and expensive they become and they become commanders and generals.' A seventeenth-century Englishman visiting Turkey described this succinctly by saying that 'the Turk loves to be served by his own, such as to whom he hath given breeding and education…and whom he can raise without envy and destroy without danger.' But the danger did exist, as the sultans of Delhi were to find out. As the ties with Ghazni and Afghanistan became increasingly fragile in the thirteenth century, the ghulams of the Bandagan-i-Khas became independent, powerful and ambitious.

When Iltutmish died in 1236, he had already been ailing for a few months and would have taken measures to ensure a smooth transition of power to his successors. Later biographers like Minhaj-i-Siraj Juzjani have claimed that Iltutmish named Raziya his successor because he is reported to have said: 'My sons are devoted to the pleasures of youth, and not one of them is qualified to be king. They are unfit to rule the country, and after my death you will find that there is no one more competent to guide the State than my daughter.' However, no textual evidence exists to back this statement and it is more likely that he promoted his oldest surviving son, Rukn al-Din, whom he appeared to be grooming for leadership, after the death of his first-born son, by giving him the governorship of Lahore. But within months of assuming power and having shifted his residence to the fortified town of Kulukhri, Rukn al-Din was facing revolt from various factions in his court including one from the senior ghulams of the Bandagan and some free amirs of the court. At the same time, his mother, Shah Terken, used her son's ascension to settle old scores in the harem and also had one of Rukn al-Din's half brothers blinded and put to death. It was when she tried to kill Rukn al-Din's half-sister, Raziya, whom she saw as a threat to her son's claim to the throne, that we first hear of the princess who would become the most powerful woman of al-Hind.

Ibn Battuta, writing a century after the event, describes the events that followed Rukn al-Din's attempt to assassinate Raziya: 'She presented herself to the army and addressed them from the roof saying, "My brother killed his brother and he now wants to kill me." Saying this, she reminded them of her father's time and of his good deeds and benevolence to the people.' With this claim to the memory of her father, Sultan Iltutmish, Raziya then asked for justice against Rukn al-Din and his mother. The crowds rallied around her, they stormed the palace and 'he [Rukn al-Din] was killed in retaliation for his brother's death.' Following this, 'the army agreed to appoint Raziya as ruler.'

When Raziya ascended the throne of Delhi in this tumultuous manner, she stood alone without a man beside her—no father, husband or son—asking men to revolt on her behalf at a time when affluent Muslim women were not meant to be seen in public. In the ninth century itself, the Iraqi theologian Al-Jahiz had categorically stated that 'the only purpose of high walls, stout doors, thick curtains, eunuchs, handmaidens and servants is to protect them [women] and to safeguard the pleasure they give.'

◆

There is very little we know about the physical appearance of Raziya, apart from her gender. Standing on the steps of the kusk-i-firuzi or royal residence, she would have been wearing a tunic with long sleeves and a loose fitting shalwar covering her legs and feet. As it was the month of spring, she may have been wearing bright silks embroidered with gold threads. At this stage of her career we know that she was 'veiled from the public gaze', so she would have had a light gauze cloth drawn across the lower half of her face. Her physical features are lost to us since biographers, perfunctory at best even in describing their male subjects, were either silent or censored such details where women were concerned. We do know, however, that she was ethnically Turkish so it is likely that Raziya had the high cheekbones, wind-blown complexion and almond eyes characteristic of the people of the steppes.

Having roused the people of Delhi and foiled the attempt on her life, Raziya now had to confront the competing interests of the free Turkish noblemen, amirs from tribes such as the Khalaj, Ghuris, Tajiks and also some Mongols. Allegiances were made and then paid for in blood when they failed to pay off. The violence that defined succession politics in the Delhi Sultanate had much to do with the particular nature of the Turkish slaves. Recruited as military mercenaries, although they were malleable and ferocious warriors they could often prove to be dangerous to those who used them.

While unquestioned loyalty to the master was one of the primary attractions of a slave retinue, there were times when the reality was different. Raziya's father Iltutmish, himself a slave, carefully promoted after years of training, acted with savage and murderous disloyalty at the death of his king and benefactor, Qutb ud-Din. Qutb ud-Din had nominated his son Aram Shah to take over as Sultan upon his death, but it was his beloved slave Iltutmish—in whom 'the signs of rectitude were, time and again, manifest and clear in his actions and thoughts'—who seized the throne for himself. Iltutmish had spent years as military commander in the provinces of the Sultanate and had acquired a large and carefully trained following of soldiers himself. Backed by these soldiers, he made his move when the time was right, despite opposition from the free amirs as well as some of the other senior ghulams, who baulked at the idea of serving under one of their own. Later chroniclers were clearly uncomfortable about Iltutmish's actions and preferred to skate over this episode, almost eliding Aram Shah from history. That a much valued and loyal slave, supposed to protect the Sultan and his family with his own life, should so quickly and unequivocally destroy his master's lineage was an abomination. Sensing the magnitude of the opposition to his move, Iltutmish added legitimacy to his claim by marrying a princess—Qutb ud-Din's daughter.

When Iltutmish died, his ghulams—especially the Bandagan-i-Khas—had to decide whether to transfer their loyalty to the heirs of their master who had trained them and raised them to positions of power. Reputations and cliques formed over a quarter of a century of negotiations and advancements suddenly disappeared overnight. The prerogative of the elite of the Bandagan-i-Khas was to maintain their power structures as fiercely as possible. This brought them immediately and violently into opposition with the free amirs and the heirs to the throne who wanted to realign the balance of power.

After Rukn al-Din had been deposed, the ghulams of the court who had rebelled against him now installed Raziya on the throne. These slaves undoubtedly believed that a woman—and one who had until then lived in seclusion—would be malleable and would maintain the status quo they had enjoyed under Iltutmish's reign. Raziya's behaviour in the coming months would prove what a grave error of judgement this was.

The first measure Raziya took was to neutralize the threat from some of the senior amirs who had challenged Rukn al-Din's authority. These powerful nobles and ghulams had fallen out of favour with Iltutmish or Rukn al-Din and were therefore interested in creating chaos that they could use to their advantage. Soon after Raziya's ascension, they laid siege to Delhi. Among this group were the senior ghulam Kabir Khan, the freeborn amirs Ala al-Din Jani and Izz al-din Muhammad Salari, and Wazir Junaidi. Raziya showed enormous skill in handling these fractious warlords. She appeased Kabir Khan with the governorships first of Lahore and then Multan and won over Muhammad Salari; when the others proved recalcitrant, she did not hesitate in using stronger tactics— she had Ala al-Din Jani killed and the wazir forced into retirement.

Once the immediate threat of revolt had been taken care of Raziya turned her attention to the junior ghulams, the so-called 'Turks of the court'. These slaves, the original Shamsi slaves of Iltutmish, became crucial players in the politics of the Delhi Sultanate. Apart from their indispensable role in the armies, some of the more valued ghulams were given high office at the court of the sultans. They had ceremonial roles such as cupbearer, holder of the royal parasol or administrator of the royal stables. Raziya rewarded loyal ghulams and amirs with these positions. Junior slaves who had supported her during the revolt of the older ghulams, obtained high office and recognition for the first time. Thus Balaban 'the Lesser' was promoted from falconer to chief huntsman. Ikhtiya al-Din Altunia, a slightly more senior slave, was given the governorship of Barain, and Ikhtiyar al-Din Aytegin was given the coveted post of amir-hajib (sometimes translated as 'Lord Chamberlain'). Aytegin and Tughril Khan, who would have been on the verge of high office at the time of Iltutmish's death, now became, in effect, the Bandagan-i-Khas. Rather ominously though, as opposed to the old Bandagan-i-Khas under Iltutmish, they did not have their power granted to them by the Sultan but rather 'reached their powerful positions by holding the Sultan [Raziya] hostage.'

While rewarding crucial members of the Shamsi ghulams, Raziya was equally careful to patronize the non-Shamsi ghulams and Turks. Like Rukn al-Din before her, she was desperate to break the monopoly of the ghulams at court. When the Turkish commander of the guard, Sayf al-Din Aybeg, died his post was given to a Ghuri Malik, Qutb al-Din Hasn. She gave the strategic governorship of Barain to the son of Hasan Qarluq, the Khwarazmian nobleman whom she had welcomed to her court.

Eminent noblemen had been drifting into the court of the Delhi Sultanate since the time of Iltutmish, fleeing the Mongols and other raiders or seeking advancement and opportunities. The Khwarazmian empire had been decimated after a Mongol caravan sent on a friendly mission was slaughtered by the Khwarazmians. Enraged, Genghis Khan himself led his armies to war and directed the destruction of the fabled cities of Samarkhand and Bukhara. When Sultan Jalal al-Din Khwarazm Shah sought sanctuary at Iltutmish's court, the Sultan refused probably wisely deciding against drawing the attention of Genghis Khan. Iltutmish also preferred to promote the 'socially dead', who would remain dependent on his patronage and were unlikely to create alternative power bases. Raziya, on the other hand, could not count on the unquestioned loyalty of the Shamsi ghulams or the free amirs. She had to maintain a delicate balance between different factions at court and in the provinces. In transferring the ghulams and amirs, she was making sure, like her father before her, that the men did not form powerful local ties within their domains.

Juzjani tells us that once these rebellions were quelled, 'the kingdom became pacified and the power of the state widely extended...all the *Maliks* and *Amirs* manifested their obedience and submission.' Even Isami, the fourteenth century historian writing a hundred years later about Raziya's reign, said that '[the] renowned woman threw herself into the tasks of administration and men of experience firmly resolved to serve her.' 'She ruled as an absolute monarch for four years,' added Ibn Battuta. 'She mounted horse like men armed with bow and quiver; and she would not cover her face.'

Raziya could now redirect her energy to ruling her kingdom and holding court at the kusk-i-firuzi at Mehrauli. The court was a public assembly and Raziya would have sat on a throne, a large, high-backed chair with a red canopy above it, flanked by a bodyguard of slaves armed with swords. In her court, there would have been Tajik bureaucrats, Persian adventurers and noblemen, holy men, scholars and Indian Muslims and other assorted Turkish and non-Turkish tribesmen. From the chronicles of the Ghaznavid Bayhaqi we can guess at what the slave guards, Central Asian men with high cheekbones and long black hair coiled in braids, would have been wearing: 'rich robes, bejeweled belts and sashes, and weapons decorated with gold and silver.' They would have been carrying maces, their traditional weapon, as well as various other items suspended from their belts, including a wallet, in the Central Asian fashion.

Isami has noted that Raziya's throne was initially separated from the courtiers and the public by a screen and that there were female guards standing next to her, as she was nominally still in purdah at the beginning of her reign. Later on, she would have sat in full view of the court, listening to her supplicants' entreaties and dispensing quick justice. In the evenings she would have attended the durbar where she would have witnessed a great alchemy of musical genres—Indian, Persian, classical and folk. There would have been scholars, artisans and performing artistes from the major centres of Islamic culture. Slaves would have walked around offering betel leaves to those present and the evenings would have culminated in banquets of chicken, goat, rice, roast beef and breads.

◆

The kingdom Raziya inherited from her father stretched from Delhi in the west to Lakhnauti in Bengal to the east. Under Raziya's reign, the autonomy of some of the eastern territories was virtually conceded to the powerful muqta of Lakhnauti, Toghan Khan. In dealing with independent powers, she was pragmatic. The fortress of Ranthambore had been under siege by the Chauhans for some time when Raziya came to power. She sent a force under Qutb al-Din Hasan to evacuate the Muslim garrison posted there and to destroy all the fortifications the Muslims had built. Similarly, in Gwalior, Sanajr-i-Qabaqulaq secured the Muslim population and brought them back to Delhi. Both Ranthambore and Gwalior passed back into the hands of Hindu kings—a reality the older Shamshis, for whom these had been major conquests, would have bitterly resented.

Iltutmish had also had a new system of coinage launched, based on the pure silver tanga which would eventually replace the dihliwals minted by the Hindu rulers of Delhi. Raziya had these coins minted with her own titles. Initially, these coins carried both her father's name as well as hers, proclaiming Iltutmish as Sultan al-Azam (the Greatest Sultan) and herself with the subordinate title of Sultan al-Mu'azzam (the Great Sultan), and reinforcing her legitimacy as Bent-al-Sultan (Daughter of the Sultan). In the early years of her reign she would have needed the weight of her father's title, but by 1238 Raziya had grown enough in confidence to have the coins minted in her own name: Al-Sultan al-Muazzam Radiyyat al-Din. Cultural historian and writer Alyssa Gabbay notes that 'she appears both on the coins and in the early histories with the gender-neutral and awe-inspiring sobriquet of Sultan: the king, the leader.' In her own lifetime, Raziya never opted for the title 'Sultana', the queen, an adjunct to the male power, the king.

At some point during her reign, Raziya abandoned purdah. Juzjani tells us that 'the sultan put aside female dress, and issued from [her] seclusion, and donned the tunic, and assumed the head-dress [of a man], and appeared among the people.' Raziya's appearance, though, would not have altered drastically as the Muslim garb for both men and women at the time was fairly similar and modest—a long tunic and loose pants. However, Raziya appeared in public with the quba (ceremonial cloak) and the kulah (pointed Turkish hat). Without her veil 'when she rode out on an elephant, at the time of mounting it, all people used, openly, to see her.' The removal of the veil was essential for Raziya to dissociate herself from being simply a female, and as such, 'naqes al-aql, deficient in intelligence, and therefore more prone to evil than men.' Without the veil the people could see more clearly the face of kingship, of power and of military strength. In the sixteenth century, Rani Durgawati dressed as a soldier to fight Akbar's Mughal troops and six hundred years after Raziya, Rani Laxmibai of Jhansi would also abandon feminine garb when she rode into battle against the British colonizers. Both Rani Durgawati and Rani Laxmibai, however, were dowager queens fighting for the rights of their infant sons. Raziya's claim to being Sultan was her conviction that she was the most capable of her siblings.

Alyssa Gabbay has argued that Raziya was part of a long line of Muslim women, including the Sassanian queens of Boran and Azarmidokht, who discarded their female attire as monarchs. In the subcontinent, however, such examples are rare. Though gender identities are more porous than those in the West, it is usually the men who cross-dress. Arjuna in the Mahabharat dresses as a woman and mistress of dance when he lives disguised as a eunuch in King Matsya's court as part of the terms of his exile. There is a great tradition of mystics, such as Ramakrishna and Chaitanya Mahaprabhu, dressing as women to symbolize the ideal devotee.

Indeed, in Sufi mysticism as in Buddhism and Hinduism, the only 'true male' or purusha is God, everyone else must approach Him with the humility of a woman. It is as though a man's virility is inviolable, sacrosanct and the wearing of women's clothes is just a game, which never fundamentally challenges that virility; but when a woman wears a man's clothes a fault line appears in society.

◆

By promoting the Ghurids and Khwarazmians and giving the powerful office of intendant of the imperial stables (Amir-i-Akhuri), to an outsider, Raziya was trying to curb the influence of her father's ghulams following his example of distributing power between loyal personages unlikely to have powerful local ties. The man she chose was an Abyssinian, an African malik called Jamal al-Din Yaqut. Therefore, when Raziya chose to elevate Malik Yaqut, she was following her father's example in distributing power between strong and loyal personages unlikely to have powerful local ties.

Financed by Indian bankers, Arab Muslim slave traders had been sending African slaves to India from East and North Africa possibly as early as the fourth century. These Habshis—derived from the old name for Ethiopians (Abyssinians)—'were employed in very specialized jobs, as soldiers, palace guards, or bodyguards: they were able to rise through the ranks becoming generals, admirals and administrators.' They were specially sought after as warriors in the Deccan, as the Delhi Sultans had called a moratorium on the use of Turkish slaves in the south. So powerful did the African Malik Ambar become in the politics of Ahmednagar, for example, that Jahangir, the Mughal emperor who was directing his attention towards the Deccan, was piqued enough to refer to him in his memoirs as 'Ambar of dark fate' and 'that crafty, ill-starred one'.

By this time Raziya had been sultan for over three years, steadily consolidating her power. Unfortunately, her decision to promote Malik Yaqut backfired—by showing favour to a rank outsider, who was not even a Turk, it created an atmosphere of uncertainty at court to which the Turkish ghulams reacted in the way they often had, with violence and blood-letting.

The first one to rebel was Kabir Khan, who had earlier been pacified by the iqta of Lahore. Affronted by what he saw as Raziya's increasing autonomy, Kabir Khan rose in revolt in Lahore, five hundred kilometres away. Faced with this betrayal, Raziya refused to make any more concessions and, in 1239, she rode to Lahore at the head of the imperial army comprising Turks, Indians and Persians, all unquestioningly following their leader against a powerful fellow ghulam, an erstwhile brother of the band. She confronted him at the Chenab River, another hundred kilometres further. Crushed on one side by Raziya's army and on the other by the threatening hordes of Genghis Khan, Kabir Khan yielded to his sultan.

The amirs and ghulams now organized a more extensive revolt. Raziya was lured out of Delhi, where she was enormously popular, by a general uprising at Tabarhindh (in modern-day Bathinda, Punjab). The amir of Tabarhindh, Altunia, had been conspiring with Aytegin, the amir-hajib at the court of Delhi. When Raziya marched out, Yaqut, who had been left behind in Delhi, was seized by the rioters and killed. Raziya herself was overpowered at Tabarhindh and imprisoned in the fort.

In the end, Raziya was undone by the game of careful brinkmanship she attempted. She was betrayed by the very men she had earlier promoted in a bid to win their loyalty—Aytegin and Altunia. After they had her imprisoned, the amirs enthroned her half-brother Muizz al-Din Bahram Shah as sultan, but only after he had agreed to the creation of the new post of 'viceroy' for the amir-hajib, Aytegin. To further secure his imperial ambitions, Aytegin married Bahram Shah's sister, much as Iltutmish had done by marrying Qutb ud-Din's daughter. Bahram Shah, however, was not unaware of these manoeuvres and he eventually had Aytegin captured and killed. Altunia, now finding himself without his main ally, unexpectedly had Raziya released and married her. This marriage was a pragmatic transaction between Altunia and Raziya—he gained an ally to replace the one he'd lost and Raziya got another chance to reclaim the throne of her father.

Despite her months of incarceration at Tabarhindh, Raziya was quick to realize that this would be her last chance to reclaim the throne of Delhi and was able to raise a considerable force that included Hindu Khokkars from Punjab, Jats and other tribes, as well as some amirs (who were still loyal) and Turks and mercenaries. Together with Altunia, Raziya marched to Delhi to confront her half-brother, the pretender to the throne, Bahram Shah. In this battle, led by Bahram himself, Raziya's army was routed, the Hindu soldiers deserted, and the surviving members scattered through the countryside. Raziya and Altunia were able to escape but were eventually overcome and killed while fleeing the neighbourhood of Kaithal in modern-day Haryana.

It is fitting that Raziya died as she had lived, fighting to regain what she saw as her lost inheritance, a warrior daughter of a slave king.

Amir Khusro, the Sufi poet and scholar, born half a century after Raziya, wrote of her:

For three years in which her hand was strong
No one laid a finger on one of her orders.
In the fourth, since the page had turned from her matters
The pen of fate drew a line through her.

Raziya's only true contemporary chronicler, Juzjani, writes generously of her talents:

She was a great sovereign and sagacious, just, beneficent,
the patron of the learned, a dispenser of justice, the
cherisher of her subjects, and of warlike talent, and was
endowed with all the admirable attributes and qualifications
necessary for kings: but as she did not attain the destiny,
in her creation, of being computed among men, of what
advantage were all these excellent qualifications unto her?

Peter Jackson has shown that there was a fortuitous confluence of circumstances at the beginning of the Delhi Sultanate that made it easier for a woman to be respected in a position of authority. The nomadic background of the Turkish ghulams, especially those from the Pontic and Caspian steppes, meant that they were used to seeing women assume a more public role. Some of the ghulams were of Khitan or Qara-Khitan stock, Mongol-type pagan converts to Islam who founded dynasties in Turkestan. They would have had the example of Koyunk Khatun, a twelfth-century daughter of a Khitan leader, who ruled Turkestan after the death of her father. The Turk ghulams of the Sultanate, many of them first generation converts from the pagan steppes, never appeared to resent her gender. Indeed, Raziya's brothers Rukn al-Din and Bahram Shah were deposed much more quickly than Raziya was when they challenged the power of the ghulams. Raziya herself seemed to have regarded her gender as no hindrance and discarded purdah when it got in the way of her governing her kingdom. Though we cannot claim with certainty that Iltutmish intended her to rule after him, it is certain that she received the same education as her brothers growing up, as her talents and skill demonstrate.

But if Raziya and her contemporaries had a gallant disregard for her gender, the same was not true of future generations. Isami was the first to write about her reign in more gender-driven terms: 'I am told that she came out of purdah suddenly, discarded her modesty and became jovial.' In case his insinuation at slighting her is not clear, Isami further adds, 'everyone high and low used to enjoy the sight of her face.' And finally Isami concludes with a rambling diatribe on the many failings of women, from the appalling ('when the passions of a pious woman are inflamed, she concedes to an intimacy even with a dog') to the more specific ('to wear the crown, and fill the throne of kings, does not benefit a woman: this is the role exclusively meant for the experienced type of man').

One could argue that Isami was writing in the fourteenth century, but the legacy of Raziya even in the twenty-first century has not fared much better. As recently as 2015, a TV series called *Razia Sultan*, purporting to be a historical drama, sabotaged the memory of a remarkable woman and turned it into an over-wrought and sensational love triangle between a scheming outsider, Yaqut, and a jealous and 'rakish' childhood love, Altunia. The show advertises Raziya as 'a lively, bright-eyed princess with no big aspirations. Just a curious little girl who grew up seeking answers… She loved her father Iltutmish the most'.

She was the daughter of a king, but Raziya, after an initial period of relying on her father's legacy, then actively distanced herself from Iltutmish and ruled unaided by any man. She became the sultan, ruling with her own titles—a remarkable achievement for a Muslim woman in the medieval world at a time when her female contemporaries in Europe, for instance, influenced by the Roman Catholic Church, were confined within the walls of their homes and kept out of all spheres of influence. The very few women of any political consequence at all were regents of their sons, or exceptions like Joan of Arc.

When Minhaj-i-Siraj Juzjani tabled the long list of rulers in Iltutmish's dynasty, he did Raziya the great honour of crediting her as the only war-leader—a Lashgarkash.

Meerabai

Dyed in Blue

It is the early decades of the sixteenth century and the hill fort of Chittor has been under siege by Bahadur Shah of Gujarat for months. Early one day, the great doors of the fort are thrown open and the bards march out, followed by thousands of horsemen, warriors of the Sisodia clan, all dressed in saffron and white with ash smeared across their foreheads. With no possibility of victory left to them, these Rajput warriors are leaving to perform the saka ritual—to fight and die an honourable death on the battlefield. As historian John Keay has written, '[W]hen all was lost, when the last scrap of food had been eaten, the last arrow fired, the last water-skin emptied...the men rode out in a still brighter blaze of glory to kill until they were killed.' The night before the saka, all the Rajput noblewomen, dressed in their bridal finery and accompanied in death by their female attendants and minor children, had committed jauhar in the underground caverns of the fort—burning themselves alive on a sandalwood pyre to protect their honour rather than risk defilement at the hands of the enemy. Liberated thus from all earthly attachment—to wives, mothers and sisters—the warriors were able to wear the saffron of sacrifice and ride into battle one last time.

Only a few years before, a woman had stepped out of a fort much like this, perhaps this very one, out of the strict purdah of her married status into the unknown dangers of the open road. A woman who defied every virtue sanctified by the jauhar: clan loyalty unto death, self-sacrifice for the community's honour, the decorum and claustrophobia of strict purdah. A noblewoman, who relinquished her birthright of luxury and comfort, a widow, who shunned sati and thought of herself as eternally married, and a daughter-in-law, who refused all the strictures of her married home and would not bow to the family deity. Her name was Meera and her enduring legacy is both a mystery and an absolution.

In medieval north India, with the disintegration of the Delhi Sultanate and then the Gurjara Pratiharas, the area of Rajputana gradually came to be dominated by a group of mixed-caste chieftains who possessed some land. These chieftains expanded their estates with a violence that would become their defining trait. They gained control of tribal territories—of the Bhil, Ahir and other tribes— and incorporated them into their republics. These small kingdoms were in a constant state of warfare with other clans as well as the Turks, and later the Mughals and the Marathas. As a result, they formed strong bonds of dependence between rulers, clans and vassals. Rajaputras, or Rajputs as they came to be called from the twelfth century onwards, was a descriptive term for men on horseback who pursued social mobility through military conquest. They built forts to defend their territories and to consolidate their power and slowly Hinduized their origins, claiming the varna status of the Kshatriyas.

The core of the Rajput army was its cavalry, the horses a symbol of great prestige. The people of Rajasthan had been breeding the Marwari—a sturdy horse, specially adapted to heat and trained to fight the war elephant, a ferocious creature that had swords strapped to its trunk—for several centuries. The Rajputs worshipped swords, believed to be made by the Hindu god of weapons and, according to Kshatriya rites, the battle itself was viewed as a sacrificial fire into which soldiers offered themselves. On such a divine battlefield, the outcome of the war hardly seemed to matter, since death was a direct conduit to heaven. In the nineteenth century, the first British official to visit Rajputana, Colonel James Tod, discovered this martial class with tales of heroism equal to anything Britain had to offer. In his voluminous *Annals and Antiquities of Rajas'than*, Tod talks as much about Mewar as all the other Rajput kingdoms combined and detailed exploits 'exemplifying chivalry, honour, fondness for opium and weakness for women.' Tod was not the only observer of Rajput valour. Upon witnessing yet another jauhar at the end of a battle, the marauding Khilji forces also 'marveled that principalities so agriculturally disadvantaged and forts so poorly endowed with treasure should occasion such passionate resistance.' Surrounded by predatory and competing tribes as well as opportunist Turks and other Muslims, the Rajput republics became closely guarded societies with increasingly ritualized and sequestered social norms and an abiding obsession with ritual and caste pollution and purity. This abhorrence of pollution was to culminate in the excesses of untouchability as when the Dalits under the Peshwa rule in the seventeenth century were made to hang a broom from their backs, to sweep away their 'polluting' footsteps and a pot below their neck to collect their 'polluting' saliva. In Rajasthan the most closeted members of Rajput society were its women—the world that Meera was born into.

Very little is known about the historical Meera. There doesn't even exist a corpus of poetry that can convincingly be associated with her. There are hundreds of poems in the Meera style but only twenty-two bearing her signature have been found in manuscripts predating 1700 and fifteen of the poems have been lost. All the details we now assume about her life have been pieced together from clues left behind in her poetry. The oldest surviving biography of Meera is Nabhadas's *Bhaktamal*, written in the beginning of the seventeenth century, some hundred years after she died. The *Bhaktamal* contains the following lines about Meera:

Meera unravelled the fetters of family
She surrendered the chains of shame to sing
Of her mountain-lifting lover and lord.

That the oldest authenticated surviving document about Meerabai is concerned with female honour—izzat, and its necessary corollary, shame (laaj or sharam in Hindi)—who possesses it and who imposes it and the ways in which women defy it, is not surprising. The patriarchal, feudal society that Meera was born into was one that placed a high value on a woman's purity. To follow her heart, Meera would have to abandon all shame and sacrifice the ties of kinship and clan that would have been branded on her consciousness since she was a child.

It is believed that Meera was born in Kudki village in Rajasthan possibly around 1498, around the time Vasco da Gama was landing in Kozhikode on the Malabar Coast. Most scholars agree that Meera was born into a noble Rathore family. One likely contender for Meera's maternal family is Rao Dudaji, a patriarch who had won the fortress city of Medta from the Muslims. Meera's mother, if she indeed was the granddaughter of Rao Dudaji, died young, and her father, Ratan Singh, was too caught up fighting in local wars to raise a child, so Meera was sent to her grandfather's palace at Medta. The birth of a daughter, in most communities, would not have been a cause for much rejoicing. Since the time of the Mahabharat, stark injunctions had been pronounced regarding this unsatisfactory outcome:

> The birth of a daughter in the families of those that are well behaved and high born and endowed with fame and humility of character is always attended with evil results. Daughters when born in respectable families always endanger the honour of their families, viz their maternal and paternal families and the family into which they are adopted by marriage.

Meera's family were Vaishnavites and the house she grew up in would have contained the familiar iconography of Krishna worship. Legend has it that when Meera was a little girl, she saw a wedding procession passing by the window and asked her mother who her own bridegroom was. Taken aback, Meera's mother pointed to a statue of Krishna and told her that He was her bridegroom. Whether Meera took this to heart or whether growing up effectively an orphan in her grandfather's palace she chose the abiding comfort of her family's favourite god, this love for Krishna would define her and would resonate through her poetry for five hundred years.

In 1516 or thereabouts, Meera was married into a noble Rajput family. There has been much conjecture about the exact identity of this family and one possibility—though Meera's poetry only refers to the oppressive patriarchal figure of a 'Rana'—is the Sisodia clan of the Mewar family so beloved of James Tod. For the constantly warring Rajputs, an alliance between the ruling Sisodias and the noble Rathores would have been crucial in consolidating the ever-fracturing unity of the Rajputs against the Muslims. Tod himself had noticed this disunity among the Rajputs. 'The closest attention to their history,' he had noted, 'proves beyond contradiction that they were never capable of uniting, even for their own preservation.' In this instance, and despite his admiration for Rajput bravery, Tod was evaluating their risk to British dreams of expansion. 'No national head exists amongst them...they are individually too weak to cause us [British] any alarm.' Marriages, therefore, were made for political gains, to strengthen unity or expand territories. By marrying into the powerful Sisodia clan, Meera would have moved up into the highest echelons of Rajput identity.

When Meera left her natal village to begin her week-long journey by horse-drawn carriage to Chittor, she would have been leaving with very little expectation of ever returning. The Rajput bride was brought up to show complete obedience and expected to adapt to all the traditions and habits of her new family.

The practice of natal alienation was not confined to Rajput women and throughout the villages and towns of India, young girls, children in many instances, were required to leave the land of their births forever. An entire genre of music, the bidaai songs—lamenting the 'farewell of a bride to her home'—is dedicated to this custom. These excessively sentimental songs allowed women to express their sorrow and vulnerability at the time of their bidaai. As Rashmi Bhatnagar has explained it, 'the *bidaai* genre naturalizes child marriage, exogamy, treating daughters as temporary residents in the natal home, and the disinheritance of daughters after marriage by the withdrawal of all that is familiar, supportive, and nurturing.' The bride's natal family was also complicit in this process, reminding the girl-child throughout her childhood that she was paraya dhan, an outsider in her own home since she was born only to belong to another man and his family.

Many years later Meera was to speak of the desolation of this experience in one of her poems:

Friend from my childhood, I long to be a renunciator,
My being resides elsewhere, here is only the empty husk
Like straw in the wind, I left behind
Mother father family
Friend from my childhood, I long to be a renunciator.

In this stanza, Meera evokes the bidaai genre of separation only to startle the listener by deciding to renounce the patriarchal system. She removes herself, '[her] being', from this failed construct to a space of greater happiness and comfort.

◆

Every Rajput kul, or small kinship unit, traced its lineage to a heroic ancestor. The goddess of the kul or kuldevi was the divine guardian of every great house of Rajasthan. One of the first duties for Meera as a young bride would have been to worship the kuldevi of the Sisodia clan. According to legend, Meera refused to acknowledge the divine authority of the kuldevi and stubbornly continued to worship her beloved Krishna instead. The ritual worship of the kuldevi by a bride was essential in ensuring her perfect condition as the sadaa-suhaagan, eternally married, never widowed. By refusing to worship the kuldevi Meera was committing the most outrageous of crimes for a married woman by leaving the preservation of her husband's life to fate and chance.

According to Rajput traditions, the husband protected the virtue of the woman through his valour as a warrior, while the bride remained true to her husband and prayed for an eternal married life. The men were exhorted not to shame their mother's milk or their wife's bangles and to be always ready to die a warrior's death for the sake of freedom. Implicit in this relationship was the understanding that the wife was always ready to sacrifice her life if her husband was no longer able to protect her honour, more specifically her sexual virtue in which was said to reside the honour of the clan. A married woman wore red—the colour of sacrifice, the colour of blood and the colour women wore when they climbed the funeral pyre to commit sati or jauhar.

We know through the poems that are attributed to Meera that she was harrassed by her mother-in-law, sisters-in-law, and a patriarch whom she calls 'Rana', for not abiding by the rules. There is no certainty regarding the identity of the Rana; in later retellings her persecutor is the husband, the father-in-law, and then finally the evil brother-in-law.

The women of noble Rajput families led sequestered lives and were not even allowed to visit the temple if it was outside the zenana. 'Mother-in-law fights, my sister-in-law teases,/ The Rana remains angry,' Meera writes. 'They have a watchman sitting at the door, and a lock fastened on it.' If women had to leave the enclosure of the palace or haveli, they had to travel in enclosed palanquins, never exposed to the defiling gaze of a man outside the immediate family. It is said that Meera had a small Krishna temple built within the zenana where she spent an increasing amount of time composing poems and singing songs in praise of Krishna. Her poetry suggests that Meera would now have sought the company of other Krishna bhakts—troubadours, devotees, travelling mendicants. It is suggested Meera even sang and danced in the company of other Krishna bhakts. She had begun her transformation from illiterate Rajput girl to the embodiment of divine love. 'Mine is the dark one, who dwells in Braj,' Meera sang, 'friends, marriages of this world are false, they are wiped out of existence.'

The exact nature of Meera's dynamic with her husband remains unclear. Some authors believe she refused all physical intimacy with her husband and doubt that she was a widow. Meera never seemed to refer to herself as a widow, talking instead about giving up silks and jewels which, as a widow, she would have been deprived of anyway. What is certain is that Meera rebelled, and articulated her rebellion, against the many ways in which women were constrained by the patriarchal society of her time.

Some modern-day Hindi scholars, struggling to reconcile Meera's reckless disregard for her marital duties with the sainthood she achieved in later life, have argued that she only turned to religion for consolation after she became a widow. 'As soon as she was separated from her *patidev*,' says Vishwanath Tripathi, 'she suddenly shattered all worldly ties, averted her attention from all else, and became even more immersed in her chosen deity.' Even the *Amar Chitra Katha* version of Meera describes her as 'an ideal Hindu wife, loved by her husband.'

As Meera struggled to fit into the role of the Rajput bride, the attacks on her became less petty and more sinister. Legend has it that several attempts were now made on her life. Meera's husband probably died within a few years of their marriage at which point she would have become a childless widow. A widow without a son to bolster her stature within the family was anathema to her in-laws. Moreover, Meerabai did not behave like a widow at all. Instead of living in the shadows or committing sati, Meera continued to sing and dance her praises of Krishna in her small temple and blasphemously claimed she was eternally married to him. This would have been an open provocation to her marital family. As she was beautiful and still young, probably only in her late twenties, her chastity was now theirs to protect. The family attempted to kill her—they sent her a basket with a snake inside it, poisoned her drink—but each time they failed and Meera survived. It could well have been the vigilance of a female attendant, perhaps a servant girl who accompanied her from her natal home, that saved her, but these incidents would only serve to add to the legend of Meera in times to come.

Meera decided to leave Chittor to seek the company of wandering mendicants and other bhakts. Her peripatetic life in the following decades would take her to Mathura, Vrindavan and Dwarka, among other places on the sacred map of Krishna mythology. However, the very first step she took out of Chittor was momentous. She was crossing the final barrier, the *lakshman rekha*, after which there could be no return to an honourable life.

Meera's heroism, then, is very different from other women—like Padmini, Karnavati and the innumerable satis—who are also part of Rajput legend. While they are venerated for conforming to the rules, sacrificing their lives to protect the honour of their families, Meera did quite the opposite. She stepped out of purdah and abandoned all familial obligations and yet she remained relevant and intriguing right into the modern era. She was the first of the Bhakti poets to be included in the *Amar Chitra Katha* pantheon and no less than ten Bollywood movies have been made about her life. Versions of her songs are sung even today in Gujarati, Bengali, Bhojpuri and Oriya.

A possible explanation for Meera's enduring popularity may lie in the very particular construct of her songs. She sang in the short, rhyming lyrics of the pada genre which were easy to remember, even for an illiterate audience. The male bhakts and the Charan bards, on the other hand, used a much longer and more complex metre. Meera composed her poems in the lyrical Brajbhasha, interspersed with Rajasthani and Gujarati dialects. The scholar Padmavati Shabnan has described Meera's padas as lokik, that is, using the folk language and literary style. Paradoxically, in nationalist and post-colonial times, Brajbhasha suffered from its association with the erotic Riti poetry of the pre-modern era and came to be associated with the nostalgic excess of the Bhakti poets. The Hindi poet Sumitranandan Pant famously remarked that in Brajbhasha, 'there was the sweetness of sleep.' Brajbhasha came to be thought of as a gentle, emasculated language somehow devalued and irrelevant. There is nothing naïve, however, in Meera's poetry:

Girls! Come form a ring.
We'll dance,

We'll turn away
From playing at what
The elders say:
We'll look within
Not go away

Not go and give ourselves away

To homes
    That are strange
    To the soul.

Jewels are false, and pearls;
The light in them is lies;

Rich silks, bright hues-those
They keep getting from the south-

    Their gleam
Just isn't there inside.

In these short arresting lines Meera talks to the women and girls
in her audience and tells them not to be taken in by the insidious
wishes of 'the elders' who mean to send them to a 'stranger's house',
lured by the promise of pearls and silks. Instead, Meera tells them
to look within themselves for true happiness and riches. When
she addresses the 'Rana' in the following pada, she is weary of the
enticements that patriarchy offers as the compensations of suhaag:

I don't like your strange world, Rana,
A world where there are no holy men,
And all the people are trash.
I have given up ornaments, given up
Braiding my hair.
I have given up putting on kajal,

And putting my hair up.
Mira's lord is Giridha Nagar: I
Have found a perfect groom.

When Meera left her marital home in search of the 'holy men', she was doing what wandering ascetics had been doing for more than two thousand years. In fact, the ancient Sanskritic tradition even had a name—Varnashrama dharma—for the stage of life when upper-caste men could renounce their social obligations and retire to the forest to meditate. Even lower-class men had the option of joining the Jain or Buddhist sects because monastic orders had long been set up to assimilate the voices of the wretched. In this way, Hindu orthodoxy had regulated the stream of disaffection. But for Meera there was no monastic order, no comforting brotherhood. For her renunciation was:

Like the casting off of the veil,
Honour, shame, family pride are disavowed
Respect, disrespect, marital, natal home
Renounced in the search for wisdom

People say Meera is maddened
Kinsfolk say she is a family annihilator
Rana sent a cup of poison
While drinking it Meera laughed

Of father, mother, brother, kinsfolk I have none
Having cast aside familial tyranny
What people say is of no consequence
Because I sought to keep company with *sadhus*
People say I have shamed the community's honour.

It is unlikely that Meera would have gone to her maternal home in Merta for shelter after leaving Chittor. She was always clear in her criticism of the Rajput tradition of alienating daughters upon their marriage. Walking alone, Meera was now truly free of society's constraints. 'I gave up all my jewels/ Unlocking the armlet I freed myself,' she sings. 'I have no use for gold or glitter/ I trade in diamonds.'

As word of her renown spread through the villages and forest communities, people came to see this highborn Rajput woman who now wore rags and beads of seeds, and danced with ghungroos tied to her feet. Meera had begun the metamorphosis that would eventually lead her followers to see in her ecstasy a divine madness. She was now Meerabai, an honoured older woman. From Vaishnav chronicles we know that Meerabai's audience included:

'the story of Ali Khan, the Pathan'
'the story of Kalavat, the washerman'
'the story of a prostitute'
'the story of a weaver's daughter'
'the story of a thief who was a Vaishnav'.

Meerabai was by no means the first person to express her religious ecstacy in this manner. By the sixteenth century, there was already an established parallel Bhakti movement that recognized a need for unorthodox expressions of spirituality. Candidasa and Chaitanya Mahaprabhu had famously cross-dressed as gopis symbolizing their intense desire for Krishna.

Unbound and exposed in the world of the forest and open road, Meerabai unbound her hair. 'If he says so, I'll let my hair grow wild,' sings Meerabai, 'I have given up ornaments, given up braiding my hair.' Unbound and unkempt hair, as we have seen in the case of Draupadi, too, was frowned upon. A married woman with unbound hair is representative of Goddess Kali, feral and frightening. The other goddess, Gauri, represented by Sita who follows her husband into the forest dressed in jewels and silk, her hair bound, is the domesticated woman—calm, composed and acceptable to society.

In an anecdote described by one of Meerabai's earliest biographers,

Priyadas, a man posing as a wandering bhakt approaches Meerabai, claiming to have been sent by Krishna himself to enjoy a romantic liaison with her. Meerabai accepts his advances on one condition. Since this is pleasing to Krishna himself, it will please all the other bhakts too, so their union must take place in full public view; she starts preparing a bed in the centre of the group of devotees. So ashamed is the man by this display of innocence and divine passion that he immediately asks for forgiveness and becomes her disciple. Clearly this story was considered too disquieting for later generations and has been expunged from many collections, including the *Amar Chitra Katha* version.

There was an ambivalence to Meerabai's situation which she herself stoked. 'If he says so, I'll colour my sari red,' says Meerabai, red of course being the blessed colour of suhaag, the colour of Gauri. 'If he says so, I'll wear the godly yellow garb,' Meerabai adds, yellow being the saffron of renunciation, of ascetics and nomads like Kali. 'If he says so, I'll let my hair grow wild.' With her talk of precious stones and coarse blankets, the listener is constantly challenged about the singer's identity. Is she a bride, or is she a sanyasin? Gauri or Kali?

◆

Vrindavan in the sixteenth century was already a lively city, attracting Krishna devotees from different parts of India. The Goswamis of Bengal were a group of aristocratic Krishna scholars, who had left behind great wealth to pursue their theological research. At the time when Meerabai arrived in Vrindavan, the youngest of them, Jiva Goswami, was in residence. He was a young scholar and writer of some repute, having dedicated his life to the study of bhakti yoga and the life of his master, Chaitanya Mahabraphu. Meerabai tried to meet Jiva Goswami, eager to discuss Krishna with someone who also shared her passion. Jiva, however, refused to meet Meerabai saying that he had undertaken a vow to never interact with women so as not to be distracted in his perfect meditation on Krishna.

This fear of the feminine harked back to the mythic rishis who were notoriously afraid of losing the power of their tapas and succumbing to the charms of a woman. Meerabai sent back word to the celibate scholar saying that she had always believed that there was only one man in Vrindavan, Krishna, and that all the others were female, gopis, in their yearning for Krishna. Jiva Goswami was immediately chastened and agreed to meet her.

At the heart of this anecdote lies the difference between how men and women were perceived in the Bhakti tradition. Although Meerabai has been given a place of honour beside the greatest Hindu bhakts that include Kabir, Tulsidas and Surdas, not only is she the only woman to be included but she has taken the form of Krishna's lover, Radha. Male devotees had to relate to God through the madhurya-bhav—taking on the role of a woman obsessively devoted to God—which for Meerabai was a lived experience. 'For those who treasure Mira's songs often feel that her words have an authenticity that no male poet can match,' is how historian John Hawley explains it. 'For them, and to a large extent for the poet as well, the distinction between Mira and the gopis who form Krishna's inner circle is blurred.'

After spending years in Vrindavan and other holy sites, Meerabai started travelling west, towards the seaside town of Dwarka.

Nothing is really mine except Krishna.
O my parents, I have searched the world
And found nothing worthy of love.
I am a stranger amidst my kinfolk
And an exile from their company,
Since I seek the companionship of holy men;
There alone do I feel happy,
In the world I only weep.

The landscape Meerabai passed on her way was overshadowed by battle. Babur, who was to found the empire of the Great Mughals in India, was leading his armies into northwestern Punjab and northern India. He defeated the Lodis at the Battle of Panipat in 1526, but there were still fractious Afghan nobles and the Rajputs under Rana Sangha who were gathering their clansmen for a final confrontation with Babur. Babur had the advantage, amongst other things, of firepower with matchlocks and cannons and the Rajput army was decisively routed. The Mughals were now commanders of northern India and in the fortified town of Chanderi the Rajput women committed jauhar when faced with imminent defeat.

While the kings waged warfare and the women burned to preserve their chastity, Meerabai fought her own lonely, sublime battle: 'Let us go to a realm beyond going / Where death is afraid to go / where the high-flying birds alight and play / afloat in the full lake of love.

Meerabai finally reached the town of Dwarka, where she spent her days attending to the famous black stone idol of Krishna in his Ranchor, deserter of war, avatar. As the years went by, and her fame spread, she won a considerable following of devotees.

While Meerabai was at Dwarka, Chittor was attacked again, this time by Bahadur Shah of the Gujarat Sultanate in 1537 and Rani Karnavati retired to the smoky underground vaults of the fortress with all her attendants to commit jauhar. Meanwhile Babur had died in an act of sacrifice that would become part of his legend. When his son Humayun fell gravely ill, Babur prayed fervently that his own life be taken in exchange for his son to be healed. It is said that soon after, Humayun began to recover while Babur fell ill and died. Humayun then spent the next decade slowly losing his father's empire, distracted by opium and the pleasure of social intercourse. A gifted and meticulous Afghan campaigner, Sher Shah of the Sur tribe, stepped into this vacuum and in his short, five-year reign, laid the foundations which would be built upon by the Great Mughals. In 1545, shortly before dying in an explosion while storming a fort, he seized the forts of Jodhpur, Chittor, and Kalinjar.

It was around this time that a delegation was sent to Meerabai from her marital home. Her reputation had spread and the

Rajputs may have blamed the series of defeats they had suffered to a weakening of their clan brought on by Meerabai's aberrant behaviour. A woman's perceived disloyalty was thought to cause enormous injury to the strength and moral character of the marital family and, consequently, the clan. The delegation of Brahmins threatened to fast unto death if Meerabai did not return to her marital home and repair the damage done to its honour. Faced with the bleak prospect of returning to a life of purdah, Meerabai composed one last bhajan—the haunting 'Hari tum Haro'—after which she disappeared. She may have walked out of the back door of the temple and into the warm, consoling waters of the ocean, but her legend said she merged into the black stone statue of her beloved Krishna.

◆

By being absorbed in the great tradition of Bhakti poets and Vaishnavite devotion, Meerabai's story was slowly sanitized and her transgressions wiped out. At every step of her life, she had baulked at what was expected of her. She was a reluctant bride who carried with her the idol of Krishna that she would love all her life. She was a disappointing daughter-in-law, refusing to worship the family goddess and, in the eyes of society, culpable for the decline of her clan. If she ever did become widowed, she was a deplorable one and refused sativrata. She threw away the symbols of her suhaag and her caste with relief and set upon the wildering path of her love for her chosen god. Two thousand years before Meerabai, the Buddhist nun Sumangalamata expressed similar joy about this freedom:

> A woman well set free! How free I am
> A woman well set free! How free I am
> How wonderfully free from kitchen drudgery
> Free from the hardship of hunger,
> And from empty working pots

Free too of that unscrupulous man,
The weaver of sunshades,
Calm now and serene I am, all lust and hatred purged,
To the shade of the spreading trees I go
And contemplate my happiness.

With the passage of time, Meerabai's human attributes were replaced by semi-divine ones. Unlike Sita, whose pious domesticity and unchallenged devotion to her husband make her an ideal Hindu wife, Meerabai becomes a woman of exception, to be admired certainly, but perhaps not to be held up as an example for one's own daughters.

Parita Mukta has argued that a gradual sanitizing and reinstating of Meerabai lore has taken place since the nationalist movement of the twentieth century. In his writings during the anticolonial struggle, Gandhi adopted Meerabai as a 'paramount satyagrahi', 'a model wife' and a woman who won over the affections of her husband by the strength of her acts. At the same time, Meerabai's history was altered so that Rana Kumbha became her supportive husband, building her the Kumbha Shyama Temple and the Sisodias incorporated her into their official history. 'Thus,' remarks Parita Mukta, 'Mira was reinstated in the bland cardboard shape of a smiling devotee in the very fortress that she had sworn never to set foot in again.' In this manner, Meerabai became a widow clad demurely in white, no sanyasin's saffron for her, piously worshipping at the family temple, a cherished member of the shrines of upper-caste middle class homes.

The legend of Meerabai survives, even today, and it is not confined to those upper-caste homes alone. It comes to us from bhajan mandalis, the lower-caste informal gatherings, in which her words are vibrantly discussed; many middle-class homes channel her through M. S. Subbulakshmi's Carnatic interpretations; and she is alive in the full-throated songs that the women sing in the temple dedicated to her at her natal home in Merta.

In Rajasthan today, there is a community of hereditary musicians who are Muslims by birth but who live and sing a blend of Sufi and Hindu mystical songs. They are the Manganiyars, who have for generations accompanied their Rajput patrons to war. Since their patrons were the Rajput nobility, some of the customs of the upper castes seeped into the ways of the Manganiyars and their women are secluded, virtually in purdah. A few women, however, have resisted this seclusion and followed their passion for singing. Bhanwari Devi is the best known of these female Manganiyars. She used to sing alongside her husband in the Bhopa-Bhopi tradition (husband-wife) but now sings alone. She is a widow but instead of retiring in contemplation, she travels around the world singing at folk festivals. Her only concession to her widowhood is that she veils her face when she appears onstage. Bhanwari Devi's voice is haunting, husky and vaults across the desert sky. It is the voice one imagines Meerabai would have had. Powerful, hoarse from singing too long in wide, open spaces, and filled with longing.

I'm coloured with the colour of dusk, oh Rana,
Coloured with the colour of my Lord.
Drumming out the rhythm on the drums, I danced,
Dancing in the presence of the saints,
Coloured with the colour of my Lord.

Jahanara Begum
In the Shadow of the Peacock Throne

In the flickering light of an oil lamp, shadows sway behind a woman kneeling on the floor of the tomb of a revered Sufi saint. Under the fine cotton fabric of her tunic, the woman's back is a tapestry of scar tissue and red welts. She has narrowly survived the terrible accident of her clothes catching fire at the Nauroz festival. No one had believed she would live, her father had been inconsolable. But she survived and has now come to give thanks. She has come here before, during the month of Ramadan, stooping to kiss the floor at every step and prostrated herself on the threshold of the tomb. In the treatise she later wrote, she referred to herself as a fakira, and a lowly woman. In another book she calls herself 'a speck of dust at the feet of the sages of Chisht.' Much later, towards the end of her long life, she will design a simple and stark mausoleum for herself inscribed with the lines, 'let nothing cover my tomb save the green grass / for grass suffices well as covering for the grave of the lowly.'

But though she refers to herself as a fakira, she has other, more exalted, names. She is Sahibat al-Zamani, Lady of the Age, Padshah Begum (Lady Emperor) and Begum Sahib (Princess of Princesses); to her family, she is simply 'Jaani'. She is Jahanara Begum (1614–1681), eldest daughter of the great Mughal emperor Shah Jahan, the Shadow of God on earth. Her father is the man behind some of the most exquisite creations ever made—the Peacock Throne and the Taj Mahal. Jahanara Begum is an enigma. She is, by her own claim, a soul obliterated. But she is also the richest woman of her age, clad in priceless silks and jewels, a princess who traces her lineage to the fearsome warlords of the Timurid dynasty.

When Shah Jahan became king in 1627, he took for himself an emblematic title. He proclaimed himself the 2nd Timur and took the title Sahib Qiran-i-Sani, Second Lord of the Auspicious Planetary

Conjunction. The original Sahib Qiran was Timur, a fourteenth-century semi-nomadic chieftain of Turkic and Mongolian ancestry. For Shah Jahan, the Great Mughal, was in fact the Great Mongol—a direct descendant of Timur, the Sword of Islam, and of Genghis Khan, the Scourge of God himself. In 1941, a Russian archeological team exhumed a body that had evidence of two healed wounds on the right hand, and was missing two fingers. This body was all that remained of Timur-i-Leng (Timur the Lame), illiterate warrior, exceptional chess player and merciless military strategist. Gifted with remorseless foresight, Timur planted barley for his horses two years ahead of his campaigns and so fierce was the loyalty he inspired that his soldiers were unpaid. Their incentive was the spoils of war: horses, metals, women and precious stones. This was the great ancestor whose memory both Shah Jahan and Jahanara, in different ways, used to cement their legacy.

Though Timur's empire did not survive long after his death, in the fourteenth century, with his Turko-Mongol hordes, he rode right up to the city of Delhi where treasures of gold, silver, jewels and precious brocades were looted and the Hindu population was either decimated or enslaved. 'Although I was desirous of sparing them,' Timur later wrote in his memoir, 'I could not succeed, for it was the will of God that this calamity should befall the city.'

More than a hundred years later, a fifth generation descendant of Timur called Zahir-ud-din Muhammad or Babur, witnessed the fall of what remained of Timur's empire to the Uzbeks at Herat. A charismatic and courageous leader from Ferghana, the fifteen-year-old Babur tried for many years to re-conquer the fabled capital city of the Timurid empire, Samarkand. It was only after he had repeatedly failed to hold Samarkand, and then Lahore, that he turned his attention to north India. Armed with the new gunpowder technology, at the head of a modest twelve-thousand strong army, and bolstered by 'a cherished but highly dubious claim to legitimate sovereignty in northern India' , because of the earlier sack of Delhi by Timur, Babur marched into India where the fragmentation of the Delhi Sultanate had exposed the vulnerability of the northern plains. This was the start of a magnificent empire that would last nearly two hundred years; the Mongols, originally synonymous with 'barbarians', would become the Mughals, whose culture would leave an indelible mark on Indian history.

Once Babur had strengthened his position in India, he consciously set about establishing a Timurid renaissance in the subcontinent in which Timurid culture would be recreated far from its original steppe environment. Babur himself was an example of the perfect dichotomy of the Timurid princes. He was raised in semi-nomadic conditions and considered himself a Turk but he was also an orthodox Sunni Muslim who wrote Persian poetry and appreciated the refined charm of the Persian gardens. As historian Stephen Frederic Dale has said, 'In his personality, sustained drinking bouts with Mughal and Turkic companions, public encounters with female relatives and other women, and explicit evocations of legitimizing Chingizid customs co-existed with a visceral distaste for Mongol and Uzbek crudity, a politically sophisticated aversion for these tribes' undisciplined rapacity and a genuine if ordinary piety marked by Babur's characteristic steppe reverence for Sufi Shayks.' It is clear from the *Baburnama*, his evocative and lively memoir, that he claimed political legitimacy from this Timurid inheritance and had a searing 'ambition for rule and desire for conquest.' Scalded by the memory of the Chingizid Uzbeks, who had wrested his beloved Samarkand from him, Babur always glorified his Timurid connection while downplaying his Chingizid one.

Over the years, because of intermarriage with Rajput and other Hindu brides, the characteristic Mongoloid features, high cheekbones and almond eyes of Babur and Humayun evolved to the sharp profiles and large eyes of Shah Jahan and Aurangzeb in succeeding Mughal generations. The mango slowly replaced the melon and the grapes of Kabul, the war elephant was assimilated into the traditional cavalry of the nomadic steppe but even so these successors maintained symbols of power linking them to their Timurid ancestry. One of these symbols, especially relevant to Jahanara, was the close alliance between the ruling dynasty and the Sufi mystic tradition.

In her Sufi treatise, *Risala-i-Sahibiyya*, Jahanara describes a religious vision she had in which she saw herself in the company of her Sufi master, a group of holy men and the Holy Prophet himself. In her vision, the Prophet acknowledges Jahanara's presence and asks the Sufi master, 'Why have you illuminated this Timurid Lamp?' She then preempts and discards all notions of gender inferiority when she adds that 'whoever is honoured by the greatest happiness of knowing and realization is the perfect human or the absolute essence of the world and is superior among all living creatures whether man or woman.'

◆

Jahanara first appears to us in historical records in 1631 when she is seventeen years old and her mother, Mumtaz Mahal, is dying. Shah Jahan has only been emperor for three years and the royal family has left the splendour of the court of Agra and is camped in a small town, Burhanpur, in the Deccan. Mumtaz Mahal is giving birth to her fourteenth child, but this time there is a complication. Desperate with anxiety and fear, the young princess starts distributing gems to the poor, hoping for divine help. After enduring a long and painful labour, Mumtaz Mahal dies giving birth to a girl, Gauharara Begum.

Shah Jahan is inconsolable at the death of his beloved wife and his grief is lavish. He goes into mourning for two years, during which time his hair and beard turn grey. 'The pleasures of worldly rule and kingship which were mine with her by my side,' he writes, 'have now become burdens and increasingly sources of grief.' With the death of her mother, Jahanara becomes, at seventeen, the first lady of the empire and head of the imperial harem. She will never marry and there will be scandalous, bazaar gossip of incest and lovers, which Italian and French adventurers will comment on with scurrilous delight.

Shah Jahan and his court returned to Agra and, for the next ten years of her life, Jahanara assumed her position as Begum Sahiba, head of the royal household. The royal residence in Agra was a monumental red sandstone fort, a walled city by the Yamuna River. Within the walls of the fort were palaces of white marble and mahals with lattice screens, water tanks, reception halls, buttresses and cupolas and with gemstone inlay work. In Agra, Jahanara was made 'keeper of the imperial seal' and 'from that day on the duty of affixing the great seal to the imperial edicts devolved upon her.' This was an honour never before conferred upon any imperial woman. She now had to supervise the social and financial upkeep of the harem, which was a city unto itself with hundreds of inhabitants—Afghan, Turk, Persian, Muslim and Hindu women—possibly a few thousand by the time of Shah Jahan. According to the traveller François Bernier, the women 'were guarded by innumerable old crones and beardless eunuchs.' There was a cacophony of languages, which the British wife of a Muslim nobleman who lived in India in the early-nineteenth century described thus: 'The buzz of human voices, the happy playfulness of the children, the chaste singing of the domenies fill up the animated picture.'

The princesses of the house, and the wives of the king, would have received sizable allowances, all of which had to be accounted for. Jahanara's quarters were close to Shah Jahan's, a sign of the enormous faith he had in her abilities. She lived close to the centre of power, in a palace with spacious rooms 'decorated with murals of flying angels, and [in which] the marble or tiled floors were covered with valuable carpets.'

At the age of twenty-two she held the role of matriarch, organizing and presiding over her brother crown prince Dara Shikoh's wedding—the most expensive ceremony ever staged in Mughal history. Dara Shikoh's wedding was meant to convey a lasting image of the magnificence and the continuity of the Mughal empire. The bride's trousseau alone cost almost a million rupees. Porters arrived at Agra for days, bearing gifts for the groom in baskets on their heads. The English traveller Peter Mundy described the fireworks: 'great elephants whose bellies were full of squibs, crackers etc, giants with wheels in their hands, then a rank of monsters, then of artificial trees (and other) inventions, all full of rockets.' Over the coming years, Jahanara would also organize the weddings of her other brothers, Murad Baksh and Shah Shuja.

The town of Agra, Shah Jahan's capital for the first half of his long reign, was an unremarkable collection of houses outside the red fort. According to the French traveller Jean-Baptiste Tavernier, it suffered from being built 'in a sandy soil, which is the cause of excessive heat in summer. The houses of the nobles are beautiful and well built, but those of private persons have nothing fine about them, as is the case in all other towns of India.' But Shah Jahan was about to change all that. He had just started work on a mausoleum for his beloved wife that would become the most exalted building of the Mughal empire. It would come to symbolize the golden age of the Mughals and a perfect synthesis of Hindu and Muslim aesthetics, 'the gateway through which all dreams must pass.'

While Jahanara spent years organizing the imperial weddings, outside the fort of Agra an endless procession of elephants dragging logs of woods was heading towards the banks of the Yamuna. An enormous foundation pit was dug below the water level of the Yamuna, and a mountain of stone poured into the pit so that any flooding from the river or instability in the mobile riverbank would never affect the monument.

At the same time that work began on the Taj Mahal, Shah Jahan commissioned the building of a throne which would reflect his glory as the Shadow of God on earth. More than a ton of gold and 230 kilograms of jewels were given to Bedadal Khan to supervise the building of what would become the single most expensive artifact ever created—the Peacock Throne. Completed by 1635, it would contain jewels so magnificent they have names of their own—the Koh-i-Noor, the Akbar Shah, the Jahangir diamonds and the Timur ruby. Their legends survived long after the stones were lost. 'The wonderful rubies,' Queen Victoria wrote breathlessly in her journal, 'they are cabochons, uncut, unset, but pierced. The one is the largest in the world, therefore even more remarkable than the Koh-i-Noor!'

◆

During the rule of Babur and Humayun's rule, when the Mughal claim to the overlordship of India was still fragile, Mughal princesses were sometimes married off to secure strong alliances. By Shah Jahan's time, however, each contender to the throne was a potentially deadly rival. With successive reigns, even as the empire grew secure, competition for the throne between male heirs increased. The Mughals never spelt out a system of imperial succession and there was no law of primogeniture so, theoretically, any ambitious son with a loyal following could stake a claim to the throne. After Akbar's reign the Mughal empire became a fabulous kingdom worth fighting for and by Shah Jahan's time it was worth murdering for. Jahangir tortured and blinded his brother to secure the throne but Shah Jahan's fratricide set a precedent that would haunt all the successive Mughal kings. From the time of Babur's clear message to his son Humayun to 'conduct yourself well with your younger brother', the Mughal kings had clashed and warred with their brothers but had obeyed this ancestral order and had never killed a sibling. Shah Jahan's action would forever haunt the process of inheritance of the Mughal kings and would lead directly to the vicious and bloody war of succession among his own sons.

For Jahanara and her younger sister Roshanara, the two oldest daughters of Shah Jahan and princesses with Timurid blood, a husband would have resulted in more heirs. Though no written law to this effect was ever made, and royal princesses did marry in each generation of Mughals, it is highly probable that the more powerful princesses were discouraged from marrying to restrict the number of claimants to the throne.

There was also a more prosaic reason for the sisters to remain unmarried—in the bloodshed accompanying Shah Jahan's ascension to the throne, all his brothers and nephews had been blinded, killed or slowly poisoned, and there were simply no royal princes suitable for Jahanara and Roshanara to marry.

◆

Of her thirteen siblings, Jahanara shared the closest relationship with Dara Shikoh, who was just a year younger to her, and the two often engaged in theological discussions. 'I love my brother Dara Shikoh extremely, both in form and spirit. We are, in fact, like one soul in two bodies and one spirit in two physical forms.'

Married at nineteen to his first cousin Nadira Begum, Dara Shikoh was devastated when his first child, a daughter, died soon after birth. The sensitive prince wrote of his despair after the tragedy: 'I was suffering from a chronic disease: for four months the physicians had not been able to cure me... [Shah Jahan] took me by the hand and with great humility and reverence entreated [Mian Mir] to pray to God for my health. The saint took my hand into his own, giving me a cup of water to drink. Results were immediate: within a week I recovered from the serious malady.' In the teachings of the elderly fakir, the young prince found comfort and by his second visit he was prostrating himself at the feet of Mian Mir: 'He threw out of his mouth a chewed clove which I gathered and ate and when the king [Shah Jahan] had left I lingered behind. I went up to him and placing my head on his foot remained in that position for some time.'

Mian Mir was a reclusive Sufi of the Qadiri order who, along with his sister Bibi Jamal Khatun, had helped spread the Qadiris' simple message of love throughout northern India. 'For those who have love's pain,' Mian Mir proclaimed, 'the only cure is seeing the Beloved.' 'Exoteric Islam has ceased to influence the mind of this fakir,' wrote Dara Shikoh, referring to himself and what he saw as the limitations of Shah Jahan's prescriptive Islam. 'The real esoteric "infidelity" has shown its face.' Dara Shikoh now introduced Jahanara to the teachings of Mian Mir and the princess was immediately captivated by the Sufi ideology.

In 1637, accompanied by Shah Jahan and Dara Shikoh, Jahanara travelled to Kashmir where she met another Qadiri Sufi mystic, Mullah Shah Badakhshi, who had reached enlightenment through gruelling breathing exercises, night vigils, fasts and meditation. He lived an austere life, with no servants to tend to him, no cooked meals and no lamps. Initially, Jahanara had been drawn to the Chishti order—which Akbar himself had favoured—but the Chishtiya order refused to initiate a woman. 'Though I am devoted to the Chishti order,' the princess wrote candidly in the *Risala-i-Sahibiyya*, 'the Chishti shayks do not show themselves in public and remain secluded. I am twenty-seven years old and did not want to lose any more time. I wanted to become a disciple of any order. I was a Chishti disciple in my heart. Now that I have joined the Qadiryya, will I achieve realization?' Jahanara accepted the Qadiryya order's stress on the importance of the purification of the self and wrote: 'When I realized that the truth for this existence requires fana (annihilation of the self), I decided to follow what my pir requires, to die before death, to not wait for death to extinguish me, to become one with the divine.'

After spending six months of spring and summer in Kashmir under the spiritual tutelage of Mullah Shah, the royal entourage returned to Agra. The city of Agra was itself in the throes of a monumental metamorphosis. Down the riverbank from the city fort, a large scaffolding was taking shape. At dusk, smoke from the nearby kilns lay over the river like dark breath from a monster's maw. Along the riverside were clusters of huts where an army of artisans, labourers, stone masons and stone carvers worked ceaselessly on an edifice that would not bear their name.

◆

'This *faqira*, only by the assistance and by the favour and approval of God the all knowing and almighty and his beloved messenger Prophet Muhammad, and with the helping grace of my revered master Mullah Shah who took my hand, I'm filled with desire to write this treatise and place it on the mantle with the other accounts of the great ones of religion and the revered ones of certainty.'

These are the opening words of Jahanara's Sufi treatise, the *Risala-i-Sahibiyya*, which she wrote soon after her encounter with Mullah Shah Badakshi around 1640. Jahanara pauses before invoking the divine mystic woman Rabi'a. 'Mullah Shah has said that about Rabi'a, she is not one woman but a hundred men from head to toe. She is entirely drowned in pain like a good Sufi and her longing and devotion on the path is equal to the piety of a hundred men.' She further quotes the Sufi biographer Attar, who justifies Rabi'a's devotion, saying, 'When a woman becomes a man in the path to God, she is a man and one cannot anymore call her a woman.'

Sufism, which arose as a reaction to the increasingly formalized structure of orthodox Islam, was generally more tolerant of female involvement. In Sufism, a woman could be seen as a symbol for the yearning soul, seeking union with God. The main traits of Sufism, such as weeping, fasting, poverty, suffering and ardent love for the Beloved or God, made it easy to accept women as personifications of the soul. The attitude towards gender in general was more nuanced, with the emphasis clearly on the soul and its potential rather than the physical attributes of the seeker. But Sufism was still within the framework of Islam, and there were reminders of the way women were seen as essentially 'defective' and of a 'weak' nature. Mullah Shah had wanted his pious and exemplary sister to succeed him but the rules of the Qadriyya order did not allow it. And when Tawakkul Beg writes the biography of Mullah Shah in the seventeenth century, he says, 'She [Jahanara] passed through all the normal visions and attained a pure union with God and gained an intuitive perception. Mullah Shah said she has attained so extraordinary a development of the mystical knowledge that she is worthy of being my representative if she were not a woman.'

Although Mullah Shah is impressed by Jahanara's mystical knowledge and devotion, it is her gender that prevents her from attaining the status of a master, a pir. Instead, Jahanara claims for herself the title pir-muridi (master-disciple). 'Even though it is not acceptable for a faqira to talk about one-self,' she begins in her treatise before adding, 'since meeting the others in my spiritual reverie last night and being blessed with eternal happiness, I need to include myself among this sacred group.'

Jahanara also makes a further claim. 'In the family of Amir Timur, only we two, brother [Dara Shikoh] and sister are honoured by this enlightened happiness. In our family no one took the step on the path to seek God or the truth that would light the Timurid lamp eternally. I was grateful for having received this great fortune and wealth. There was no end to my happiness.'

When Jahanara spoke about the 'Timurid lamp', she was harking back to her ancestor Timur. Timur didn't have any Chingizid blood himself and he never laid claim to the nomadic honorific 'Khan', but he married Chingizid wives to stake a claim to some of Genghis Khan's legacy. Genghis Khan, who put together the largest empire in the world, had said that 'God has designated him (Chingiz Khan) the sole legitimate ruler of the world, and that he had transmitted sovereignty to his descendants.' Such was the fear that Genghis Khan inspired that even after his death and the break-up of his empire, the only real contenders to power were Chingizid princes. As Timur had married Chingizid wives, the Mongol term Guregen, son-in-law, became one of his official titles. Although Timur's empire was smaller than Genghis Khan's, he was an extremely successful military campaigner. Morever, he fused the Islamic tradition with his native Turco-Mongol one to forge the Timurid legacy. To reinforce his legitimacy as an Islamic king, Timur commissioned mosques and madrasas, patronized the Yasavi order of Sufis and built shrines at Sufi holy places. Although he called himself a pious Muslim—linking his name to the Sayyids, respected members of the Ulama—Timur maintained his Genghis legacy. With supreme pragmatism, Timur welded together people of different faiths and beliefs who answered only to his leadership. 'He had in his army Turks that worshipped idols and men who worshipped fire, Persian magi, soothsayers and wicked enchanters and unbelievers.' In time, this became a powerful model of Perso-Islamic/Turco-Mongol rule. After Timur's death, his descendants would no longer require the Genghis Khan name as it had been replaced by the equally powerful Timurid one.

When the Uzbek confederation finally defeated the Timurid empire in Central Asia at the beginning of the sixteenth century, they took over the cities of Herat, Tashkent, Bukhara and Samarkand, and killed or forced into exile the entire Timurid aristocracy. For the next two hundred years, the descendants of these refugees yearned for their lost homeland. 'In this exile my heart has not been gladdened,' wrote Babur, after he had laid claim to north India. 'No one can be comforted at all in exile.' Nonetheless, despite his deep nostalgia for Samarkand, Babur would lay the foundations in India of an empire that would outweigh even the magnificence of Genghis Khan's.

Timur's successors continued the patronage of Sufi orders, including the Naqshbandis, renowned for their 'particular sobriety' and zikr (silent repetition of the name of God). In later years, Akbar and Jahangir favoured the more socially liberal order of the Chishtis who were patronized by both Hindus and Muslims.

In her anthology of the Chishti saints, the *Mu'nis al-Arvah*, Jahanara describes the scepticism of Shah Jahan regarding the authority of the Chishti order and her own role in influencing him. 'The current emperor, the father of this weak one, did not know the truth of the importance of his path. Because of this, he was always wondering about it and was floundering. And me, the faqira, I constantly told him that Chishti was a Sayyid but he did not believe me until he read the *Akbar-nama*.'

Although Timurid women had often been used to publicly performing acts of piety, Jahanara's quest was more personal. 'My beloved came easily into my arms on the nights of parting without efforts,' she wrote, 'I was a crazed lover... My pir, my God, my religion, my refuge, without you there is no one, my lord, my friend.'

In the two books attributed to Jahanara—the *Mu'nis al-Arvah*, written in 1639-40, and the *Risala-i-Sahibiyya*, written in 1640-41—she offers up the spiritual truths as 'guides' and blessings for the reader: 'Because of my deep beliefs and convictions, the idea behind this manuscript is to guide you and I hope that the readers and listeners of this manuscript will benefit and understand the ideas and thoughts of Chishti in the best way.'

Jahanara was held in high esteem by her father—a fact noted by all the foreign travellers who came to Shah Jahan's court. 'Among all these ladies, the most esteemed and respected was Begum Sahib, because she obtained from her father whatever she liked,' noted Niccolao Manucci, the Italian adventurer. 'Her ascendancy in the court of the Mongol should have been nearly unlimited,' added the French physician, François Bernier. 'She should always have regulated the humors of her father, and exercised a powerful influence on the most weighty of concerns.' Bernier also notes that she was fabulously wealthy and was courted with presents by all those who wished to influence the court. 'This princess accumulated great riches by means of her large allowances, and of the costly presents which flowed in from all quarters, in consideration of numberless negotiations entrusted to her sole management.'

Unlike her near contemporary, Empress Nur Jahan, the Persian wife of her grandfather, Jahangir, who, despite her enormous talent and charisma, managed to alienate as many people as she charmed, Jahanara was respected even by those whom fate dictated would not be on her side. Her younger brother, Aurangzeb—who would later be ensnared in a bloody succession battle against Jahanara's favourite, Dara Shikoh—would always show her the love and respect due to an older sister. The grace with which she wielded her authority is commented on by the court poet Abu Talik Kalim: 'Though the princess is on the apex of sovereignty of the sun of fortune (Shah Jahan), she is always hidden behind the cloud of chastity.' Whereas Nur Jahan's behaviour was often considered controversial, her hunting skills and brazen desire for power suspect and even 'unfeminine', Jahanara was admired for her humility.

Because of their nomadic origins, Timurid women played a more active role in society than in other Muslim cultures. Timurid noblewomen participated freely in the politics and culture of the court, and had access to literary and artistic production. Even young, childless women were able to wield considerable influence in Timurid society. The harem, at the time of Timur, was not an enclosed space but, as noted by a Castilian envoy, Ruy Gonzalez de Clavijo, a series of unwalled gardens containing sumptuous tents described by the envoy as 'pavilions of silk'. The women of the court drank alcohol in mixed groups of men and had veils of gauze that allowed observers to see their features closely. By the time of Akbar, however, women were leading more sequestered lives in the zenana.

Jahanara was conscious of the rules of behaviour and was appropriately self-effacing in her worship. She kept a modest distance even from her own pir, during ritual events and ceremonies. She interacted with him through letters and acts of piety like the contemplation of the pir's portrait, and sending meals to Mullah Shah's hut.

Until quite recently, almost no certain pictorial representations of Jahanara Begum were thought to exist. In 2012, the scholar Jeremiah Losty reinterpreted the Dara Shikoh Album—the only imperial Mughal album that has survived with all its original miniatures more or less intact—and identified two paintings that are likely depictions of Jahanara, painted at a time when the princess was very young, between sixteen and eighteen. Though the royal women were in purdah and the artists would have had no direct access to them, the paintings do give us glimpses of this 'invisible' princess. Both the portraits show a slim woman with very long, black hair, fine, large eyes and a slight smile. In one image, she is holding out a book to a Sufi saint, painted on the opposite page. In the other image she is 'shown holding *paan*, of which apparently she was inordinately fond and to pay for which, we are told, her father transferred to her the income from Surat, the chief port in western India, from his father's widow Nur Jahan'.

In both portraits Jahanara wears a long dupatta of such diaphanous muslin that her striped and patterned shalwars are clearly visible. She wears the most magnificent jewels of all the women in the album. 'Her two pearl chokers are interspersed with large gemstones while a short pearl necklace below has four jeweled pendants dangling from it, including a carved ruby or spinel and an enormous sapphire. A single rope of huge pearls surrounds them all. The sapphire and ruby are possibly inherited from her mother, half of whose estate went directly to her, when her father gave her the title of Padshah Begum.' From the time of Babur the title of Padshah Begum, an honorific term denoting great authority, had been given to a greatly respected royal woman. In the initial years of the Mughal empire, the Padshah Begum was always an older woman, a great-aunt or an older sister. Later on, the Padshah Begum was sometimes a favourite wife of an emperor, but Jahanara was the first unmarried daughter to be given this title, one which Aurangzeb also returned to her when she was reintegrated in the Mughal court after the death of Shah Jahan.

◆

The central mausoleum of the Taj Mahal was completed by 1643 and while the travellers and citizens of Agra were chastened by the magnitude of their emperor's grieving which had resulted in such magnificence, Shah Jahan's family was struck by another tragedy. In 1644, while attending the celebrations for Nauroz, the fine muslin of Jahanara's kameez brushed against a floor lamp and instantly caught fire. Two maids died trying to put out the flames that had engulfed the princess. Although Jahanara survived, she suffered severe burns all over her body. Shah Jahan was distraught and desperate to find a cure for his much-loved daughter. He called upon the Sufi saints to offer prayers and distributed alms to the poor. Physicians and healers from every corner of the empire were summoned to Agra, driven by the fortune to be made if the princess was healed. There were western physicians, English and French, hakims with their arsenals of potions and mendicants with dubious reputations. After months of uncertainty, when Jahanara finally recovered, Shah Jahan's relief and gratitude were so great that he had her weighed in gold which was then distributed to the poor. The weighing of a person in gold had been, until then, an exclusively male royal prerogative. It was at this time that Shah Jahan also gifted the port of Surat and its massive annual revenues to Jahanara. The *Sahibi*, Jahanara's ship, sailed the waters flying the princess's colours and made her one of the richest women of her age.

In 1643, after she had recovered sufficiently, Jahanara made a pilgrimage to the tomb of the Sufi saint Moinuddin Chishti in Ajmer. After experiencing a mystical trance at the tomb, Jahanara ordered the construction of a marble pavilion exclusively for female devotees in front of the tomb, known even today as the Begumi Dalan.

Jahanara also had a congregational mosque built in Agra which was completed in 1648. Inayat Khan records in the *Shah Jahan-nama* that, 'Jahanara begged that this sacred place might be erected out of her personal funds and under her auspices.' Leading up to the prayer hall is an inscription, praising the patron of the mosque: 'It [the masjid] was built by her order who is high in dignity...the most revered of the ladies of the age, the pride of her gender, the princess of the realm...the most honoured of the issue of the head of the Faithful, Jahan Ara Begum.'

By having a mosque built, Jahanara set a unique precedent. Royal Mughal women were linked to the building of gardens, tombs and madrasas, but the building of mosques was a male prerogative. Her acknowledged Sufi status became the fulcrum upon which Jahanara was able to transgress certain boundaries.

Shah Jahan now wanted to build a capital city that would be a true reflection of his splendour. In 1648, Agra was abandoned—it would never again be the capital of India—and the entire Mughal court shifted to Delhi. Here he would build a city bearing his name—Shahjahanabad, the seventh capital city of Delhi. In addition to the old residential city, Shah Jahan built the Red Fort, the Jama Masjid and spacious houses for the nobility with hidden flower gardens, women's quarters, high-ceilinged verandas and libraries and reception areas.

Jahanara used her wealth to add to the lustre of Shahjahanabad. Indeed, the buildings of the imperial women, the wives and daughters of Shah Jahan and later of Aurangzeb, dominated the landscape of the city. Of all the women, Jahanara was the greatest single builder, responsible for five out of the nineteen buildings of Shahjahanabad. She built a mansion in her father's palace compound overlooking the Yamuna and a central marketplace which contained more than fifteen hundred shops. The Paradise Canal ran through the centre of the market and shimmered on moonlit nights, giving it the name Chandni Chowk. Bernier described Chandi Chowk as having 'arcades on both sides...only in bricks and the top serves for a terrace. The spaces between which are open shops, where, during the day artisans work, bankers sit for the dispatch of their business and merchants exhibit their wares. Within the arch is a small door, opening into a warehouse in which these wares are deposited for the night. The houses of the merchants are built over these warehouses at the back of the arcades: they look handsome enough and appear tolerably commodious within.'

People came from distant lands to trade goods and ideas. There were Armenians and Turks, Persian poets and Italian merchants. There were coffee houses along the tree-lined streets for the rich that used imported beans from Persia and there were shops selling Chinese eyeglasses, gems, and even eunuchs. There were merchants from Zanzibar, Syria, England and Holland selling rubies from Badakshan, pearls from Oman, fruit from Kashmir and Central Asia, and exotic animals, including cheetahs, elephants, horses and camels.

A second branch of Paradise Canal watered a garden, also built by Jahanara, the Sahiba ka Bagh, the largest garden in the city. To the west of Chandni Chowk, Jahanara built a caravanserai that was considered 'the most imposing structure in the city after the Jami Masjid'. The scholar Lisa Balabanlilar has pointed out that unlike the more anonymous women builders of the Ottoman and Safavid courts, who also commissioned mosques and madrasas, Jahanara not only wanted to add to the glory of her father's court, but she wanted personal recognition for it. She was 'that Timurid girl,' who wanted to build a serai 'large and fine like no other in Hindustan'. 'The wanderer who enters its courts will be restored in body and soul and my name will never be forgotten', she wrote.

A hundred years after Chandni Chowk was built the great poet Mir Taqi Mir would write:

The streets of Delhi were, in fact, the pages
of a painter's book
Every figure that I saw seemed a work of art.

As Shah Jahan's reign stretched on, each royal prince became more independent and experienced in military matters. Shah Jahan was the first Mughal king to spill royal blood for the throne and now, according to François Bernier, 'not only was the crown to be gained by victory alone, but in the case of defeat life was certain to be forfeited. There was now no choice between a kingdom and death.' The main contenders in the war of succession were two very different personalities—Dara Shikoh and Aurangzeb.

Dara Shikoh was Shah Jahan's chosen successor and, as we have seen, Jahanara was very close to her older brother. 'I wanted to talk to my brother about my deep love and admiration for the Qadriyya order but father sent Dara Shikoh to Kabul. When separating, I was overcome with disappointment, sadness and restlessness and my brother was greatly saddened,' she writes, in one instance. Dara Shikoh was also a great patron of the arts and a scholar of Persian, Arabic and Sanskrit. In fact, he translated fifty Upanishads from Sanskrit into Persian and wrote a treatise describing the similarities between Vedanta and Sufism. For the orthodox Muslims at court, and later for his brother Aurangzeb, this very erudition would be Dara's undoing and they would use his syncretic beliefs to condemn him.

For almost forty years, Dara Shikoh and Jahanara, the cherished older children of Shah Jahan, lived a resplendent life at the court of the emperor where they were respected and beloved above everyone else. Aurangzeb, on the other hand, was 'very different from the others, being in character very secretive and serious, carrying on his affairs in a hidden way, but most energetically. He was of a melancholy temperament, always busy at something or another, wishing to execute justice and arrive at appropriate decisions. He was extremely anxious to be recognized by the world as a man of wisdom, clever and a lover of the truth.' He was also, however, determined, talented and single-minded and no one at this stage could have imagined that he would rule the empire for fifty years and expand it to such a point that the Mughal empire would implode after his death. In this bitter rivalry for the throne, Jahanara's younger sister, Roshanara, was Aurangzeb's committed supporter.

Aurangzeb was jealous of Shah Jahan's clear preference for Dara Shikoh despite his own, considerably superior, military skills and remained angry with his father for decades. Through all the years of suspicions and treachery, however, Aurangzeb displayed consistent respect and love for his sister Jahanara. Even though Roshanara was Aurangzeb's clear ally in the war of succession, Jahanara was the one he wrote to, complaining of Shah Jahan's treatment of his sons, despite knowing that Jahanara and Dara Shikoh were very close. In 1652, while visiting Shahjahanabad, Aurangzeb wrote tenderly of his eldest sister, whom he addresses with a combination of love and respect as Nawab Begum Sahib Jiu—'After inspecting the mosque, [this murid] came to the garden of Nawab Begum Sahib Jiu, and spent a little time strolling about that charming place.' Then, adds Aurangzeb, '[This murid] took his eldest sister to his own mansion.' After this visit, Aurangzeb would return to his war camp and would not see Jahanara again for fifteen years, until after the death of their father.

In 1653, Aurangzeb wrote to Jahanara:

> If his majesty [Shah Jahan] wishes that of all his servants I alone should spend my life in dishonor and die in obscurity, I cannot but obey. It is better that by order of his majesty I should be relieved from the disgust of such a life so that no harm may reach the state and other people's hearts may be at rest.

In 1657, Aurangzeb wrote to Jahanara again, betraying his enormous resentment towards his father.

> Despite twenty years of service and loyalty, he [Aurangzeb] is not considered worthy of the same level of confidence as Suleiman [Dara Shikoh's son].

Jahanara used all the influence she had at court to prevent a war of succession. She was appalled at the thought that her brothers would fight over the empire knowing, as she did, that the victor would leave no one alive. She offered a compromise by suggesting a partitioning of the empire between the warring brothers. In 1657, as Shah Jahan fell ill and was thought to be dying, Jahanara wrote Aurangzeb a last, passionate letter, exhorting the rights of Dara as the elder brother:

> You should yourself judge how impolite it is on your part to encounter and draw the sword against your own father, in whose obedience lies the pleasure of God and His Prophet, and to shed blood of innocent people. Even if your expedition

is due to the antagonism to Prince Dara Shikoh it cannot be approved by the principal of wisdom, for according to the Islamic law and convention the elder brother [Dara Shikoh] has the status of father...for the life of a few days in this transitory and evil world and its deceitful and deceptive enjoyments are no compensation for eternal infamy and misfortune...you should refrain from shedding the blood of the followers of Islam during the auspicious month of Ramadan. You should submit yourself to the orders of your benefactor and your ruler, as the commandment of God in that respect refers to obedience to the emperor.

In the same letter, Jahanara then praises Aurangzeb and appeals to his better instincts and high character:

The unbecoming and improper action of this wise and prudent brother [Aurangzeb], who is endowed with an elegant disposition, a noble mind, amiable manners and mildness of temper...the strife and hostile contest begun by this sagacious and high minded brother [Aurangzeb], who is esteemed for his laudable demeanor, praiseworthy behavior and generous disposition, and who has always endeavored to fulfill the wishes of the holy and blessed Emperor.

Jahanara's letter is a model of diplomacy and eloquence, and also of the authority she wielded over her brothers. Though Aurangzeb rejected the suggestion of partitioning the empire, he received Jahanara in his royal apartments, as befitted her imperial status as a royal woman of high authority. Many years later, on his own deathbed, he would make similar plans for the partitioning of his vast empire between his three warring sons.

For now, however, there would be no reconciliation. In 1658, Aurangzeb deposed his father and imprisoned him in Agra Fort. Jahanara, now forty-four years old, accompanied Shah Jahan into exile and spent the next seven years in prison with the once magnificent king of the world. In Delhi, Aurangzeb made a grand entry at the head of a parade of elephants bedecked with gold and silver. He sat on the Peacock Throne, distributed robes of honour and adopted the name Alamgir—Seizer of the Universe. Dara Shikoh was charged with apostasy, and paraded through the streets of Delhi before being killed. His son, Suleiman Shikoh, was slowly poisoned with opiates and died months later. There are no letters or diaries from this time that describe the terrible desolation Jahanara must have felt at the murder and desecration of her beloved sibling.

For the next seven years, the ambitious and talented Roshanara would attain the kind of recognition and glory she had fought so long for, though she was never given the title of Padshah Begum. The elephants, the endless retinues, the cavalry and the royal magnificence were at last hers to command.

Shah Jahan died after seven years of captivity at Agra, at the age of seventy-four. He had become, by the end, a man undone by the betrayal of his son and the frailty of his body. After his death Jahanara, now over fifty years old, was brought back to Delhi by Aurangzeb and installed in the grand mansion of Ali Mardan Khan, a dead Persian nobleman, in the relative freedom of Shahjahanabad outside the fort. This was bitterly resented by Roshanara, herself confined within the harem at the Red Fort. Aurangzeb gave Jahanara an annual pension of 1.7 million rupees and for the rest of her life she would bear the title of Padshah Begum. Unlike Nur Jahan, who effectively lost all power after the death of her husband, Emperor Jahangir, Jahanara retained her influence at the court. She led a socially and politically engaged life, arranging the marriage of her niece, Jahanzeb Banu Begum—Dara Shikoh's daughter, whom she had taken in upon his death—to Aurangzeb's third son, Azam. According to Manucci, 'To the seed pearls which issued from [Begum Sahib's] eyes at thus losing her beloved niece, added lovely pearls and handsome jewels as a marriage present.'

The local rajas of Kumaon, Garhwal and Sirmaur would write

to her over the years, asking for small concessions from the emperor and send her gifts of herbs, musk, honey, exotic birds and animals. 'The taste of honey was delicious and pleasing,' Jahanara wrote back to the Raja of Garhwal. And elsewhere, 'Procure one more pheasant and send it to us. As a favour, from our regal chambers, a robe of honour is being sent to you as a reward. Consider me to be your benefactor.'

Over the next few decades, Jahanara would see the gradual return of orthodox Islam to the court of Delhi. Aurangzeb prohibited alcohol, gambling and beards longer than 'four finger breadths'. Court music was outlawed, as was the office of the poet laureate. Even the rose beds in the imperial gardens were frowned upon. The infamous jizya or religious tax on non-Muslims was brought back, despite Jahanara's efforts to dissuade Aurangzeb.

Jahanara died in 1681, aged sixty-seven, having outlived her sister Roshanara who was never quite able to match the splendour of Jahanara's presence. Aurangzeb, who was in the Deccan at the time, commanded that she be referred to in court documents as Sahibat al-Zamani.

Jahanara designed her own final resting place, a stark contrast to the grandeur of the Taj Mahal—which originally had a blanket of pearls covering Mumtaz Mahal's tomb, long since looted—an open-air tomb of white marble, enclosed in lattice screens. The inscription on Jahanara's tomb reads:

> Let nothing cover my tomb save the green grass for
> grass suffices well as a covering for the grave of the lowly.

Her tomb lies a few feet away from that of the great Sufi saint Nizamuddin Auliya at his dargah in Delhi.

◆

Jahanara Begum was one of the most influential women of her age, and even though her legacy can be seen in some of the great monuments she built with her personal fortune, her caravanserai in what is now Old Delhi, that was meant to ensure that her name would never be forgotten, was destroyed. It was razed to the ground by the British after the Uprising of 1857 as a hated symbol of past Mughal grandeur. Jahanara's hamaam was also destroyed as was the Begum Ka Bagh and the mosques of some of Shah Jahan's wives. Chandni Chowk today is unrecognizable and Jahanara's reputation has been besmirched by Europeans who made aspersions about her love for her father.

Jahanara claimed for herself a glory as lustrous as that of her great ancestor Babur when she called herself 'that Timurid girl'. Her impeccable ambition in writing her very personal Sufi biographies, in which she claims the blessing of the Prophet Muhammad Himself, is quite unparalleled for a Muslim woman. With the casual negligence of time, Jahanara's memory is almost forgotten today. If she is remembered at all, it is paradoxically as a 'shadow princess' which in her own lifetime she most emphatically was not. However, there are still places where her memory survives—in the Agra mosque, where women gather every Thursday evenings in the zenana prayer halls she had built. 'They dip their palms in henna and leave the "mark" of their spiritual devotion on the *qibla* wall.' And at the Nizamuddin Auliya Dargah in Delhi. When the Sufi qawwalis soar and vault into the pewter dusk, the name of Jahanara, buried just a few steps away from the saint, is perforce strewn with reflected glory.

Rani Laxmibai

The Accidental Heroine

The Rajput chiefs who ruled the plains of Bundelkhand were engaged in skirmishes with the Mughals from the time Babur arrived in India in the early sixteenth century. In the seventeenth century, the Rajput Bundela chief Bir Singh Deo struck up a friendship with the young Prince Salim, later Emperor Jahangir, and added the Jahangir Palace, celebrating this friendship, to the imposing red stone fort of Orchha. He ordered a string of forts to be built, forming a defensive barricade around his principal city Orchha. Legend has it that he pointed out one of the new forts to a visiting friend, the Raja of Jaitpur, from the roof of Jahangir Palace. The Raja of Jaitpur searched the horizon, shading his eyes from the remorseless sun and finally muttered, 'Jhainsi', shadowy. This was the unassuming beginning of a city over which much blood would be spilled in the coming years, the home to one of India's greatest heroines—Rani Laxmibai.

Bundelkhand, which straddles the modern-day states of Rajasthan and Uttar Pradesh, is a land of harsh climate and poor soil. In the relentless Indian summer, the streams dry up completely and the dusty topsoil of the countryside is swept away by the desert winds. The monsoon rains cut deep gorges and ravines into the terrain which is blighted by a prehistoric weed called kans whose roots penetrate deep into the ground, making the soil even harder to plough and till.

In 1742, the Marathas took Jhansi from Orchha state and gained a foothold in the Bundelkhand region. Old rivalries between Jhansi and the Orchha chieftains simmered, however, aggravated by a lack of clear borders. What was noteworthy about Jhansi was its location—immediately south of Delhi, Agra and Gwalior and leading into the Deccan. The roads leading to these towns were used by traders of cotton, grain, sugar and salt, and by the mid-nineteenth century, Jhansi made a modest revenue from transit duties on these goods. Its location, so close to the Grand Trunk Road leading to Kanpur and Meerut, was what made Jhansi so important to the British colonizers in the years to come.

When they first arrived in Delhi, many of the British East India Company officials were fascinated by, and enthusiastically adapted to, the local culture. By 1760 after the three Carnatic Wars, the British had defeated their old enemy, the French, and had become the paramount colonial power in the world. Along with the arrogance of power came the certitude of evangelical Christianity and it was no longer considered acceptable to cohabit with local bibis and adopt Indian ways. The Indians were no longer the inheritors of a great and ancient civilization. They were now 'poor benighted heathens' awaiting conversion and the benign influence of Western progress. The magnificent Mughal empire, which had ruled the country for more than two hundred years, was undermined to the extent that the Mughal emperor, the Shadow of God on earth, had been demoted to the humble 'King of Delhi' by 1835 and coins were no longer minted with his likeness on them. Local chieftains formed alliances with the East India Company, which provided them military protection while retaining the rights to their trading profits and land revenue collection. By the 1850s, the Company had transformed itself from being a trading monopoly working to the shared advantage of English merchants and the Indian elite to becoming an administration with the right to the land revenues of princes and farmers.

Around the mid-nineteenth century, Lord Dalhousie, who at thirty-six was the youngest Governor General to come to India, had devised the provocative 'Doctrine of Lapse' to take advantage of India's age-old system of the adoption of children when rajas died without an heir. 'I cannot conceive it possible for anyone to dispute the policy of taking advantage of every just opportunity which presents itself for consolidating the territories that already belong to us, by taking possession of states which may lapse in the midst of them,' Dalhousie wrote in 1847, 'for thus getting rid of these petty intervening principalities which may be made a means of annoyance.' Jhansi, the small Maratha buffer state between Scindia, Gwalior and Rajput Bundelkhand, was just such a 'petty principality' and Rani Laxmibai, the reigning queen, was going to become a 'means of annoyance' far greater than Dalhousie could ever have anticipated.

By the turn of the nineteenth century, Maratha power had weakened and the Peshwa's authority was being challenged by his own officers, especially Holkar and Scindia. Forced to seek British help, the Peshwa fled his capital in Pune and conceded all his territorial claims in Bundelkhand, including Jhansi, to British forces in 1817. The ruling Newalkar family of Jhansi signed a separate treaty with the East India Company in the same year, recognizing Ram Chand Rao, the ruler at the time, as the hereditary ruler of Jhansi and raising his standing to maharaja. After this treaty, the successors of Ram Chand Rao ruled Jhansi with varying degrees of ineptitude but a steadfast loyalty to the British and were given the right, in 1833, to fly the British flag from the fort of Jhansi. The rulers of Jhansi from 1817 right upto 1857 'inherited a tradition of benevolence and dependence upon the British government.'

After the death of Ram Chand Rao in 1835, several rulers died without heirs and each time the East India Company intervened to decide on the issue of succession. When Raghunath the Leper died after three years, the Company appointed Gangadhar Rao as the Raja of Jhansi in 1838. Several years of drought and bad harvests had brought crushing poverty to Jhansi, exacerbated by the indifferent rule of Raghunath the Leper. Gangadhar Rao was unable to restore order among the Rajput people who resented their Maratha ruler and so, in 1839, the British occupied Jhansi Fort. Gangadhar became the titular king of Jhansi and was given a monthly allowance for upkeep by the British. Bereft of any power, he consoled himself with the arts, patronizing painters and musicians and participating in theatre and plays. British rule gradually brought back prosperity to the state and in 1842 Gangadhar Rao, now a middle-aged man whose first wife had died without giving him any heirs, took for his second wife a young Brahmin girl. Her name was Manikarnika and she was about fifteen years old.

There is very little that is known about Manikarnika before she took the name Laxmibai at the time of her wedding to Gangadhar Rao. Her father was Moropant Tambe, a Brahmin, and adviser to the brother of the deposed Maratha Peshwa and then a member of the Peshwa's retinue. A few details can be gleaned from this background: she was born in Varanasi; her mother an illiterate but intelligent woman called Bhagirathi died when she was very young and Manikarnika was raised in the court of the exiled Peshwa. Deprived of her mother's influence, Manu was raised among the boys of the court. She learnt how to read and write—unusual accomplishments for a girl of her time—and even learnt how to ride a horse and use the sword. Some traits of her personality can arguably be traced back to this unconventional upbringing: her self-confidence, her unencumbered vivacity and ability to hold forth in the company of men, even foreign men, and her impatience with the restrictions of purdah.

In 1843, the year in which the young Laxmibai married Gangadhar, the British returned Jhansi to its ruler. They maintained a military force called the Bundelkhand Legion in a piece of land outside Jhansi, which would later become the cantonment. Five years later, the condition of Jhansi having improved, the Bundelkhand Legion was disbanded and only a small force of British soldiers remained stationed in the town.

An unusual element of Laxmibai's wedding was that her father, Moropant Tambe, accompanied her to her marital home and continued to stay with her in Jhansi. Laxmibai lived as Rani of Jhansi for ten years, until Gangadhar's death in 1853. Despite British claims about his incompetence, the crime rate in the region had dropped during Gangadhar's reign. Further evidence that belied the claims of the British that the situation had worsened was the fact that, as we have seen, the Bundelkhand Legion was eventually disbanded and Jhansi returned to its ruler. What sources appear to agree on was that Gangadhar was a volatile, sometimes sullen, leader, given to meting out harsh punishments for minor infractions. Another, no doubt bewildering for the British, idiosyncracy of his was his penchant for dressing up in woman's clothes. Vishnu Bhatt Godshe, who came to Jhansi at this time, wrote in his memoirs about Gangadhar:

> It was rumoured that every once in a while, Gangadhar Baba would start behaving like a woman. When the urge struck him, he would suddenly go to the roof of the palace, remove his male attire and return dressed as a woman in a resplendent *zari choli* and sari, with a colourful silken braid attached to his topknot, bangles on his wrists, pearls around his neck, a nose ring and jingling anklets.

What Laxmibai thought of this, let alone what she thought of her husband overall, we will never know, as there are no surviving documents from her.

In 1853, as Gangadhar Rao lay on his deathbed, Laxmibai found herself childless and about to be widowed. Before dying, Gangadhar adopted a five-year-old boy, Damodar Rao, and invited Major Ellis, the political agent in Jhansi, and Captain Martin to his bedside so they could officially witness the adoption.

> God willing, I still hope to recover and regain my health. I am not too old, so I may still father children. In case that happens, I will take the proper measures concerning my adopted son. But if I fail to live, please take my previous loyalty into account and show kindness to my son. Please acknowledge my widow as the mother of this boy during her lifetime. May the government approve of her as the queen and ruler of this kingdom as long as the boy is still underage. Please take care that no injustice is done to her.

Gangadhar Rao also provided documents furnishing the record of the Newalkar family's long-standing loyalty to the British government. Accordingly, when Major John Malcolm, senior political agent, wrote to Dalhousie at Fort William with the news of Gangadhar's death and the adoption of his heir, he said that the Rani was 'a woman highly respected and esteemed and...fully capable of...assuming the reins of government in Jhansi.'

By all contemporary accounts, Rani Laxmibai, who was probably in her mid-twenties when her husband died, did not submit to the restrictions on the dress and habits of a Hindu Brahmin widow. She did start wearing white saris but continued wearing jewellery, including the pearls she was especially fond of, until her death. She did not shave her head, as was the custom for widows, but performed an expiatory puja every morning with holy Ganga water to atone for this sin. She was seen in public by her people and also visited the Lakshmi temple in town every day. It was only in the presence of British men that she remained in purdah.

As we know, soon after his arrival in India in 1848, Lord Dalhousie had brought into effect the 'Doctrine of Lapse', a ruling so controversial that it would bring about the end of his career and would forever be associated with his name. Dalhousie's ruling, which allowed the British to annex all lands in which a ruler died without an heir, had already made an exile of the adopted son of the Maratha ruler Peshwa Baji Rao II, Nana Sahib. Rani Laxmibai would not have been unaware of the resentment and disquiet around this issue and the need to quickly cement Damodar Rao's claim to the throne. In December 1853, Rani Laxmibai initiated talks with Major Robert Ellis who would later be reprimanded and transferred for allowing 'a doubt as to the finality of the decision of the government regarding the lapse of the state of Jhansi to rest on the mind of the ranee.' Rani Laxmibai would have also known of the accepted practice of sending appeals to the British government and this is what she did after consulting with Major Ellis. In her petitions, Rani Laxmibai stressed the fact of the loyalty of the Rajas of Jhansi to the British and referred to a long history of mutual respect and appreciation between the two. She also pointed out that the custom of adoption was prevalent 'in every part of Hindustan'.

Despite her appeals, Lord Dalhousie refused to recognize the adoption of Damodar Rao, deeming that Jhansi was not an 'ancient hereditary kingdom' and, therefore, existed at the behest of the British. 'The adoption of a boy by any man when he is almost in the last agonies,' wrote Dalhousie, 'is liable to suspicion.' There was also a more pragmatic reason for the annexation of Jhansi: 'The possession of it as our own will tend to the improvement of the general internal administration of our possessions in Bundlecund.' The Doctrine of Lapse was used to annex Punjab, Sikkim, lower Burma, Awadh and Udaipur. The land-collection revenues of the princely states thus annexed by Dalhousie added up to more than four million pounds per year, as he himself declared to the House of Commons in 1856 upon his return from India.

Even after Jhansi's lapse had been made official, Rani Laxmibai continued to write appeals to the Governor General, reminding him 'how loyal the Rajas of Jhansi have ever been: how loyal are their representatives.' She also described Jhansi as 'a powerless native state' and her husband Gangadhar Rao as 'not keeping up even the semblance of a warlike state.' Finally, '[h]elpless and prostrate,' she wrote for a month's grace, entreating 'your Lordship to grant me a hearing.' After Damodar's adoption had been declared void, the British made Rani Laxmibai vacate her palace in Jhansi Fort and shift into the Rani Mahal, a modest three-storey haveli in Jhansi town.

Rani Laxmibai now hired the services of a lawyer, John Lang, who had recently won a case against the British on behalf of an Indian plaintiff which became a cause célèbre. His speech was described by a contemporary as 'one of the most impudent perorations ever delivered before a British tribunal.' Lang was an eccentric Australian who ran a newspaper called the *Mofussilite* in

Meerut. He was mistakenly identified as an Englishman by most Indian contemporary accounts and it is likely that Rani Laxmibai presumed he was English too. John Lang used his newspaper to publish gossip and satire and excoriate attitudes of the British wherever possible. He learnt how to speak Persian and Hindustani and was 'generally regarded as a gadfly, a thorn in the side of "John Company" and the British administration.'

The manner in which John Lang was received in Jhansi is a testament to Laxmibai's keen sense of statecraft—the Rani needed to prove to him that Jhansi was capable of ruling itself. Lang was brought from Agra in a horse-drawn carriage accompanied by the Diwan of Jhansi and a butler who carried a bucket of ice containing water, beer and wine. A servant stood outside the palanquin on a footboard and fanned the men with a punkah. Upon reaching Jhansi, an escort of fifty horsemen carrying immense spears accompanied the palanquin to a garden where a large tent had been set up.

Rani Laxmibai sat behind a curtain at one end of the tent which had been carpeted with flowers for the occasion. John Lang later wrote of this meeting in his report. Since at one point the young Damodar Rao, perhaps urged by his mother, moved aside the purdah, Lang was able to provide a description of the Rani:

> She was a woman of about the middle size rather stout, but not too stout. Her face must have been very handsome when she was younger, and even now it has many charms— though according to my idea of beauty, it was too round. The expression also was very good, and very intelligent. The eyes were particularly fine, and the nose very delicately shaped. She was not very fair, though she was far from black. She had no ornaments, strange to say, upon her person, except a pair of gold earrings. Her dress was a plain white muslin, so fine in texture and drawn about her in such a way, and so tightly that the outline of her figure was plainly discernible—and a remarkably fine figure she had.

When her son exposed her by drawing the curtain, the Rani 'was, or affected to be, very much annoyed; but presently she laughed, and good-humouredly expressed a hope that a sight of her had not lessened my sympathy with her sufferings nor prejudiced her cause.' John Lang gallantly replied, 'On the contrary. If the Governor-General could only be as fortunate as I have been...he would at once give Jhansi back again to be ruled over by its beautiful Queen.'

The Rani and John Lang carried out their talks from six in the evening to two o'clock the next morning. Every time the Rani would list her grievances against Lord Dalhousie's ruling, the entourage of women sitting behind the purdah would let out a loud chorus of lament. There is no mention of any male advisers, or the presence of the Rani's father at this meeting. The Rani herself argued her case to Lang, listened to his suggestions, and discussed the options available to her. Allowing Lang to see her could well have been a deliberate move on her part—so he could see the poignancy of her widow's whites, the lack of ornaments and also her physical charm—to win over someone she thought could be invaluable to her case.

In June 1854, with the help of John Lang, Laxmibai drew up a comprehensively argued appeal, reminding Lord Dalhousie of the treaties of 1804, 1817 and 1832 which guaranteed to Ram Chand Rao and his successors the right to rule Jhansi. She mentioned the precedence of recognized adoptions in the past, both in Jhansi and in other similarly placed kingdoms. Lord Dalhousie, however, ruled the Rani's request 'wholly inadmissible'. Laxmibai responded with fresh arguments, and passionately worded appeals, talking of her dispossession as a 'gross violation and negation of British faith and honour.' She also wrote of her distress at the loss of her 'authority, rank and affluence' and being reduced to a state of 'subjection, dishonour and poverty.'

But Lord Dalhousie was part of a new corps of British officers in India characterized by 'an impatience at the existence of any native state...and often insane advocacy of their absorption'. Jhansi lapsed to the British in May 1854 and a new superintendent, Captain Alexander Skene, was appointed; a pension was recommended for the Rani and the British resumed the collection of Jhansi's land revenues. Gangadhar Rao's private property and a pension was decreed for Laxmibai on the understanding that she should also be responsible for the outstanding debts of the state with respect to its assets. Laxmibai was furious at this treatment, arguing that the debts were state debts, not personal ones contracted by herself. She refused the pension and considered leaving Jhansi to return to her native Varanasi. The British were concerned enough about the effect of such a move by Laxmibai to ask Sir Robert Hamilton, agent to Dalhousie, to visit with the Rani.

Laxmibai received Robert Hamilton and the two new officers, Skene and Gordon, in full durbar, in the presence of her father Moropant Tambe and her other advisers. Robert Hamilton later wrote that she was 'civil and polite, quite the lady, and easy in manner and in conversation.' Hamilton enquired if she would accept the pension offered by the British and Laxmibai said she could not as it would mean accepting the lapse of Jhansi. Hamilton convinced her not to leave Jhansi—it was clearly crucial to the keeping of the peace—and Laxmibai agreed. Hamilton would later write that 'she was a clever, strong-minded woman, well able to argue and too much for many. There was a complete command of patience and temper'.

It was probably around this time that Laxmibai resumed her childhood habit of horseriding and physical exercise. She rode around Jhansi on horseback and in the afternoons held a daily court at Rani Mahal. The many gifts she received were almost all distributed amongst her attendants. Laxmibai usually wore white chanderi saris but occasionally donned the more practical male attire of loose pyjamas, a fitted coat, and a turban covering her long hair.

Hamilton visited Jhansi again in April 1855. This time the Rani received him alone in the durbar room, where she sat behind a curtain. She proposed, 'very cleverly and clearly', that she be placed under his authority rather than any other arrangement. Laxmibai made no mention of the lapse of Jhansi, or her resentment towards the British. She was concerned, according to Hamilton, about the maintenance of her dignity as the widow of a king. Laxmibai later wrote to Hamilton saying 'you are well aware that as a fallen party, whose state had been lost, I have stretched out my supplicant hands for the protection and favour of this Government'. She reiterated her abhorrence at the thought of 'being looked down upon' by neighbouring chiefs and that the financial arrangements that the British had afforded her were 'a disgrace, which renders it quite impossible...to live from day to day'.

Until January 1856, Rani Laxmibai continued to send requests and pleas to the British but the government remained unresponsive. Gangadhar Rao's debts had been deducted against the Rani's pension, cow slaughter had been allowed in Jhansi despite an earlier ban, and the revenue from two villages associated with the Lakshmi temple was to be paid to the British. As far as they were concerned, Jhansi was an inconsequential state and Laxmibai's dogged pursuit of justice and honour was swept aside by the increasingly autocratic way in which the colonial power was beginning to function.

As a portent of things to come, Lord Canning, who was soon to replace Dalhousie as Governor General of India, addressed the court of directors of the East India Company in London in August of 1855: 'We must not forget that in the sky of India, serene as it is, a cloud may arise, at first no bigger than a man's hand, but which, growing bigger and bigger, may at last threaten to overwhelm us with ruin.'

◆

Years of oppressive rule, the introduction of recent Christian evangelical laws, British interference in local customs and religious practices and many other political, economic and social factors are cited by historians as the reasons that led to the Revolt of 1857. What precipitated the Uprising, however, was the introduction, in February 1857, of the Enfield rifle, the cartridges of which were greased with cow and pig fat—a grave insult to both Hindu and Muslim soldiers who had to bite these cartridges in order to make them ready for use. The rebellion started in May 1857 in Meerut—one of the largest cantonments in India at that time—with the massacre of English officers, women and children, and quickly spread throughout north India.

Jhansi was strategically located at the junction of four important roads, to Kanpur, Lucknow, Agra and Delhi—all major centres of the rebellion—and the garrison posted at Jhansi comprised only Indian troops. Moreover, many of the Bundela Rajput chiefs despised British rule and saw the chaos of the Uprising as a way to settle old scores. In 1855, when Robert Hamilton had reported on the relations among the houses of Bundelkhand, he had described the armies of the chiefs as an 'assembly of idle, dissipated men in parties independent of each other, under no proper control, and ready for any broil.' In Almora, an Englishman noted, 'There were several gangs of robbers in Bundelkhand just waiting for an opportunity to plunder.'

The British superintendent Skene reported a week after the Meerut massacre: 'The troops here, I am glad to say, continue staunch and express their unbounded abhorrence of the atrocities committed at Meerut and Delhi.' A few days later he added, 'All will settle down here...on the receipt of intelligence of success...' The British attitude in other centres of the Uprising was no different from Skene's—the colonial masters could simply not believe their own loyal troops could mutiny. But revolt they did, and on 5 June 1857 a company of the Twelfth Native Infantry occupied the Star Fort in the cantonment outside Jhansi, stormed the jail and released all the prisoners.

The British population of the cantonment rushed to Jhansi Fort for safety and sent messages to Rani Laxmibai asking for assistance. But Laxmibai was vulnerable herself, sequestered in her small city palace with only a force of one hundred and fifty bodyguards to protect her. Laxmibai was about to find herself stranded in the eye of a storm she hadn't seen coming. Within three days, all the British men, women and children would be massacred in an area called Jokhun Bagh after surrendering to the sepoys upon a promise of safe conduct.

In mid-1857, with Delhi, Meerut, Kanpur and Jhansi already stoked by the Uprising, the rebels now began to intimidate the Rani so that her main concern was the safeguarding of the autonomy of Jhansi. The rebels even considered allowing a Newalkar relative, Sadasheo Rao, to claim the throne of Jhansi until the Rani offered them money and aid to placate them. The rebels left for Delhi, but not before issuing a final proclamation: 'The people are God's, the country is the Padhshah's, and the Raj is Ranee Luchmee Baee's.'

Laxmibai wrote to Major Walter Erskine, commissioner of the Sagar area, the day after the rebels left Jhansi for Delhi and reported that the government troops 'through their faithlessness, cruelty, and violence killed all the European civil and military officers, the clerks and all their families.' She added that the rebels had 'behaved with much violence against herself and servants and extorted a great deal of money from her...to save her life and honour.' In a second letter to Erskine she talked of the breakdown of law and order in Jhansi which she asserted she would not be able to control 'without a competent Government force and fund.'

Despite the later British certainty that Laxmibai was complicit in the massacre of the British civilians at Jhansi, there is no actual proof to this effect. In fact, Erskine replied to Laxmibai authorizing her rule of Jhansi and assured her that she would be recompensed for the losses she had incurred and that the British would 'deal liberally' with her. Moreover, Erskine felt sufficiently confident of the Rani's loyalty to forward her letters to the central government reassuring them that her letter 'agrees with what I have heard from other sources.'

Even Sir Robert Hamilton, who having met the Rani at length, felt he had some insight into her personality, later wrote: 'not a paper incriminating the Ranee did I find nor did there appear any evidence that she desired or was privy to the murder of any Europeans... The Ranee was not present nor any man on her behalf.'

As soon as the rebels had left Jhansi, Laxmibai directed her attention to the defence and safety of her city. The British were too occupied with the numerous incendiary revolts that were taking place throughout Bundelkhand following the massacre at Jokhun Bagh to attend to the relief of Jhansi and so Laxmibai found herself, for the first time, solely in charge of Jhansi. She moved back into her palace inside Jhansi Fort, where she held court every day, attending to the city's affairs personally. She resumed the manufacture of all weapons—guns, cartridges and gunpowder—and used her troops to restore peace. She also opened a mint, and distributed food and clothing to the poor.

It was around this time that she began wearing clothes which 'symbolically combined the elements of a warrior with those of a queen: jodhpurs, a silk blouse with a low-cut bodice, a red silk cap with a loose turban around it. She wore diamond bangles and large diamond rings on her small hands: but a short bejwelled sword and two silver pistols were stuck into her cummerbund.' According to Nathu Godse, her hair 'was either tied in a large bun or hung below her waist in a long plait... She looked like the avatar of a warrior goddess.'

In less than a year, Rani Laxmibai wrought her legend into the Bundelkhand countryside. 'The ranee was remarkable for her bravery, cleverness and perseverance,' Sir Hugh Rose, commander of the Central India Force, was to write of her later. 'Her generosity to her subordinates was unbounded.' But for her transformation into a national heroine, further sacrifices would have to be made. Already, as 1857 lurched into 1858, a storm was gathering on the distant horizon.

The first threat to Jhansi came not from the British, but from the regent queen, a Rajput, of the neighbouring state of Orchha. Jhansi was besieged for two months by the Orchha troops before

Laxmibai was able to break the siege and force the enemy to retreat to their lands. Shaken by the vulnerability of her small state, Laxmibai began building up her troops, strengthening her army to a total of around fifteen thousand troops.

Meanwhile, news of the brutality of British reprisals against the cities which had dared to rebel began to trickle in. The 'poor benighted heathens' needing conversion to a civilizing Christian religion, which was the earlier British narrative, were now people whose religion consisted only of 'bestiality, infanticide and murder... the rankest filth that imagination ever conceived.' From the Delhi Ridge, Brigadier-General Nicholson (later to become the 'Hero of Delhi' of Victorian novels, and the 'Butcher of Delhi' to Indian historians) a self-proclaimed clairvoyant, declared, 'let us propose a bill for the flaying alive, impalement, or burning of the murderers of the women and children at Delhi. The idea of simply hanging the perpetrators of such atrocities is maddening.' Nicholson's call was met with enthusiasm with the killing of an Indian becoming 'best sport'. Thousands died at Varanasi, 'their corpses hanging from branches and signposts all over town.' Scores of others were blasted from the mouths of cannons after they were 'smeared with the blood of the Englishmen murdered by the rebels. When the gun was fired, the head of the victim, hardly disfigured, would fly through the smoke and then fall to the ground slightly blackened, followed by the arms and legs, which would also only be partially mutilated.' As each town in the north was retaken by the British forces, the surviving rebels fled and Bundelkhand became the last stand of the Indians against the British.

When Laxmibai heard that her sympathetic interlocutor Robert Hamilton had returned to India, she wrote him an imploring letter in January 1858: 'I beg you will give me your support in the best way you can, and thus save myself and the people who are reduced to the last extremity and are not able to cope with the enemy.' For Laxmibai, even eight months after the beginning of the Uprising at Meerut, and well after the worst of the atrocities committed in reprisals by the British, the 'enemy' was still anyone who threatened the safety of Jhansi, including her ancient rivals in Orchha. The Rani was far from the 'Goddess of Swaraj' or the embodiment of Bharat Mata of later narratives. There is no evidence that she was colluding with the Maratha leaders of the Uprising such as Nana Sahib or Tatya Tope. She was simply fighting for her son's birthright, her widow's prerogative—her honour and her land.

As news of the massacres of white women and children reached Great Britain, any sympathy for the Indians was replaced by fear and hate. The Uprising of 1857 was now the 'epic of the race' and most Britons were united in their loathing of 'native' cruelty. Even Charles Dickens weighed in, imagining himself addressing the Indian people: '[I] have the honour to inform you Hindoo gentry that it is my intention...with all merciful swiftness of execution, to exterminate the Race from the face of the earth.'

Laxmibai received no reply from Robert Hamilton, nor to any other missive she sent to the central government. In the violence of 1857, the British had decided that Laxmibai was complicit in the murder of the British at Jokhun Bagh. Even Erskine, who had earlier believed the Rani's version of events, now assured Hamilton in January 1858 that Laxmibai 'should be hanged when caught'. Rebel soldiers meanwhile continued to stagger into Jhansi, bringing stories of carnage and of the approaching British armies.

Sometime in the early months of 1858, Laxmibai finally accepted that she had been abandoned by the British and decided, instead, to prepare for war. She started repairing and strengthening the city walls and the bastions and turrets were manned day and night. The manufacture of munitions was ramped up and the fort was stocked with supplies of flour, ghee and sugar. Laxmibai had all the trees around the fort and town cleared, so that the British soldiers, when they arrived, would be tormented by an absence of shade as the days got steadily hotter.

As the certainty of war approached Jhansi, some people panicked and started deserting the town. Sensing the mood, Laxmibai organized a lavish ceremony, a haldi kumkum rite for all the women of the town. 'I have never witnessed such a spectacular celebration anywhere' wrote Vishnu Bhatt Godshe. 'From two in the afternoon till late at night, streams of women dressed in all their finery kept arriving at the palace.' As the gunners on the city ramparts mounted the twelve cannons that would defend the city to the end, in the Rani's palace 'all the chandeliers [were] aglow, [and] the vast room dazzled the eyes.' As women and children from different castes walked into the palace, they 'were all welcomed with sprays of perfume and showered with fragrant flower petals.'

Meanwhile, fresh troops brought in from Great Britian especially to quell the Uprising were now heading towards Jhansi. The leader of this Central India Field Force, General Sir Hugh Rose, was a distinguished career soldier, son of a diplomat and a seasoned veteran of many conflicts, including the Crimean War. He was brought to India in 1857 to deal with the Uprising in Bundelkhand and what he had seen so far of fighting on the Indian side had not impressed him. 'If they stand at Jhansi,' he wrote dismissively, 'they must have improved since the last ten days, as it has been one general uninterrupted run.'

Hugh Rose set up cavalry camps and had trenches dug all around Jhansi so that no one could escape. An army surgeon, Dr Thomas Lowe took note of the Rani's tactic of using the unbearable heat against the British: 'The country about Jhansi was as bare as a desert, they had evidently done all they could to starve us.' But even in this fight for the freedom of Jhansi, Laxmibai was shackled by the lack of cooperation between the Indian parties. 'We found friends in Scindia and the Rani of Orchha,' Dr Lowe explained, 'and from them we obtained grass and firewood and vegetables for the troops.'

When the siege of Jhansi began, the British forces struck the granite walls of Jhansi with eighteen-pound cannons. Laxmibai and her gunners resisted with ferocious bravery so that even Hugh Rose was impressed enough to write: 'The chief of the rebel artillery was a first rate artilleryman...the manner in which the rebels served their guns, repaired their defences and reopened fire from batteries and guns repeatedly shut up was remarkable. From some batteries they returned shot for shot.'

In the late afternoon, the Rani could be seen riding her horse along the broad summit of the fort walks, stopping to inspect and encourage her troops. The gunners of Jhansi resisted the siege for longer than was thought possible with their ancient guns. 'We had silenced several of their guns and as often as they were silenced, so often did they re-open from them to our astonishment,' wrote Dr Lowe. The Rani herself was the subject of intense speculation amongst the British soldiers. 'The dauntless bravery of the Ranee was a great conversation in the camp,' an army surgeon later reminisced. 'Far-seeing individuals thought they saw her under an awning on the large square tower of the fortress...watching the progress of the siege.' In the historical records of the 14th Light Dragoons Laxmibai is described as 'a perfect Amazon in bravery...just the sort of daredevil woman soldiers admire.'

But there was a limit to the resistance of these ancient cannons and gallant defenders and soon the guns of Jhansi fell silent. The British were now perilously close to entering the fort. For a few hours, the people of Jhansi dared to hope, when news of the arrival of the guerrilla leader Tatya Tope reached the city. But the next day, Tatya Tope and his troops suffered a disastrous defeat at the Betwa River and it became certain that Jhansi now stood alone.

'Sometimes,' wrote Vishnu Bhatt Godshe succinctly, 'a sense of desperation lends a strange sort of courage to the losing side. By now, the army of Jhansi knew that the fall of their city was imminent and once the British entered the city they would show no mercy.' Even in these grim circumstances, 'the Rani summoned her generals and said to them that since the Peshwa's army had failed to defend Jhansi, they must guard the fort themselves; they all agreed.'

The British forces scaled the walls of Jhansi on 3 April 1858, and it is clear from Dr Lowe's description that the soldiers and people of Jhansi tried to stop them with whatever projectiles and weapons they had: '(A)mid the chaos of sounds of volleys of musketry and roaring of cannons and hissing and bursting of rockets, stink pots, infernal machines, huge stones, blocks of wood and trees' were thrown at the British soldiers. 'The Rani, dressed in male attire with a sword in her hand, began her rounds to boost the morale of her men,' wrote Vishnu Bhatt Godshe, but Jhansi's walls were breached, and the British soldiers stormed through the streets of the city and 'they fought from house to house in hand-to-hand combat. Skirmishing continued in the streets and houses as the English cut their way toward the palace against obstinate resistance.'

From the fort of Jhansi, the Rani looked down at the city and 'saw scenes of devastation...[the city] was still smouldering. Cries and moans filled the air. Guns roared and the howls of hundreds of stray dogs, along with the panic-stricken cries of dying cattle and mules, made our hair stand on end.'

Contemplating the desolation of her city, Laxmibai realized that her dream of ruling Jhansi was over. She would realize, too, that the British would not easily forgive her for taking up arms against them. According to Vishnu Bhatt Godshe, 'The Rani was deeply distressed by the humiliation of her beloved subjects and sat mourning for them in her living quarters.' This desecration of her people's honour was unbearable for her and for a bleak moment she considered ending it all. 'She would blow herself up, along with the empty fort,' wrote Vishnu Bhatt Godshe of the Rani's decision, preferring death to capture by the British.

Despite the enduring representation of the Rani jumping off the walls of Jhansi Fort on horseback, charging at a distant enemy with her adopted son strapped to her back, this was not the way Laxmibai could have left the city. The walls of the fort were too high to make this a feasible route and even if Laxmibai survived the jump, her horse would not have, and she would not have been able to take her soldiers with her.

Instead, on 3 April 1858, in the middle of the night, the

Rani and a few hundred soldiers gathered in the fort's courtyard, mounted their horses and rode out into the open countryside. It is in this precipitous moment that Laxmibai stepped into legend and immortality. Although it is popularly believed that Laxmibai had her adopted son, now ten years old, strapped to her back on the horse, Damodar Rao himself had no memory of this. The image of the Rani that is etched in legend is that of a young woman on a silver horse, silver sword girded to her side and a necklace of pearls glinting in the moonlight.

Throughout the next few weeks of battle, the Rani lived on the road, in the blighted countryside of Bundelkhand where the heat was now so great that 'big tears trickle[d] down the cheeks of the patient elephants and the very camels groaned.' The days were leaden wastelands of roiling red dust and shimmering sun. Even during this headlong and desperate escape from Jhansi, Laxmibai maintained some semblance of her old opulence and Hugh Rose was later to describe her war tent as 'very coquettish'.

Finally the Rani and her soldiers reached Kalpi, about a hundred and fifty kilometres away in the modern-day state of Uttar Pradesh, where the remaining rebels had gathered. Here they found Tatya Tope, and Rao Sahib, nephew of Nana Sahib, the last Peshwa's dispossessed son, and readied themselves for battle. Horrified to discover that the Rani had escaped, Hugh Rose pursued the rebels and engaged with them at Koonch and at Kalpi. In heat so terrible— the morning temperature was already close to 40 degrees Celsius— the Enfield rifles would not load and the rebels were routed after putting up a fierce resistance. A British officer present at the battle noted that 'after the firing, down went the musket and out came the sharp-cutting native sword. They cut and slashed our horses and men so long as one of their band remained alive.'

Vishnu Bhatt Godshe, who met her on the road to Kalpi, described in his memoir one of the last authenticated records of the Rani of Jhansi. 'She was dressed as a Pathan male,' he wrote, 'and looked exhausted, dusty and tense. Her face looked sad and flushed.' The rebels had just been routed at Koonch despite desperate bravery and would be summarily defeated at Kalpi within a few days.

Rani Laxmibai, Tatya Tope and Rao Sahib escaped from Kalpi after the defeat of the rebel army and made the unexpected move of capturing the great fortress of Scindia at Gwalior. The young maharaja, Jayaji Rao, fled from his fortress to the safety of the British garrison at Agra, but his troops and soldiers all went over to the rebel forces. The Rani was gifted a 'priceless' pearl necklace from Scindia's treasury. The absent Nana Sahib was proclaimed Peshwa of the Maratha Confederacy and, for a few days, the rebel leaders feasted and celebrated their victory.

Conspicuous by her absence from these celebrations was Laxmibai, who had left the fort and shifted to the Phoolbagh sector of Gwalior with Damodar Rao and a few female attendants. Here she spent the next few days dressed in an army uniform, 'continually on horseback, armed with sword and pistol, at the head of 300 horse.'

When Hugh Rose, accompanied by a squadron of the 8th Hussars, reached Gwalior the first obstacle they came upon was the Rani and her band of soldiers at the Kotah ki Serai. Laxmibai was wearing her pearl necklace along with her armour, her sword in its jewelled scabbard. It is claimed that she took as her motto for this last battle the famous verse: 'If killed in battle we enter the heavens and, if victorious, we rule the earth.'

The Rani was killed in the confrontation with Hugh Rose's soldiers in the month of June 1858. Although the exact manner of her death is not known, three independent accounts written immediately after her death agree she was mortally wounded as a result of a blow received during hand-to-hand fighting. Captain Clement Walker Heneage of the 8th Hussars who was present at the battle wrote:

> There was no pretence of resistance any longer except from
> a slight, fully-armed figure that was helplessly whirled along

in this cataract of men and horses. Again and again this one leader, gesticulating and vociferating, attempted to stem the torrent of routed rebels, but all in vain. There was no possibility of holding up the broken Mahrattas and at last a chance shot struck down, across his (*sic*) horse's neck, this one champion of the retreating force. A moment later the swaying figure was overtaken, and one stroke from a Hussar's sabre ended the whole matter...it was discovered that it was the Rhani of Jhansi herself who had thus ended her meteoric career.

A similar account was found among Lord Canning's papers:

> Killed by a trooper of the 8th Hussars, who was never discovered. Shot in the back, her horse baulked... She then fired at the man and he passed his sword through her. She used to wear gold anklets and Scindia's pearl necklace. The army mourned her for two days. The infantry attacked the cavalry for allowing her to be killed. The cavalry said she would ride too far in front.

Sir Hugh Rose and the 8th Hussars, at whose hands she was probably killed, praised the outstanding courage and intelligence of the Rani. 'In her death,' said the regimental history of the 8th Hussars, 'the rebels lost their bravest and best military leader.'

Laxmibai was quickly removed from the scene of the battle and cremated by her men before her body could fall into the 'polluting' hands of the enemy. With the death of the Rani, the rebels lost heart and Gwalior fell to the British. Nana Sahib managed to escape but Tatya Tope was captured and hanged. Bundelkhand returned to the control of the British after more than a year of resistance and the 1857 Uprising effectively came to an end.

Rani Laxmibai's death on the battlefield made her a prominent star of the nationalist movement. There would be minor variations, especially within the British narrative, as they struggled to decide whether she was a licentious 'Jezebel', a brave and worthy foe equal to Joan of Arc, or a murdering fiend slaughtering innocent women and children. She was the subject of numerous 'mutiny novels' in subsequent years and, in India, her legend grew through the oral tradition of folksongs and ballads.

◆

'In the Greek myths [the warrior women] Amazons always die young and beautiful. But a short, splendid life and violent death in battle was the perfect *heroic* ideal in myth,' writes historian Adrienne Mayor. But if Rani Laxmibai led her troops and died a heroine's death, she was also a woman sometimes assailed by doubt. After Hugh Rose's forces had scaled the walls of Jhansi, and were engaged in hand-to-hand combat through the streets of the city, Laxmibai is said to have wept and considered leading her corps of bodyguards into a last suicide attack.

For a Hindu Brahmin widow, her decision to not shave her head nor renounce her pearls and diamonds was revolutionary for its time. She dressed like a man, argued with men, rode horses and wielded a sword as well if not better than most men—all of which were unthinkable activities for a widow. When Gandhi spoke of the role of women in India's nationalist movement, he spoke of them as the 'embodiment of sacrifice, silent suffering, humility, faith and knowledge.' In speaking of role models for women within the freedom struggle, Gandhi never spoke of the unflinching Laxmibai or, for that matter, other warrior queens—Bhima Bai Holkar, who fought the British in 1817 or Hazrat Mahal of Awadh (of whom we shall hear in the next chapter). Both these women ruled kingdoms and resisted their enemies in battle, but neither of them, arguably, achieved the sort of posthumous fame Laxmibai did.

It is sometimes forgotten that Rani Laxmibai chose to fight after her repeated attempts to solve the problem diplomatically had failed—she was a reluctant participant in the drama that made her a heroine. Whether Laxmibai would have joined the Uprising if the British hadn't taken over Jhansi is a matter of conjecture. Her priority throughout her short life was Jhansi, and she died fighting as the rightful queen of her kingdom.

As the Indian nationalist movement came into being in the early decades of the twentieth century, the Rani's legend was appropriated and she was made a national icon whose image began to appear 'on postage stamps, the names of streets and buildings and historical and literary texts'. It was conveniently forgotten that she had been forced into rebellion following the Jokhun Bagh massacre. Her story was made into a rallying cry for the nationalists and she became a symbol of sacrifice for freedom—Bharat Mata or the Goddess of Swaraj herself.

For the more radical elements in the nationalist movement (precursors to the Hindu national movement that is now known as Hindutva) too, she was an appropriate symbol. They incorporated her iconography—along with other martial women such as Durgavati and Padmavati—as the emphasis shifted to strong women of the 'virangana' genre. After Independence, moreover, the threatening 'Other' was no longer the imperialist British but the Muslim, and the Rani, with her impeccable Brahmin Hindu lineage, was a perfect role model.

One of the ballads immortalizing Laxmibai reimagines her as an amalgamation of various goddesses:

Though Lakshmi you are Durga
Like the Ganga you purify all evil
In war you are Bhairavi and Chamunda
You are Kali,
Forgiving and protector of kindred
Death-axe to the British enemy.

In becoming arguably the greatest Indian woman legend, Rani Laxmibai lost some of her humanity which makes her an authentic and believable heroine. History has merged with myth to obliterate the traits which resonate even today—the small vanities, the despair, the occasional doubt. She had the pistols and swords, certainly, but also the pearl necklace and the diamond scabbard. She was haunted constantly by her lost honour, but she watched over the dignity of all Jhansi's people—the Hindus, as well as the Muslims. She was a complicated, ardent woman who never baulked at the full extent of the sacrifice asked of her. Laxmibai asked of her destiny what the worth was of a dispossessed Indian widow. The price she was willing to pay was blood, a kingdom, and defiance of the most powerful empire on earth.

Hazrat Mahal
The Making of a Rebel Begum

On 3 July 1857, a grand procession is entering the Chandiwali Barahdari, a pavilion in the immense central garden of the Kaiserbagh Palace in Lucknow. At the centre of the procession is a fourteen-year-old boy, slim and dark, who is being led by his mother. Surrounding them is an entourage of women, co-wives and servant girls in their sparkling shararas and veils. They are on their way to the coronation ceremony of the young boy, Birjis Qadr, son of the recently exiled Nawab Wajid Ali Shah, the last King of Awadh. His mother is Begum Hazrat Mahal, one of the innumerable wives of the deposed Nawab, and one of the nine women he had divorced long before leaving Lucknow the year before.

'This was no token ceremony by a group of rebels, as the British would have liked to believe,' writes Llewellyn-Jones, 'but a solemn occasion that brought together the leaders of groups alienated since annexation and now confirmed in their determination to regain the lost kingdom.' For after the sepoy uprisings at Delhi, Meerut and Kanpur, Lucknow and Awadh too had committed to the cause of the rebellion in 1857. All the other begums of Wajid Ali Shah had been asked for their consent in appointing Birjis Qadr and he was to become the visible symbol in whose name orders could be given and legitimacy ensured for the fractious rebels. 'We affect to disbelieve his legitimacy,' admitted war journalist William Howard Russell, 'but the zemindars, who ought to be better judges of the facts, accept Birjeis Kuddr without hesitation.' The overall sovereign, however, was still the old Mughal emperor in Delhi, Bahadur Shah Zafar, who, although considerably enfeebled, was still a rallying force for the rebels, his appeal cutting across religion and caste. Historian Rudrangshu Mukherjee has pointed out that Birjis Qadr's coronation too evoked glimpses of a lost Mughal world 'witnessed by the pomp and ceremony that accompanied the coronation, in the offer of nazranas, the gift of khilats, and the establishment of the durbar.' The Emperor himself, petitioned by Birjis Qadr, bestowed the title of wazir on the young boy and asked him to rule in Awadh as his representative.

Birjis was crowned with a simple turban of silk with gold thread, called a mandeel, as the crown jewels—along with the rest of Wajid Ali Shah's treasure, weapons and jewellery—had been lost the previous month when the British plundered Kaiserbagh Palace. The loot from the palace was spirited away to the Residency where Captain F. M. Birch commented on the 'certainly very impressive' crown jewels which 'would make a pleasant addition to army prize money... There were some very fine pearls and emeralds, some of them being as large as eggs.'

The sparks of the revolt were lit in Lucknow on 30 May when troops in the Marion cantonment of the city set fire to the officers' bungalows and killed three British soldiers. Chief Commissioner Lawrence immediately ordered all European women and children to the Residency complex and began arresting and hanging officers and sepoys suspected of being part of the Uprising. For a month the city of Lucknow waited in a state of suspended terror while garrison after garrison in north India blazed. On 30 June, Lawrence was informed that rebel troops, some 5,000 officers and soldiers, were marching towards the city. Lawrence rode out to meet them with 600 soldiers, British and Indian. The troops clashed at Chinhat, six miles outside Lucknow, and the British forces were decisively routed. Lawrence would later recall:

> It was one moving mass of men. Regiment after regiment of the insurgents poured steadily towards us, flanks covered with a foam of skirmishers, the light puffs of smoke from their muskets floating from every ravine and bunch of grass in our front. As to the mass of the troops, they come on in quarter distance columns, their standards waving in their faces and everything performed as steadily as possible. A field day on parade could not have been better.

The siege of Lucknow began with the rebels moving into the city and settling in the sprawling gardens of the rich noblemen. The air was filled with the metallic smell of musket shots and the shouts of the sepoys.

Three days later, watching the coronation of the young Birjis, apart from a throng of curious civilian onlookers, were most of the rebel leaders and sepoys and a crowd of taluqdars. There were two men in particular who would leave their imprint on the Lucknow Uprising. The first was Raja Jailal Singh, a taluqdar of Faizabad district and a prominent courtier during the time of Wajid Ali Shah. He was appointed collector of revenue and would later act as liaison between Hazrat Mahal's court in Kaiserbagh Palace and the rebel army, which was stationed in the Khurshid Manzil. The second was Mammu Khan, superintendent-in-charge of the Begum's political offices. Raja Jailal Singh and Mammu Khan, along with another twenty men—members of the old Nawabi court as well as soldiers and officers of the rebel army—formed the new government of Awadh. Since Birjis Qadr was a minor, the government owed its allegiance to his mother, Begum Hazrat Mahal. Over the next few months, taluqdars from the Awadhi countryside, some of whom were minor rajas of their areas, would answer the Begum's call to arms in great numbers.

◆

If an exalted birth were a prerequisite for a heroic fate then Muhammadi Khanum, as Hazrat Mahal was known before she was discovered by Wajid Ali Shah, was born for obscurity and even squalor. It was a fortuitous mix of Hazrat Mahal's beauty, keen intelligence and the fin de regime decadence of the culture of the nawabs of Lucknow that brought Hazrat Mahal into the coronation hall at Chandiwali Barahdari in 1857.

Muhammadi Khanum was born to a slave of African origin called Umber, who was owned by a certain Ghulam Ali Khan. Her mother was Maher Afza, Umber's mistress. At some stage of her adolescence she was sold by her parents to a courtesan. In another city or at another time this could have meant a slow descent into ignominy but Lucknow up until the mid-nineteenth century was a city that valued and honoured tawai'fs or courtesans as expert practitioners of music and dance, in addition to providing companionship to the discerning gentry of the city. With the slow disintegration of the court of Delhi from the eighteenth century onwards, musicians, dancers and poets began drifting into the Awadhi capital of Lucknow, renowned as a centre of culture and refinement. According to the French traveller François Bernier, who attended a dance performance in the seventeenth century, 'the seraglio singing and dancing girls called Kenchens were not indeed the prostitutes seen in bazaars, but those of a more private and respectable class... Most are handsome and well dressed and they dance with wonderful agility.' The tawai'fs were, moreover, discerning upholders of the exquisite Lakhnavi etiquette or tehzeeb, which entailed elaborate rituals, for instance, for the eating of paan, greeting an elder or dressing for an evening. Young men from good families were sent to esteemed courtesans to be burnished by their charm and grace. According to Abdul Halim Sharar, 'Until a man had association with courtesans, he was not a polished man.'

By the mid-nineteenth century, the feudal court-city of Lucknow was the most prosperous precolonial city in India. The once-great Mughal capitals of Delhi, Lahore and Agra had been reduced to shadows of their earlier glory. But the sun was a long time setting on the Mughal empire. Even a hundred and fifty years after the death of the last of the Great Mughals, Aurangzeb, provincial governors in Punjab, Bengal and Awadh continued to operate through institutions inherited from the Mughals even as they became increasingly autonomous. Prayers were said in the Emperor's name and coins were struck proclaiming his glory.

Lucknow thrived on revenues from the Awadh countryside, derived primarily from the grain trade. This supported the lavish lifestyles of the nawabs of Awadh. Artisans, craftsmen, jewellers and tradesmen flourished around the court supplying the growing demand for luxury goods. While the court at Kaiserbagh was the vibrant heart of city life, military and administrative functions were concentrated around the Machhi Bhawan Fort in lesser palaces. The nobility, loath to be outdone by their nawab, built their own residential palaces and created mohallas with their own mosques and bazaars, attracting an army of merchants and suppliers. Even in the countryside, wealthy landowners aspired to the style of the royal court. William Howard Russell, who accompanied Colin Campbell's forces into Lucknow in 1857, struggled to describe the place: 'There is a city more vast than Paris as it seems, and more brilliant, lying before us,' he wrote in his diary. 'Is this city in Oude? Is this the capital of a semi-barbarous race, erected by a corrupt, effete and degraded dynasty? I felt inclined to rub my eyes again and again.'

When the East India Company (EIC) expanded from trade to administration, they fought successive battles in the eighteenth century for which they deployed a combination of local troops and small companies of European mercenaries. The British Indian force, led by European officers, came into being around the 1760s and was known as Lal Paltan, or the Red Battalion, owing to their red jacket uniform.

Through the late eighteenth to early nineteenth century, the EIC slowly brought a swathe of north India under its control. Lucknow, initially a convenient buffer state between the EIC's holdings in Bengal and the Mughal emperor in Delhi, gradually became an irritant to the EIC's ambition. To undermine the potentially dangerous allegiance of the nawabs of Awadh to the Mughal emperor in Delhi, the nawabs were given the derisory and largely empty title of king from 1819 onwards. There was a more malicious intent in the apparent granting of autonomy to the rulers of Awadh and one of the conditions was the acceptance of British indirect control by the kings of Awadh. Now a British Resident and sepoys were to be stationed in Lucknow, at the king's expense, with the Resident essentially controlling the government.

As money drained out of the Awadh treasury towards the British coffers, the kings of Awadh were increasingly cloistered within a fraught situation in which 'they had responsibility without power. The real power vested with the Resident who curbed any initiative that the Nawab showed for governance.'

From the nineteenth century onwards, as described by the historian T. R. Metcalf, 'the nawabs one after the other increasingly abandoned the attempt to govern and retired into the zenana, where they amused themselves with wine, women and poetry. The sensuous life did not reflect sheer perversity or weakness of character on the part of the nawabs. Indolence was rather the only appropriate response to the situation in which the princes of Awadh were placed.'

Nawab Wajid Ali Shah, who ruled Awadh from 1847, was a flamboyant character and a much-maligned king. Speaking of him, the British Resident at Awadh said, '[his] character holds out no promise of good.' John Shakespeare, writing to Lord Elgin with barely disguised contempt, said, 'By all accounts his temper is capricious and fickle, his days and nights are passed in the female apartments and he appears to have resigned himself to debauchery, dissipation and low pursuit.' Despite contemporary British accounts highlighting his incompetence, Wajid Ali Shah initially made attempts to rule his kingdom. He lobbied to have the telegraph installed in Lucknow and tried to organize his army, forming cavalry regiments to which he gave poetic names like Banka, Dandy, Tircha and Fop. He also laid the foundations for the Kaiserbagh complex, which had palaces, pavilions, temples, parks and ponds. Fanny Parkes, an Englishwoman who travelled through Awadh in the 1830s, wrote: 'The subjects of his Majesty of Oude are by no means desirous of participating in the blessings of British rule. They are a richer, sleeker and merrier race than the natives in the territories of the Company.'

Consistently undermined by the British Resident, however, Wajid Ali Shah slowly retreated into the world of poetry, music and dance and the ephemeral charm of beautiful women. Eventually, in February 1856, a year before the Uprising, Wajid Ali Shah was asked to hand over the administration of Awadh to the EIC. Lord Dalhousie justified this outrageous demand by claiming there was a breakdown of law and order in the state, a situation, in fact, brought about by the EIC's curtailing of the nawab's powers. Wajid Ali Shah stoutly refused to sign the treaty whereupon Awadh was formally annexed to the British empire.

In the decade preceding the annexation of Awadh, while the EIC siphoned increasing amounts of money from Awadh's treasury, Wajid Ali Shah spent his days and nights writing poetry and organizing plays so elaborate they would often last up to a month. Photographs taken of him show 'a stout, probably tall man with a double chin, prominent breasts and sturdy arms.' As a younger man, the king had 'long, luxuriant hair flowing over his shoulders in ringlets.' Soon after his coronation, Wajid Ali Shah began writing a candid autobiography called the *Pari Khana* (House of Fairies). The *Pari Khana* shows what the King thought of himself: 'a lover who was irresistible to women, and who could not resist them either.' Infatuated by women in general and always searching for talented dancers for his plays and entertainments, Wajid Ali Shah acquired a large harem of singers and dancers by using a Shi'a variant of Islamic marriage called mu'tah wherein a temporary contract could be drawn up between a man and a women for a specific amount of time in exchange for gifts or money. According to Sharar, the king 'fell in love with a large assortment of female palanquin bearers, courtesans, domestic servants, and women who came in and out of the palace, in short with hundreds of...beautiful and dissolute women.' It wasn't just the king but most of the nobility, too, who became patrons of musicians and dancers with 'the inevitable result,' said Sharar, 'that not only did their style and clothing acquire a female element but they even adopted feminine mannerisms...and most other people [followed] their example.'

Having married women of high birth and important political connections through the traditional nikah, Wajid Ali Shah then went on to contract temporary arrangements through mu'tah. In addition to his four nikah wives, by this stage he is said to have married an additional twenty mu'tah wives. The lowest in the heirarchy of his mu'tah wives were the khilawati, domestic servants essentially, who did menial jobs around the palace. Then there were the unveiled begums, who had not yet given birth to any of the king's children. Once they had given birth to children, the wives were given the title 'mahals' and were allowed to live in purdah.

Nawab Wajid Ali Shah had 'all kinds of wives,' wrote Elihu Jan, hookah bearer to the mother of Wajid Ali Shah. 'Some of them princesses to whom he had been married in his father's lifetime, but when he became king he had black women, Abyssinians, high caste and low, young and old, Mussulman and Hindu.'

In addition to these wives, Wajid Ali Shah had also set up the institution of the pari, or fairy. These were young girls and women who were patronized by the king, trained by professional dancers and singers so as to provide recruits for his theatre. If they were 'talented' enough, they might be taken on as mu'tah wives. They were recruited from the lower classes including the tawai'fs who lived in the old city. This was how Muhammadi Khanum, now reborn as Mahak Pari, came to the king's attention.

It can be gleaned from the paintings in the *Ishqnamah* (Chronicle of Love), an autobiographical collection of paintings and poems, that Wajid Ali Shah was particularly attracted to dark-skinned women. There are various women in the paintings who are of obvious African origin, such as Yasmin Mahal and Ajaib Khanum. Mehak Pari also appears once in the *Ishqnamah*—the only authentic portrait known of her—wearing wide, pleated pyjamas, a tight, cropped choli and a gauze-like dupatta. Her hair is pulled back into a high plait looped up at the crown of her head and covered with brocade. 'Wajid Ali Shah was completely besotted by Hazrat Mahal, writing her many poems,' we are told.

In 1845, Mahak Pari became pregnant and gave birth to a son. She was allowed to veil her face and given the more suitable title of Iftikhar-un-nissa, Dignified Among Women. Her fortunes, at least within the zenana, were immediately transformed:

> The establishment with which a mother of a son was endowed comprised an annual payment from the treasury, larger or smaller in proportion to the favour in which she was held, but never to my knowledge less than Rs.12,000/- a year. Handsome jewels and clothes were sent to her. She was dressed as a mulika, or queen. Guards, attendants, slaves, were appointed for her, and she became at once the mistress of a household.

Hazrat Mahal now had servant girls of her own and an income as a cherished wife and mother of an heir. Her meals were sumptuous, spiced pulaos, rich mutton kormas and kebabs, with a hookah following every meal. She had access to the whole palace, including the flower gardens, and would have attended some of the endless plays her husband wrote.

In 1850, Hazrat Mahal was divorced by Wajid Ali Shah— probably at the instigation of the queen mother who abhorred the low-born among the king's wives. She retired quietly to a house in Lucknow along with Birjis Qadr, living on the pension provided to her by her ex-husband.

If Wajid Ali Shah had not been king at the time of the annexation of Awadh and the subsequent Uprising, Hazrat Mahal would have arguably remained in the shadows of history, becoming a courtesan, perhaps, after her divorce, or the mistress of a nobleman. But in keeping with Lord Dalhousie's desire 'to overthrow this fortress of corruption and infamous misgovernment...as a parting coup', Wajid Ali Shah found himself a king without a kingdom. Five weeks later, he left Lucknow in tears, never to return. There was no talk at all, at this stage, of mutiny or revolt. Fearful of the consequences for his people, Wajid Ali Shah urged the people of Awadh to follow the laws of the English. The British may have had no regard for him or his rule, but Wajid Ali Shah was deeply mourned by his people. They wept for their disgraced, generous and cultured nawab and followed him all the way to Kanpur, reciting dirges written by him.

Only three of the king's wives accompanied him into exile in Calcutta while the others, including Hazrat Mahal, remained in Lucknow. This was how it came to be that as the begums and mahals and erstwhile paris cowered unhappily in the city, Begum Hazrat Mahal embraced her destiny and stood in for the imperial authority of the Mughal emperor. 'Hazrat Mahal showed such courage that the enemy was terrified,' later wrote Begum Sayda, a co-wife, admiringly to the exiled Wajid Ali Shah. 'She turned out to be very daring. She has brought name to the Sultan Alam.'

By July 1857, the sepoy Mangal Pandey had already been hanged at Barrackpore for attacking British officers; Meerut, Kanpur and Delhi were burning and a reluctant Rani Laxmibai was struggling to control Jhansi after the massacre of British women and children at Jokhun Bagh. In Lucknow, meanwhile, as news of the British defeat at Chinhat spread, rebels started pouring into the city, drawn also to Birjis Qadr's standard, symbol of a charmed past. Seven thousand rebel sepoys had arrived in Lucknow by July 1857. In addition to the sepoys, there were numerous taluqdars whose forts dotting the countryside around Lucknow the British had demolished after the annexation of Awadh. They, too, presented themselves at the Begum's court at Kaiserbagh along with the peasants and other foot soldiers they had rallied. The coronation of Birjis Qadr had given all these parties hope. They 'called Birjis Qadr from the palace,' said an onlooker, 'embraced him and said, "You are Kanhaiya".'

Through the month of June, soon after the Uprising had begun, the British started razing to the ground all the structures they considered unnecessary and obstructing. The Khas Bazaar, or luxury market, and the trading places between palaces, were all demolished. 'The English like grass better than bazaars,' wrote the hookah-bearer to the old queen mother of Awadh, Janab-i-Aliyya, in a moment of intercultural prescience.

For the next eight months, until March 1858, when the British finally recaptured Lucknow, the Begum headed the operations in Lucknow, directing the siege of the Residency for three months. Inside the Residency were some three thousand people, British children, soldiers and civilians as well as Indian soldiers, camp followers and servants. Relief forces were sent for by the British and then abandoned because of 'the warlike population of Oude... swarmed by mutinous troops' was thought to be 'too strong' to contend with. Through the four and a half months of siege, nearly half the British population fled or was killed. William Howard Russell wrote: 'The sepoys, during the siege of the Residency, never came on as boldly as the zamindarie levies and nujeebs (irregulars). This Begum exhibits great energy and ability. She has excited all Oudh to take up the interests of her son and the chiefs have sworn to be faithful to him.'

From the time of Birjis Qadr's coronation the Begum had been issuing proclamations, either in her name or in that of her son, exhorting people to join the cause against the British:

> ...as God has given us back our hereditary dominions to us we must exterminate those English heathens and work together to kill their remnants at the Bailly Guard. Therefore exhibit your bravery. God willing you will be endowed with jagirs and rewards even better than in the old days. All those who kill them will be allowed a half of the Jama of their jagirs free.

In September, a relieving force under Havelock and Outram finally managed to enter the Residency but were unsuccessful in their effort to retake it as their forces were too small in number. Since the British had retaken Delhi around this time, a surging mass of men had arrived to join the rebel troops in Awadh. Havelock wrote to the Commission Chief of his abandoning the Residency with 'great grief and reluctance' as 'an advance to the walls of Lucknow involves the loss of this force.' With the fall of Delhi and the capture of Bahadur Shah Zafar, Awadh had now become the last outpost of resistance. The Begum called upon her compatriots 'in the name of Khuda to help her, and they joined in the fight immediately, infusing new enthusiasm into the rebel camp.'

In November, a force under Colin Campbell was finally able to reach the Residency and evacuate the besieged population, but far from discouraging the rebels, 'it was then proclaimed in the city that the Europeans had abandoned the place and addresses to the same purport were sent to the district authorities and to the king of Delhi... Councils of war are constantly being held.'

In December 1857 came a slow realization that the tide was turning. Mutinous towns were being recaptured by the British and subjected to extreme violence. In Varanasi, Colonel James Neill had spread terror among the people because of his infamous 'hanging parties' with amateur executioners boasting about the number of suspected mutineers they were able to hang from mango trees, using elephants for drops. Allahabad was set on fire and the inhabitants blown away by grapeshot. At the Delhi Ridge, General Nicholson— for whom the thought of hanging the mutineers was too lenient— was a murdering fury.

A source of constant indignation for the Begum and her troops was the continued presence of James Outram and a small band of soldiers at Alambagh, a small palace to the south of Lucknow. Nine times the Awadhi troops attacked the Alambagh palace, which was defended only by a low wall and garden, but were unable to dislodge the British or cut off their supply lines from Kanpur. Hazrat Mahal joined the soldiers herself during one of these attacks, riding an elephant, trying to bolster the courage of her men and directing the swirling mass of soldiers. The Begum had clearly realized by now that with all the other centres of the rebellion having fallen, Awadh would soon become the next target of the British. At a famous speech she gave during a meeting of the war council in December, she said:

> Great things were promised from the all-powerful Delhi,
> and my heart used to be gladdened by the communications
> I used to receive from that city but now the King has

been dispossessed and his army scattered: the English have bought over the Sikhs and Rajahs, and have established their Government West, East and South and communications are cut off: the Nana has been vanquished: and Lucknow is endangered: what is to be done? The whole army is in Lucknow, but it is without courage. Why does it not attack the Alumbagh? Is it waiting for the English to be reinforced, and Lucknow to be surrounded? How much longer am I to pay the sepoys for doing nothing? Answer now, and if fight you won't, I shall negotiate with the English to spare my life.

The chiefs at the war council, who had all heard of the violent retribution being meted out to bystanders and mutineers alike, replied:

Fear not we shall fight, for if we do not we shall be hanged one by one: we have this fear before our eyes.

The Begum also made a sharp point about the 'Sikhs and Rajahs' who had been bought over by the British. She too was offered a guarantee of one lakh rupees as yearly pension and a treaty with Queen Victoria by General Outram if she would surrender. According to Lucknow historian Llewelyn-Jones, Outram's letter 'was tossed contemptuously aside.' However, there were other fighters, the Begum realized, whose honour was not as unimpeachable as hers and who would be swept along with the changing tides of the Uprising. Moreover, many of the taluqdars and rebel leaders had conflicting interests and were not always prompt in obeying proclamations. Once British fortunes began turning, some taluqdars quietly returned to their fortresses, abandoning Lucknow.

The greatest threat to the Begum's authority, however, did not come from any irascible Rajput chieftain or even the sepoy army but from Maulvi Ahmadullah Shah—a self-styled holy man who claimed to have received divine orders to throw out the British from India. The charismatic maulvi claimed to be a disciple of a Sufi holy man from Gwalior, Mehrab Shah. According to an account in Rudrangshu Mukherjee's *Awadh in Revolt*:

> Ahmadullah Shah preached as a fakir in Agra and in other parts of N.W.P., propagating a holy war against the British. He was around forty at the time of the outbreak: a man of little learning, having a smattering of Persian and Arabic and some English.

The maulvi had begun his activities a few years before the Uprising, travelling between Agra, Aligarh, Lucknow and Faisabad and preaching the need to unite against the infidel, in this case, the British in India. During the Uprising, he was present with his followers at the battle of Chinhat after which he went to Lucknow and took part in the siege of Lucknow. For a while, the Begum and the other leaders tried to keep the maulvi out of Lucknow and the war council but as they began to suffer losses, his incendiary messages became difficult to ignore:

> As rebel reverses increased and the troops grew dissatisfied with the conduct of the court party, his forceful personality, holy character and military judgment commanded increasing support from all sections of the army. Jailal Singh and Hazrat Mahal were forced to agree to his return to Lucknow, where he began to style himself Vice-regent of God and to pose a serious threat to the pre-eminence of the court faction.

By early January 1858, there were effectually two camps within the rebel forces. The Awadh regiments supported Begum Hazrat Mahal and Birjis Qadr and on the other side were the sepoys from Delhi and other towns supporting the maulvi, who now wanted to be acknowledged as king. Accusations and rumours flew between the two camps, and some skirmishes took place too. But contending with the fiery maulvi was only part of Hazrat Mahal's challenge—relentless columns of British forces were all marching towards Awadh, and Lucknow, unlike Delhi, was not a walled city.

Lucknow was 'a curious mixture, often remarked upon, of European-style houses, huge religious buildings and tortuous narrow alleys that led through the mohalls, the clusters of smaller and often poorer houses.' An ambitious plan was made to build a defensive wall around the city and additionally fortify all the major complexes. Hazrat Mahal appointed Raja Jailal Singh supervisor of the fortifications, and allocated five lakh rupees, even selling some of her own jewellery, for the constructions. Walls were strengthened and a huge earthen embankment was built with openings for guns, primarily around the southeastern part of the city. The British were clearly taken aback by these fortification plans: 'Sir Colin takes long looks through his glass; he says he is surprised at the size of the works. They look, indeed, like heavy railway embankments.' The Kaiserbagh complex, the Moti Mahal Palace complex and the Khurshid Manzil were all fortified and some of the main streets of Lucknow were blocked with stockades and parapets. 'It appears from the energetic character of these ranees and begums,' wrote Russell, clearly referring to Laxmibai as well as Hazrat Mahal, 'that they acquire in their zenanas and harems a considerable amount of actual mental powers and, at all events, become able intriguantes.' According to General Grant, the inhabitants of Lucknow 'had fortified their stronghold to the utmost extent of which they were capable. The Kaiser Bagh constituted the citadel.' Suddenly, there came news of a far more deadly foe marching towards them—the dreaded Gurkha fighters of Jung Bahadur had joined the British forces and were heading towards Lucknow. So fearsome was the reputation of these fighters, with their vicious, curved khukris, that some of the chiefs deserted at this point rather than face the Gurkhas in combat.

Jung Bahadur's diplomacy had allowed Nepal to remain independent through the nineteenth century even as the British gradually tightened their hold over the Indian subcontinent. The Begum learnt that the British had offered Jung Bahadur the town of Gorakhpur, in addition to the anticipated loot of Lucknow, in return for his Gurkha troops. Keen to counter this threat, Hazrat Mahal sent out two of her men from Lucknow with a counter-offer for Jung Bahadur—she would give him the towns of Azamgarh, Arrah, and Varanasi, in addition to Gorakhpur, if he would stand by her and fight against the British. But the Begum's emissaries, disguised as Qalandari fakirs, were intercepted by the British and murdered. The Gurkha troops continued their inexorable march towards Lucknow.

Another bitter betrayal for the Begum was the desertion, in February 1858, of the important taluqdar Man Singh. An enormous British force under Campbell, almost 60,000 men strong, now advanced towards the heart of Awadh. Ultimately, despite the Begum's forces putting up a gallant resistance in certain parts, Lucknow capitulated to the British forces. The notion that India was won by a few, heroic men in the face of overwhelming odds, according to historian Jon Wilson, 'was a myth.' In the end, India was reconquered by the arrival of 40,000 soldiers brought in from Europe. Kaiserbagh was the last to fall, the sepoys 'fighting desperately to the last.' An increasingly admiring Russell now compares Hazrat Mahal to the Amazon warriors of mythology; 'Penthesilea, the Begum, is still undaunted. The Kaiserbagh is the stronghold but, after all, it is merely a series of open courts and stucco palaces.' The fiercest fighting was at the Begum's palace, which was given up only 'after an obstinate resistance by Pandy.' 'The begum alone stands undismayed,' Russell remarked in his diary. 'A fine dramatic figure, this black Semiramide—ardent, intriguing, subtle, courageous, devoted to her son.'

Before the British forces could get to Kaiserbagh, where the Begum was stationed, she was able to make her escape on 15 March 1858 along with her remaining supporters and established herself at Musa Bagh, a country house outside Lucknow. Clearly for General Colin Campbell the escape of the Begum and her supporters was a huge blow. 'At dinner this evening Sir Colin was rather silent,' wrote Russell, 'perhaps he was thinking that people at home would not be satisfied that more of the rebels had not fallen for he knew that it was now impossible to prevent the greater number of them escaping.' At Musa Bagh, Hazrat Mahal and her forces made their last stand to defend Lucknow on 21 March alongside Maulvi Ahmadullah Shah. The rebels continued to fight even as they fell back before the advancing British: 'It was reported to us this morning that the enemy actually had the audacity to make an attack in great force on the garrison of the Alumbagh yesterday at the time Outram was driving them before him in the city.' Several hundred of Lucknow's last defenders died fighting Outram's forces. Once the rebels had been routed at Musa Bagh—their last stronghold—they dispersed into the countryside. In their isolated fort strongholds, or in bands of small groups, they resisted the British with varying degrees of success, so that for the entire year, in 1858, Awadh was a wasteland of insurgency. These rebel soldiers and fighters were a thorn in the side of the British who were trying desperately to regain control over the country. The maulvi escaped and headed towards Rohilkand where he continued to engage in skirmishes with the British until he was betrayed and beheaded in June 1858.

The Begum turned down yet another offer of surrender with honour from Outram. From Musa Bagh, Hazrat Mahal along with her son and remaining supporters, fled towards the Nepalese border. The Begum crossed the Gogra River and set herself up in a fort at Baundi, in Bahraich district. She was joined here by, amongst others, Nana Sahib, the Maratha leader who had managed to escape from Bundelkhand, where he had fought beside Rani Laxmibai.

The Begum's army at this point was still surprisingly strong:

[A] force is encamped on all sides of the Fort, numbering about 15 or 16,000 including followers. Among these, there are 1500 cavalry and 500 mutineer sepoys, the rest are nujeebs and followers. There are also about 60 or 70 shutre sowars (soldiers on camels)…and 17 guns.

Even in this untenable position, for the better part of a year, the Begum tried to maintain a semblance of administration. She frequently held councils of war in a 'cutcherry' parliament and orders were issued under the name of Birjis Qadr. Revenue was collected in as orderly a way as possible and salaries were distributed. Despite the presence of clashing groups, such as the Muslim clerics and the army sepoy faction, without the Begum 'no orders had any authority, nor any plans any chance of execution.'

Desperate to win back the taluqdars to their fold so that governance could be restored, the British circulated their infamous Awadh Proclamation in March 1858, guaranteeing the safety and the restoration of rights to landholders who agreed to submit to the British Government. Very few taluqdars responded to this call as Russell's diary entry shows:

> At present all Oudh may be regarded as an enemy's country, for there are very few chiefs who do not still hold out, and defy the threats of the Proclamation. The capture of Lucknow has dispersed the rebels all over the country, and reinforced the hands which the rajahs and zemindars have collected around their forts.

Since it was recognized that the British forces were too large and well-organized for the rebels to attack outright, a new manner of harassment was devised:

> Do not attempt to meet the regular columns of the infidels, because they are superior to you in discipline and *bunderbust*, and have big guns: but watch their movements, guard all the ghauts on the rivers, intercept their communications, stop their supplies, cut up their daks and posts, and keep constantly hanging about their camps: give them no rest.

What is notable is that the Begum could have quite easily, and with some honour, surrendered to the British at this point as they were only too willing to re-establish all the leaders as long as they did not have British blood on their hands. But the Begum not only dismissed every attempt by the British at reconciliation, but she orchestrated a veritable war of terror on all the taluqdars who dared to surrender. When Man Singh, an important landholder, surrendered, the Begum confiscated all his property and settled it with other claimants.

All the while the rebel leaders Beni Madho, Mehndi Hussein, the maulvi and others were scattered all around Awadh and extensive planning was carried out by the Begum to try and organize a major attack against the British forces. Though ultimately impossible to implement, these plans are a testament to the rebels' tenacity in the face of increasingly overwhelming odds.

There is no doubt that the Begum could have surrendered even at this stage—her life would have been spared and she would have been granted a pension by the British authorities. Queen Victoria had issued a proclamation in November 1858 safeguarding the safety and the right to religious freedom to all her 'native princes'. Hazrat Mahal responded to the Queen's declaration with a counter-proclamation of her own:

> In the Proclamation it is written that the Christian religion is true, but no other creed will suffer oppression, and that the laws will be observed towards all. What has the administration of justice to do with the truth or falsehood of a religion?...
> To eat pigs and drink wine, to bite greased cartridges, and to mix pigs' fat with flour and sweetmeats, to destroy Hindoo and Mussulman temples on pretence of making roads, to build churches, to send clergymen into the streets and alleys to preach the Christian religion, to institute English schools and to pay people a monthly stipend for learning the English sciences, while the places of worship of Hindoos and Mussulmans are to this day entirely neglected: with all this, how can the people believe that religion will not be interfered with? The rebellion began with religion and for it, millions of men have been killed.

Let not our subjects be deceived; thousands were deprived of their religion in the North-West and thousands were hanged rather than abandon their religion.

Begum Hazrat Mahal's questioning of the commitment of the British to religious equality was remarkably prescient, given that as Queen Victoria was issuing her proclamation, Brigadier Napier of the Bengal Engineers 'was executing his master plan in Lucknow that converted the main Muslim holy places into temporary barracks: the Friday mosque permanently ceased to be the Muslim center for prayer and ritual.'

Hazrat Mahal then questioned the good faith of the British government, and listed the long list of rajas and landowners whom they had deprived of their ancestral lands in the preceding years, as well as the vast sums of money the EIC had appropriated from Wajid Ali Shah as 'loans' that were never repaid. She then added:

> If our people were discontented with our Royal predecessor, Wajid Ally Shah, how come they are content with us? And no ruler ever experienced such loyalty and devotion of life and goods as we have done? What then is wanting that they do not restore our country?

It was only when all hope of resisting had ended and determined to avoid an ignominious capture by the British that Hazrat Mahal sought refuge in Nepal, defiant to the end. The Begum continued to agitate, even while on Nepalese soil, as is evident from the Resident's complaints:

> [T]he Begum's followers have been fighting against us and making raids into our provinces, and that lady has herself applied to him (Jung Bahadur) for armed assistance, for the purpose of making conquests within the British provinces.

Resident Ramsay finally persuaded Jung Bahadaur to address a letter to the leaders Mummo Khan, Nana Sahib and Beni Madho, asking them to leave Nepal though the Resident was dissatisfied with the tone of the letter, calling it 'objectionable' and 'more calculated to encourage than to dishearten them.' Regarding Hazrat Mahal, Jung Bahadur declared from the beginning 'that he will not allow any violence to be used towards that lady but that if she persists in remaining in Nepal she shall be permitted to do so.'

In the end, Mummo Khan surrendered to Jung Bahadur while Beni Madho died fighting. Bala Rao also died, sometime in 1860, while Nana Sahib disappeared in Nepal, his escape remaining a mystery to this day. Hazrat Mahal lived the rest of her life in exile in Nepal, the only remaining leader of the Uprising who did not submit to the British.

Wajid Ali Shah, meanwhile, was horrified at the role his erstwhile Begum had played in the Uprising and complained bitterly in a letter to Colonel Cavenagh that he had been unaware of the use that had been made of his name by Hazrat Mahal. He added that 'henceforth he dismissed both her and her son, Birjis Kudder.' Wajid Ali Shah lived the rest of his days in Matia Burj, near Calcutta, where he built a miniature kingdom and lived off a generous pension the British government paid him. He never ceased to bemoan his exiled existence when compared to the extravagance of his past: 'There was a time when showers of pearls were trodden underfoot,' he wrote piteously, 'now I feel the cruel sun above and pebbles underfoot.'

When the British troops recaptured Lucknow in March 1858, they brought the curtain down on the era of the nawabs of Lucknow and the refined culture of the Awadh court, a process that had begun with the annexation of Awadh and the exile of the nawab. The British troops were allowed to plunder the city with a rapacity that was famously captured by William Russell:

> The scene of plunder was indescribable. The soldiers had broken up several of the store-rooms, and pitched the contents into the court, which was lumbered with cases, with embroidered clothes, gold and silver brocade, silver vessels,

arms, banners, drums, shawls, scarfs, musical instruments, mirrors, pictures, books, accounts, medicine bottles, gorgeous standards, shields, spears, and a heap of things... Through these moved the men, wild with excitement, "drunk with plunder". I had often heard the phrase, but never saw the thing itself before. They smashed to pieces the fowling-pieces and pistols to get at the gold mountings and the stones set in the stocks. They burned in a fire, which they made in the centre of the court, brocades and embroidered shawls for the sake of the gold and silver. China, glass, and jade they dashed to pieces in pure wantonness; pictures they ripped up, or tossed on the flames; furniture shared the same fate.

The Kaiserbagh Palace was particularly targeted as a loathsome symbol of the Begum's resistance with one officer later 'revelling in the pock-marking of the Kaiserbagh and gloating at the ubiquity of British graffiti'. There is a list which details items seized from one set of 'female apartments' of the Kaiserbagh Palace where some of Wajid Ali Shah's wives resided. It runs into more than twenty pages of exquisite items: gold and silver ornaments studded with precious stones, embroidered cashmere wool and brocade shawls, bejewelled caps and shoes, silver, gold, jade and amber-handled fly whisks, silver cutlery, jade goblets, plates, spittoons, hookahs, and silver utensils for serving and storing food and drink and valuable furnishings. These items evoked the life of the countless wives of Wajid Ali Shah—for a time, they were the gilded accessories that defined the luxuries and restrictions of Hazrat Mahal's life in the zenana, before she became a warrior queen.

More insidious was the destruction of all the papers and documents found in Kaiserbagh Palace. This is why no physical evidence—no surviving 'mutiny papers' for Lucknow unlike those that exist for Delhi—remains of the four months during which the Begum ruled Lucknow and directed the efforts of the rebel troops after the removal of the besieged British population at the

Residency. This destruction was more damaging and lasting than the shameful purloining of jewels and plundering of buildings—all that remains are the accounts of witnesses recorded during the trials that followed the recapture of Lucknow and the proclamations issued by Hazrat Mahal.

The world that Hazrat Mahal had fought for was the precolonial Mughal world of tradition that involved ancient loyalties and feudal patronage. It was a world in which an accomplished courtesan was the heartthrob of a city and a king was mourned with the writing of poignant verse. But that world was destroyed forever in the aftermath of the Uprising. 'Now there is not a shadow of a doubt,' said the old Emperor Bahadur Shah, 'that of the great House of Timur I am the last to be seated [on] the throne of India. The lamp of Mughal domination is fast burning out.'

When Hazrat Mahal died in 1879, she had already become a remote memory of the past. The British government had refused her wish to return to India and her grave in Nepal became a neglected roadside memorial over the years. Hazrat Mahal's tomb is 'not with a line carved, not a stone raised, and left alone in her glory.' Even with the rise of the Indian nationalist movement in the early decades of the twentieth century, her memory, unlike that of Rani Laxmibai or Meerabai, was never resurrected. It is possible that as the nationalist movement shaped itself, Hazrat Mahal's past as a courtesan could not be accommodated in its narrative. Her association with Wajid Ali Shah, himself a vocal British supporter, was embarrassing, and being a Muslim woman she was quickly forgotten.

Treasured courtesan, an unassailable begum, mother of a boy king, leader of the largest army raised to counter the British in India—these are the words we use, like 'a diamond-cutter's tools', to shape the memory of Hazrat Mahal in our collective consciousness. To all these words we need to add a final one—heroine.

EPILOGUE

India is a young republic in an ancient land. For most Indians, both these ideals coexist harmoniously, one taking precedence at a certain season, the other perhaps at a different stage of life. A complex, ancient wisdom rubs shoulders with an exuberant new nation. Sometimes, in the chasm that forms between the two, fragile stories fall through and are forgotten. Or they are warped beyond recognition. In the stories that I have chosen to tell, I have not included any women from our modern history, namely the nationalist movement and the twentieth century. There have been remarkable Indian women in the modern age, naturally, but women have carved their luminous destinies in India for far longer than we choose to remember. Indira Gandhi's iron will and astounding destiny as only the second woman leader of the modern age in the world have made her omniscient in the collective memory while we have almost forgotten Raziya Sultan and her ferocious destiny. Forgotten that India gave birth to this proud daughter of a slave king, the first and only woman to occupy the throne of Delhi. Before the scrappy and passionate arguments of Arundhati Roy there were women philosophers from the very dawn of time, Gargi, Sulabha, Maitreyi, who held their own against Brahmins and theologians.

The stories of the great women of India are notoriously hard to come by. In *Incarnations*, his recent book on Indian personalities who have shaped the idea of India, Sunil Khilnani included only six women in a collection of fifty lives. Primary sources for the lives of women are hard to come by, explains Professor Khilnani, and this is true enough. The sources are rare and moreover they are often tainted and biased and opaque. What we have, often, is the mangled memory, or elusive shadow, of what a great woman must have been like. Precious documents, when they are written by women, are considered somehow not as eloquent or significant and their testimony is disregarded. And so Begum Gulbadan's extraordinary account of her brother Humayun's life was lost to us for centuries until it was discovered and translated into English from the original Persian in 1902. It is no coincidence that of the eight women studied in my book six were queens and another was a noblewoman. These were almost all elite women, whose history and achievements had some small chance of surviving the disregard of time. For the innumerable heroic non-elite women, even these fragments of material are missing. For these women, and for women's stories in general, the sources are more nebulous and elusive. They can be found in folk songs, in inscriptions, in ballads and in their desolate absence from the public record.

There has been a quiet flaring of interest in the works of women, both elite and subaltern, in the past few decades. Their contributions and lives are being revisited; in one example, Ruby Lal studies the very concept of the harem in the Mughal world and its continued misuse through the centuries in her seminal work, *Domesticity and Power in the Early Mughal World*. If not quite a groundswell, then there is definitely a sustained ripple of interest in the world today in the affairs of women. Glass ceilings are cracking and male bastions are being stormed in countless places. There is a sense that a reckoning must come and an imbalance redressed in the affairs of the world. In India, these upheavals are sometimes accompanied by backlash and yet more repression. In the seventy years since India has been a free country, India's child-sex ratio has plummeted to its worse ever rate of 919 girls to every 1,000 boys. Literally millions of female children are missing from India in what eminent science writer Siddhartha Mukherjee calls 'grotesque eugenic programs' through infanticide and selective sex abortion.

In the twenty-first century reality for Indian women, it is more important than ever to remember the stories of our heroic women.

To remember that women having been standing up against injustice and oppression for thousands of years, with courage and grace. For the countless daughters of India who would be astronomers and scientists, artists and entrepreneurs, it is essential that there are heroic role models who are human in their fallibility and sublime in their ambition. Real women, with weaknesses to overcome, not impossible goddesses complacent in their divine superiority. As women forge new identities for themselves in a changing country, they must be able to take comfort and courage from heroines who blazed an incandescent trail in similarly fraught times. So there is Draupadi's celebrated dark beauty, as a bulwark against the Bollywood queens of today and the arsenal of skin-lightening creams that would seek to make the daughters of India ashamed of their dusky complexion. There is Meerabai's elegiac song against a stifling patriarchy to remind us that women have long struggled against the forces that would restrict and suppress their creativity and desires. And beyond these eight heroines there are countless more who deserve to be counted and remembered. They form the great tribe of women who give form to our dreams and a voice to our hopes. As we strive to broaden the horizons for our daughters it is important to remember who we once were, to provide the springboard to what they can, once again, become.

ACKNOWLEDGEMENTS

For their fierce loyalty and suspiciously prejudiced reading of my manuscript, my friends and family: Ayesha Mago, Caroline Juneja, Anjuli Bhargava, Ashoke Mukhoty, Brijesh Dhar Jayal and Manju Jayal.

For their patient help with questions and clarifications, Professors Rudrangshu Mukherjee and Sunil Kumar.

For her sympathetic reading and feedback, my editor Simar Puneet at Aleph Book Company.

For everything else, and much more besides, Mohit Dhar Jayal, thank you.

NOTES AND REFERENCES

Chapter 1. Draupadi: Dharma Queen

2   **'The heroes are dead. The evil is done':** James L. Fitzgerald (trans., ed), *Book of Peace, Part One*, Chicago: University of Chicago Press, 2004.

2   **Arjuna, one of the Pandava brothers and the greatest warrior of his age:** Benu Varma, 'Plenitude of the Singular: Draupadi in Literature and Life', SERC (Socio-Economic Research and Consultancy), New Delhi.

2   **'that the Pandavas waged a war reluctantly in support of a dubious claim':** Gurcharan Das, *The Difficulty of Being Good: On the Subtle Art of Dharma*, New Delhi: Penguin Books, 2009.

3   **Heroes [are] of many kinds:** Ibid.

3   **'For this foul man, disgrace of the Kauravas, is molesting me, and I cannot bear it':** Draupadi in the hall where the game of dice is being held, when Dusshasan is attempting to disrobe her. Taken from Gurcharan Das, *The Difficulty of Being Good*.

3   **'extolled as the perfect wife-chaste, demure, and devoted to her husbands':** Ashok Yakkaldevi, 'Role of female identity in the ancient Indian stories', *European Academic Research*, Vol. I, Issue 10, 2014.

3   **She has been gambled and lost by her husband Yudhishthira:** In Vedic times, gambling with dice was considered a sacred ritual. Just as no king could ignore a challenge to a duel or a call to a battle, no king could turn down an invitation to a gambling match. Taken from Devdutt Pattanaik, *Jaya: An Illustrated Retelling of the Mahabharata*, New Delhi: Penguin Books, 2010.

4   **'She is not too short, nor is she too large, nor is she too dark':**

Sally J. Sutherland, 'Sita and Draupadi: Aggressive Behaviour and Female Role Models in the Sanskrit Epics', *Journal of the American Oriental Society*, Vol. 109, No. 1, 1989.

5   **'Whom did you lose first, yourself or me?':** Shalini Shah, *The Making of Womanhood: Gender Relations in the Mahābhārata*, New Delhi: Manohar Publishers & Distributors, 2012.

5   **The bleak truth is that at the time that the Mahabharat was written:** Consensus amongst Indologists now point towards the Mahahbarat as being a heterogeneous work which was created over a span of six to eight hundred years, from the third or fourth century BCE to the third or fourth century CE.

6   **'what irked the most was not losing the kingdom or the exile of my sons':** Pradip Bhattacharya, 'Five Holy Virgins, Five Sacred Myths, Part IV', *Manushi*, 2004.

7   **I shall never forgive the Kauravas for doing what they have done to me:** Devdutt Pattanaik, *Jaya*.

7   **Draupadi uses two powerful symbols, unbound hair:** Unbound hair is not only a symbol of the undomesticated woman, as represented by Kali, but also a symbol of widowhood.

7   **Despite the inability of any of the men present to answer Draupadi's question:** According to the scholarly Pune Critical Edition of the Mahabharat, the episode of the endlessly unfurling sari and Krishna miraculously saving Draupadi is a later interpolation. In the original version, Draupadi saves herself by her own agency, and her belief in the righteousness of her cause.

8   **Up till now we have heard of many beautiful women:** Irawati Karve, *Yuganta: The End of an Epoch*, New Delhi: Orient Longman, 2006.

8   **'That day Krishnaa [Draupadi]':** Pradip Bhattacharya, 'Five Holy Virgins'.

9   **And also a Pancali girl arose from the middle of the sacrificial altar:** Alf Hiltebeitel, *Rethinking the Mahabharata: A Reader's Guide*

to the Education of the Dharma King, Chicago: University of Chicago Press, 2001. (It is of note that Draupadi's dark complexion is said to be the colour of the Gods themselves.)

10 **'is an abominable crime in itself':** Alf Hiltebeitel, *Rethinking the Mahabharata*.

10 **'Because of her, a great fear will arise for the Ksatiryas':** Ibid.

12 **Draupadi's cutting reply is that among her in-laws:** Pradip Bhattacharya, 'Five Holy Virgins'.

12 **Though she is won by Arjuna during her swayamvar:** Many explanations have been given for Draupadi's polyandrous marriage to the Pandavas. It is likely that Kunti realized that all the Pandavas, and especially Yudhishthira, were smitten by the beautiful princess and her marrying Arjuna would have caused lifelong bitterness and jealousies.

13 **An ideal wife or pativrata must be:** Robin Roland, 'Pativratya: The Theology Behind the Ideology', paper uploaded to the Luther College, Iowa website, http://www.luther.edu/religion/asian-studies/resources/papers/pativratya/.

13 **The pativrata wife par excellence in Hindu mythology is Sita:** Prabhati Mukherjee, *Hindu Women Normative Models*, Hyderabad: Orient Blackswan, 1994.

13 **'Her loyalty and steadfast devotion to Rama':** For an alternate explanation of Sita's behavior, see Sally J. Sutherland, 'Sita and Draupadi'.

13 **Scholarship regarding the character of Sita has shown her to be not entirely the subservient wife:** Irawati Karve writes in *Yuganta: The End of an Epoch* that Draupadi's arguments in the assembly hall are foolish and pointless, that she would have done better to beg and plead and throw herself upon the mercy of her elders.

14 **After the episode of the gambling hall:** Alf Hiltebeitel, *Rethinking the Mahabharata*.

14 **'This saying is well known in the world':** Simon Brodbeck and

Brian Black (eds.), *Gender and Narrative in the Mahabharata*, New Delhi: Routledge, 2007.

15 **This blessed God, the self-existent great-grandfather':** Sally J. Sutherland, 'Sita and Draupadi'.

16 **Krishna, why was a woman like me, wife of the Parthas:** Ibid.

16 **I blame only these strong Pandavas:** Ibid.

16 **I have no husbands, no sons, no brothers, no father, no relatives':** Ibid.

18 **'How do [my] strong and illustrious husbands, like eunuchs, endure me–their dear and faithful wife':** Ibid.

18 **Her anger, when her sexual chastity is repeatedly questioned by Ram:** Ibid.

18 **'How can you, Partha,' Draupadi asks Bhima:** Irawati Karve, *Yuganta*.

18 **'my enemy is dead, now let me feast my eyes on his corpse':** Sally J. Sutherland, 'Sita and Draupadi'.

19 **Were a man to desire a woman, she would be like this one:** Ibid.

19 **She 'serves her husbands without regard for her own likes and dislikes…':** Simon Brodbeck and Brian Black (eds.), *Gender and Narrative in the Mahabharata*.

19 **I avoid excessive mirth (arrogance) or excessive vexation and anger:** Sally J. Sutherland, 'Sita and Draupadi'.

19 **While Duryodhana and his friend Karna:** Karna is the son Kunti had before she married Pandu. He is the eldest brother of the Pandavas but is a steadfast and powerful friend to Duryodhana. He will learn of his birth mother just before the war at Kurukshetra.

20 **The only true heir, apart from the Pandavas themselves:** Arjuna and Subhadra's son, Abhimanyu, dies on the battlefield of Kurukshetra but his young wife Uttara, daughter of King Viraat of Matsya, is pregnant at the time of the battle. She will give birth

to Parikshit who is crowned king when the Pandavas retire to the mountains at the end of the epic.

21 **Yudhishthira is crowned dharma-raj at an elaborate and bloody Ashvamedha yagna:** Performed for the consecration of a king, this horse sacrifice involved the sacrifice of many animals, including horses, goats and deer.

Chapter 2. Radha: Illicit Goddess

24 **In the beginning, Krishna, the Supreme Reality, was filled with the desire to create:** John Stratton Hawley and Donna Marie Wulff (eds.), *The Divine Consort: Radha and the Goddesses of India*, New Delhi: Motilal Banarsidass Publishers, 1982, p. 57.

25 **According to Diana L. Eck, 'it is a fine country...':** from Manmatha Nath Dutt (trans.), *Harivamsha*, Calcutta: Elysium Press, 1897; quoted in Diana L. Eck, *India: A Sacred Geography*, Harmony Books, 2012, p. 354-355.

25 **When the gopis go to meet Krishna, they must, therefore:** Manmatha Nath Dutt, *Harivamsha*.

26 **Clouds thicken the sky:** Jayadeva, *Gita Govinda*, New Humanity Books, 1990.

27 **As David Kinsley has noted:** David Kinsley, *Hindu Goddesses: Visions of the Divine Feminine in the Hindu Religious Tradition*, Berkeley: University of California Press, 1988.

28 **Now assuming a steadfast pose:** Rupa Gosvami, *Vidagdhamadhava*, Murshidabad: Radharamana Press at Baharamapura, 1307.

29 **When spring came, tender limbed Radha wandered:** Jayadeva, *Gita Govinda*.

29 **Your drowsy red eyes:** Ibid.

29 **My heart values his vulgar ways/ Refuses to admit my rage:** Ibid.

30 **'Krishna, removing cow-dust from Radhika':** Barbara S. Miller, 'Radha: Consort of Krishna's Vernal Passion', *Journal of the American*

Oriental Society, 1975.

31   **Saavan clouds are pouring down, fields are flooding but I burn with viraha:** From Malik Muhammed Jayasi's *Padmavat*.

32   **'their erotic love play made a transition from the refined':** Pavan K. Varma, *The Book of Krishna*, New Delhi: Penguin Books, 2009.

32   **Casting away/ All ethics of caste:** David Kinsley, *Hindu Goddesses*, p. 88.

32   **I throw ashes at all laws/ Made by man or God:** Ibid, p. 88.

33   **If I go to Krishna I lose my home:** Ibid, p. 86.

34   **He promised he'd return tomorrow:** Vidyapati, 'Love Songs to Krishna', translated by Azfar Hussain, from *Reading About the World*, Volume 1, published by Harcourt Brace Custom Books for Washington State University, 1999.

34   **Radha appears before me on every side:** David Kinsley, *Hindu Goddesses*, p. 90.

34   **She reddens her lips with the betel leaf of intense attachment:** from Raghunatha Dasa Gosvami's *Stavavali*, quoted in *The Divine Consort*.

35   **So pretty! Who are you?' he asks:** J. S. Hawley, 'A Vernacular Portrait: Radha in the *Sur Sagar*', in *The Divine Consort*, p. 43.

36   **The embodiment of beauty/ Young, intelligent:** Karine Schomer, 'Where Have All the Radhas Gone? New Images of Woman in Modern Hindi Poetry', Ibid, p. 92.

36   **'shattering the pride of haystack, dome, mountains and even Himalaya':** Ibid, p. 92.

36   **'the cows are well fed and rich in milk':** Pavan K. Varma, *The Book of Krishna*.

38   **Women's sexual purity became synonymous with Indian culture:** Ratna Kapur, *Erotic Justice: Law and the New Politics of Postcolonialism*, New Delhi: Routledge, 2013.

38   **Heidi Pauwels has pointed out that in Ramanand Sagar's:** Heidi R.

M. Pauwels, *The Goddess as Role Model: Sita and Radha in Scripture and on Screen*, Oxford: Oxford University Press, 2008.

Chapter 3. Ambapali: The Glory of Vaishali

42   **Nearchus's description is admiringly detailed:** Nearchus, quoted in Arrian's *Indica*,16; J. W. McCrindle, *Ancient India as Described by Megasthenes and Arrian*, p. 219.

43   **'she went for a night for fifty kahapanas':** *The Book of the Discipline (Vinaya Pitaka)*, I. B. Horner (trans.), published for the Pali Text Society by Oxford University Press, 1938.

43   **To cease from evil/ To do what is good:** Ibid.

46   **'should do nothing independently even in her own house':** Manu, *The Laws of Manu*, F. Max Müller (ed.), Oxford: Clarendon Press, 1886.

46   **'You yourself must know,' the Buddha adds:** *Kalama Sutta: The Buddha's Charter of Free Inquiry*, Buddhist Publication Society, 1981.

46   **'Subject to birth, old age, and disease, extinction will I seek to find':** Story of Sumedha from Henry Clarke Warren, *Buddhism in Translations*, Cambridge: Harvard University Press, 1922.

48   **'pleasant disposition, beautiful and otherwise attractive':** Mallanaga Vatsyayana, *Kamasutra: Oxford World's Classics*, Wendy Doniger and Sudhir Kakar (trans.), Oxford: Oxford University Press, 2009.

49   **'have temples and reservoirs built, arrange pujas and offerings to the gods':** Ibid.

50   **Tradition has it that Ajatashatru set a bizarre and abominable precedent:** Romila Thapar, *The Penguin History of Early India: From the Origins to AD 1300*, London: Penguin Books, 2015.

50   **'large-sized catapult used for hurling rocks':** Ibid.

52   **Though these nuns were contemporaries of the Buddha:** The *Therigatha* poems were composed around 6 BCE. They remained in

the oral form and were added to for about three centuries. They were finally written down around 80 BCE.

52 **'Black and glossy as a bee and curled was my hair'**: See *Therigatha*, (in Oldenberg and Pischel's Pali Text Society edition), London, 1883, pp. 252-270.

53 **'O free indeed, O gloriously free am I'**: Mrs Rhys Davids, *Psalms of the Early Buddhists*, London 1909.

53 **'So thoroughly free am I'**: Psalm of Sister Mutta, translated from the Pali by Thanissaro Bhikkhu.

54 **It is only in 1948 that she is resurrected:** *Vaishali ki Nagarvadhu* by Acharya Chatursen, 1948.

Chapter 4. Raziya bint Iltutmish: Slave to Sultan

59 **'were like bandit raids—he fought several quick battles'**: Abraham Eraly, *The Age of Wrath: A History of the Delhi Sultanate*, London: Penguin Books, 2015.

59 **'consumed the body as easily as flame melts a candle'**: Ibid.

59 **'O people, know that you have committed great sins'**: Sunil Kumar, *The Emergence of the Delhi Sultanate: 1192-1286*, New Delhi: Permanent Black, 2007.

62 **The historian Sunil Kumar has pointed out that by the end of Iltutmish's reign in 1236:** Sunil Kumar, 'Service, Status, and Military Slavery in the Delhi Sultanate: Thirteenth and Fourteenth Centuries', in *Slavery and South Asian History* by Indrani Chatterjee and Richard M. Eaton (eds.), Bloomington: Indiana University Press, 2006.

62 **'reputation at least, during moments of military crisis'**: Ibn Khaldun, *The Muqaddima*, Franz Rosenthal (trans.), Princeton: Princeton University Press, 1967.

62 **'natal alienation and social death'**: Minhaj-i-Siraj Juzjani, *Tabakat-i-Nasiri*, Lahore: Sang-e-Meel Publications, 2006.

62　'his comeliness, his fairness, and agreeable manners': Sunil Kumar, *The Emergence of the Delhi Sultanate*, New Delhi: Permanent Black, 2007.

62　'the further (the Turk slaves) are taken from their hearth': Ibid.

63　'the Turk loves to be served by his own': Bernard Lewis, *The Middle East: A Brief History of the Last 2,000 Years*, New York: Simon and Schuster, 2009.

63　'My sons are devoted to the pleasures of youth': Minhaj-i-Siraj Juzjani, *Tabakat-i-Nasiri*.

63　Ibn Battuta, writing a century after the event: Mehdi Hussain (trans.), *The Rehla of Ibna Battuta (India, Maldive islands and Ceylon)*, Oriental Institute Baroda, 1976.

64　'the only purpose of high walls': Guity Nashat and Lois Beck (eds.), *Women in Iran from the Rise of Islam to 1800*, Chicago: University of Illinois Press, 2003.

64　'veiled from the public gaze': Minhaj-i-Siraj Juzjani, *Tabakat-i-Nasiri*.

65　'the signs of rectitude were, time and again, manifest': Kumar, 'Service, Status and Military Slavery in the Delhi Sultanate', Indrani Chatterjee and Richard M. Eaton (eds.), *Slavery and South Asian History*, Champaign: Indiana University Press, 2006.

67　'reached their powerful positions by holding the Sultan [Raziya] hostage': Ibid.

68　'the kingdom became pacified and the power of the state widely extended': Isami, *Futuh al-Salatin*, A. S. Usha (ed.), Madras: University of Madras, 1948.

68　'[the] renowned woman threw herself into the tasks of administration': Minhaj-i-Siraj Juzjani, *Tabakat-i-Nasiri*.

68　'She ruled as an absolute monarch': *The Rehla of Ibna Battuta*.

68　'rich robes, bejeweled belts and sashes': Peter Jackson, 'Turkish Slaves on Islam's Indian Frontier', in Indrani Chatterjee and Richard

M. Eaton (eds.), *Slavery and South Asian History.*

69 **'she appears both on the coins and in the early histories':** Alyssa Gabbay, 'In Reality a Man: Sultan Iltutmish, His Daughter, Raziya and Gender Ambiguity in Thirteenth Century Northern India', *Journal of Persianate Studies,* Vol. 4, Seattle: University of Washington, 2011, pp. 45-63.

70 **'the sultan put aside female dress, and issued from [her] seclusion':** Minhaj-i-Siraj Juzjani, *Tabakat-i-Nasiri.*

70 **'when she rode out on an elephant, at the time of mounting it':** Alyssa Gabbay, 'In Reality a Man'.

70 **'naqes al-aql, deficient in intelligence, and therefore more prone to evil than men':** Minhaj-i-Siraj Juzjani, *Tabakat-i-Nasiri.*

70 **Raziya was part of a long line of Muslim women:** Alyssa Gabbay, 'In Reality a Man'.

71 **'were employed in very specialized jobs, as soldiers, palace guards, or bodyguards':** Vikas Pandey, 'Africans in India: From Slaves to Reformers and Rulers', www.bbc.com, 19 December 2014.

71 **'that crafty, ill-starred one':** B. N. Goswamy, 'Malik Ambar: A Remarkable life', *The Tribune,* 13 August 2006.

73 **Raziya and Altuniah were able to escape:** Peter Jackson, 'Sultan Radiyya bint Iltutmish', Gavin R. G. Hamley (ed.), *Women in the Medieval Islamic World: Power, Patronage, Piety,* New York: St. Martin's Press, 1998.

73 **'For three years in which her hand was strong':** Alyssa Gabbay, 'In Reality a Man'.

73 **'She was a great sovereign and sagacious, just beneficent':** Minhaj-i-Siraj Juzjani, *Tabakat-i-Nasiri.*

74 **They would have had the example of Koyunk Khatun:** Gabbay, 'In Reality a Man'.

74 **'everyone high and low used to enjoy the sight of her face':** Isami, *Futuh al-Salatin.*

74   'to wear the crown, and fill the throne of kings': Alyssa Gabbay, 'In Reality a Man'.

75   **When Minhaj-i-Siraj Juzjani tabled the long list of rulers**: Urvi Mukhopadhyay, 'Imagining the Powerful "Other"', Diana Dimitrova (ed.), *The Other in South Asian Religion, Literature and Film: Perspectives on Otherism and Otherness*, Routledge, 2014.

Chapter 5. Meerabai: Dyed in Blue

78   **'[W]hen all was lost, when the last scrap of food had been eaten'**: John Keay, *India: A History*, **New York:** Grove/Atlantic, Inc., 2011.

79   **'exemplifying chivalry, honour, fondness for opium and weakness for women'**: Ibid.

79   **'marveled that principalities so agriculturally disadvantaged'**: Ibid.

80   **This abhorrence of pollution was to culminate in the excesses of untouchability:** Shoaib Daniyal, 'Was Aurangzeb the most evil ruler India has ever had?', www.scroll.in, 2 September 2015.

80   **'Meera unravelled the fetters of family'**: Nabha-das, *Bhaktamal*.

81   **The birth of a daughter in the families:** The Udyogaparva of the Mahabharat.

82   **'The closest attention to their history'**: John Keay, *India*.

82   **'No national head exists amongst them'**: Ibid.

82   **'the *bidaai* genre naturalizes child marriage'**: Rashmi Dube Bhatnagar, Renu Dube and Reena Dube, 'Meera's Medieval Lyric Poetry in Postcolonial India: The Rhetorics of Women's Writing in Dialect', 2004.

83   **'Friend from my childhood, I long to be a renunciator'**: Ibid.

84   **'Mother-in-law fights, my sister-in-law teases'**: Madhu Kishwar and Ruth Vanita, 'Poison to Nectar: The Life and Work of Mirabai', Women Bhakta Poets (special issue), *Manushi*, January-June 1989, pp. 50-52.

84 **'Mine is the dark one who dwells in Braj':** Ibid.

84 **Meera never seemed to refer to herself as a widow:** Ibid.

85 **'As soon as she was separated from her *patidev*':** Ibid.

85 **'an ideal Hindu wife, loved by her husband':** Anant Pai (ed.), Kamala Chandrakant (author), Yusuf Bangalorewala (illustrator), 'Mirabai', *Amar Chitra Katha*, Volume 535, Amar Chitra Katha Pvt. Limited, 1974.

86 **The scholar Padmavati Shabnan has described Meera's padas:** Rashmi Dube Bhatnagar, Renu Dube and Reena Dube, *Female Infanticide in India: A Feminist Cultural History*, Albany: State University of New York Press, 2005, p. 39.

86 **'there was the sweetness of sleep':** Sumitranandan Pant, *Pallav*, Delhi, 2006.

86 **'Girls! Come form a ring':** Shama Futehally, *In the Dark of the Heart: Songs of Meera*, Rowman Altamira, 2003.

87 **'I don't like your strange world, Rana':** Madhu Kishwar and Ruth Vanita, 'Poison to Nectar'.

88 **'Of father, mother, brother, kinsfolk I have none':** Rashmi Dube Bhatnagar, Renu Dube and Reena Dube, *Female Infanticide in India*.

89 **'I gave up all my jewels/ Unlocking the armlet I freed myself':** Rashmi Dube Bhatnagar, Renu Dube and Reena Dube, 'Meera's Medieval Lyric Poetry in Postcolonial India'.

89 **'the story of Ali Khan, the Pathan':** Madhu Kishwar and Ruth Vanita, 'Poison to Nectar'.

89 **'If he says so, I'll let my hair grow wild':** Sandra M. Gilbert and Susan Gubar, *The Madwoman in the Attic: The Woman Writer and the Nineteenth-Century Literary Imagination*, New Haven: Yale University Press, 2000.

89 **'I have given up ornaments':** John Stratton Hawley, Mark Juergensmeyer, *Songs of the Saints of India*, Oxford: Oxford University Press, 2007.

89   'If he says so, I'll let my hair grow wild': Parita Mukta, 'Mirabai in Rajasthan', *Manushi*, pp. 94-99.

91   'For those who treasure Mira's songs often feel that her words have an authenticity': John Stratton Hawley and Mark Juergensmeyer, *Songs of the Saints of India*.

91   'Nothing is really mine except Krishna': Igor Kononenko, *Teachers of Wisdom*, Dorrance Publishing, 2010.

92   'Let us go to a realm beyond going': John Stratton Hawley and Mark Juergensmeyer, *Songs of the Saints of India*.

93   A woman well set free! How free I am: Uma Chakravarti and Kumkum Roy (trans.), *Shura Darapuri*.

94   'Mira was reinstated in the bland': Parita Mukta, 'Mirabai in Rajasthan'.

95   'I'm coloured with the colour of dusk, oh Rana': John Stratton Hawley and Mark Juergensmeyer, *Songs of the Saints of India*.

Chapter 6. Jahanara Begum: In the Shadow of the Peacock Throne

98   'a speck of dust at the feet of the sages': Jahanara Begum, *Mu'nis al-Arvah*, Persian Manuscript Collection, British Museum, London.

99   'Although I was desirous of sparing them': John Keay, *India*.

99   'a cherished but highly dubious claim': Ibid.

100 'In his personality, sustained drinking bouts with Mughal and Turkic companions': Stephen Frederic Dale, 'Steppe Humanism-The Autobiographical Writings of Zahir al-Din Muhammad Babur', 1483-1530, *International Journal of Middle East Studies*, Volume 22, 1990.

100 'ambition for rule and desire for conquest': Ibid.

100 Scalded by the memory of the Chingizid Uzbeks: Gulbadan's *Humayun Nama*, British Museum, London.

101 'Why have you illuminated this Timurid Lamp?': Jahanara, *Risala-i-Sahibiyya*.

101 'whoever is honoured by the greatest happiness of knowing': Ibid.

101 'The pleasures of worldly rule and kingship': Annemarie Schimmel, *The Empire of the Great Mughals: History, Art and Culture*, London: Reaktion Books, 2004.

102 **In Agra, Jahanara was made 'keeper of the imperial seal':** Inayat Khan, *Shah Jahan-nama* (an abridged history of the Mughal Emperor Shah Jahan, compiled by his royal librarian : the nineteenth-century manuscript translation of A.R. Fuller), Oxford: Oxford University Press, 1990.

102 'were guarded by innumerable old crones and beardless eunuchs': Annemarie Schimmel, *The Empire of the Great Mughals*.

102 'The buzz of human voices, the happy playfulness of the children': Meer Hassan Ali, *Observations on the Mussulmans of India*, Austrian National Library, 1832, Digitized: 22 Oct 2015, p. 312.

102 'decorated with murals of flying angels': Annemarie Schimmel, *The Empire of the Great Mughals*.

103 'great elephants whose bellies were full of squibs': Diana Preston and Michael Preston, *A Teardrop on the Cheek of Time: The Story of the Taj Mahal*, London: Doubleday, 2007.

103 'in a sandy soil, which is the cause of excessive heat in summer': Jean-Baptiste Tavernier, *Travels in India*, Valentine Ball (trans.), Cambridge: Cambridge University Press, 2012.

104 'The wonderful rubies, they are cabochons, uncut, unset, but pierced': 'Story of the Timur Ruby', GemSelect, 23 May 2008.

105 'to conduct yourself well with your younger brother': *The Baburnama: Memoirs of Babur, Prince and Emperor*, translated, edited and annotated by Wheeler M. Thackston, Oxford: Oxford University Press, 1996.

105 'I was suffering from a chronic disease': Waldermar Hansen, *The Peacock Throne: The Drama of Mogul India*, New Delhi: Motilal Banarsidass, 1986.

105   'He threw out of his mouth a chewed clove': Ibid.

105   'For those who have love's pain': Samina Quraeshi (ed.), *Sacred Spaces: A Journey with the Sufis of Indus*, Cambridge: Harvard University Press, 2010.

106   'Though I am devoted to the Chishti order': Jahanara, *Risala-i-Sahibiyya*.

107   'When I realized that the truth for this existence requires fana': Ibid.

106   'This faqira, only by the assistance': Ibid.

107   'Mullah Shah has said that about Rabi'a': Ibid.

107   'when a woman becomes a man in the path to God': Sofia Kim, 'A Sufi Approach to Issues of Gender and Reconciliation', *St Francis Magazine*, Vol. V (1), February 2009.

107   In Sufism, a woman could be seen as a symbol for the yearning soul: Ibid.

107   Mullah Shah had wanted his pious and exemplary sister to succeed him: Afshan Bokhari, 'The "Light" of the Timuria: Jahan Ara Begum's Patronage, Piety, and Poetry in 17th-century Mughal India', *Marg*, Vol. 60 (1), September 2008.

107   'She [Jahanara] passed through all the normal visions': Jahanara, *Risala-i-Sahibiyya*.

108   'Even though it is not acceptable for a faqira': Ibid.

108   'In the family of Amir Timur': Lisa Balabanlilar, 'The Lords of the Auspicious Conjunction: Turco-Mongol Imperial identity on the Subcontinent', *Journal of World History*, Vol. 18 (1), 2007, pp. 1-39.

108   Although he called himself a pious Muslim: Ibn Arabshah, *Tamerlane or Timur the Great Amir*, J. H. Sanders (trans.), London: Luzac & Co, 1936.

109   'He had in his army Turks that worshipped idols and men who worshipped fire': *The Baburnama*.

109   After Timur's death, his descendants would no longer require

the **Genghis Khan**: Lisa Balabanlilar, 'The Lords of the Auspicious Conjunction'.

109 **'In this exile my heart has not been gladdened'**: Ibid.

109 **'The current emperor, father of this weak one'**: Jahanara, *Mu'nis Al-Arvah*.

110 **'My beloved came easily into my arms'**: Ibid.

110 **'Because of my deep beliefs and convictions'**: Ibid.

110 **'Among all these ladies, the most esteemed and respected was Begum Sahib'**: Niccolao Manucci, *Storia do Mogor or Mogul India, 1653-1708*, William Irvine (trans.), Calcutta: Editions Indian, 1965.

110 **'This princess accumulated great riches by means of her large allowances'**: François Bernier, *Travels in the Mogul Empire*, Volume 1, Archibald Constable (trans.), Oxford: Oxford University Press, 1891.

110 **'Though the princess is on the apex of sovereignty'**: Taken from Afshan Bokhari, 'Gendered "Landscapes": Jahan Ara Begum's (1614-1681) Patronage, Piety and Self-Representation in 17th C Mughal India.'

111 **Even young, childless women were able to wield considerable influence**: Lisa Balabanlilar, 'The Lords of the Auspicious Conjunction'.

111 **'shown holding *paan*, of which apparently she was inordinately fond'**: Jeremiah Losty, 'The Dara Shikoh Album: A Reinterpretation', British Library Add. Or. 3129, New Trends of Research, Vienna 26-27 May, 2014.

112 **'Her two pearl chokers are interspersed'**: Ibid.

113 **'Jahanara begged that this sacred place might be erected'**: Taken from Afshan Bokhari, 'Gendered "Landscapes"'.

113 **'It [the masjid] was built by her order who is high in dignity'**: Ibid.

114 **'arcades on both sides, only in bricks'**: François Bernier, *Travels*

in the Mogul Empire.

114 **There were coffee houses along the tree-lined streets**: Raza Rumi, *Delhi by Heart*, New Delhi: HarperCollins, 2013.

115 **'The wanderer who enters its courts will be restored in body and soul'**: Lisa Balabanlilar, 'The Lords of the Auspicious Conjunction'.

115 **'not only was the crown to be gained by victory alone'**: François Bernier, *Travels in the Mogul Empire.*

115 **'I wanted to talk to my brother about my deep love and admiration'**: Jahanara, *Risala-i-Sahibiyya.*

116 **'very different from the others, being in character very secretive and serious'**: Niccoloa Manucci, *Storia do Mogor.*

117 **'If his majesty [Shah Jahan] wishes that'**: Aurangzeb, *Adab-i-Alamgiri.*

117 **Despite twenty years of service and loyalty**: Ibid.

117 **You should yourself judge how impolite it is on your part**: Bokhari, 'Gendered "Landscapes"'.

118 **The unbecoming and improper action of this wise and prudent brother**: Ibid.

119 **'To the seed pearls which issued from [Begum Sahib's] eyes'**: Niccoloa Manucci, *Storia do Mogor.*

119 **'The local rajas of Kumaon, Garwhal…'**: Ajay Bahadur Singh, 'Gifts for a Princess', *Sunday Tribune*, 24 October 2010.

Chapter 7. Rani Laxmibai: The Accidental Heroine

125 **They were now 'poor benighted heathens'**: William Dalrymple, 'The East India Company: The Original Corporate Raiders', *The Guardian*, 4 March 2015.

125 **'I cannot conceive it possible for anyone to dispute the policy'**: George Malleson, *History of the Indian Mutiny*, Volume 1, London: Longman, Green, & Co., 1986.

126 **'inherited a tradition of benevolence and dependence upon the**

British': Ibid.

126 **By the turn of the nineteenth century:** Antonia Fraser, *The Warrior Queens*, London: Knopf Doubleday, 2014.

128 **'It was rumoured that every once in a while':** Vishnu Bhatt Godshe Versaikar, *1857: The Real Story Of The Great Uprising*, Mrinal Pande (trans.), New Delhi: HarperCollins, 2015.

128 **God willing, I still hope to recover and regain my health:** Harleen Singh, *The Rani of Jhansi: Gender, History, and Fable in India*, Cambridge: Cambridge University Press, 2014.

129 **'A woman highly respected and esteemed':** Joyce Lebra-Chapman, *The Rani of Jhansi: A Study in Female Heroism in India*, Honolulu: University of Hawaii Press, 1986.

129 **already made an exile of the adopted son of Peshwa Baji Rao II, Nana Sahib:** A future leader of the Uprising, some accounts claim Nana Sahib was a childhood companion of Manikarnika at the court of the deposed Peshwa Baji Rao II. This is considered improbably by R. C. Majumdar in his *An Advanced History of India* as his chronology places Nana Sahib eighteen years older than the future Laxmibai.

129 **'a doubt as to the finality of the decision of the government':** Joyce Lebra-Chapman, *The Rani of Jhansi: A Study in Female Heroism in India*, Honolulu: University of Hawaii Press, 1986.

130 **the custom of adoption was 'prevalent in every part of Hindustan':** Ibid.

130 **'how loyal the Rajas of Jhansi have ever been:** Ibid.

130 **'one of the most impudent perorations ever delivered before a British tribunal':** Venkat Ananth, 'The Story of John Lang', *LiveMint*, 19 November 2014.

131 **She was a woman of about the middle size-rather stout:** Rainer Jerosch, *The Rani of Jhansi, Rebel Against Will: A Biography of the Legendary Indian Freedom Fighter in the Mutiny of 1857-1858*, James A. Turner (trans.), New Delhi: Aakar Books, 2007.

132   'On the contrary. If the Governor General': Ibid.

132   'gross violation and negation of British faith and honour': Joyce
       Lebra-Chapman, *The Rani of Jhansi.*

132   'an impatience at the existence of any native state': William H.
       Sleeman, *A Journey Through the Kingdom of Oudh*, Asian Educational
       Services, 1996.

133   'she was a clever, strong-minded woman, well able to argue':
       Joyce Lebra-Chapman, *The Rani of Jhansi.*

134   'you are well aware that as a fallen party, whose state had been
       lost': Ibid.

135   'assembly of idle, dissipated men in parties independent of each
       other': Ibid.

135   'There were several gangs of robbers in Bundelkhand': Ibid.

135   'All will settle down here...': Ibid.

132   'The people are God's, the country is the Padhshah's': Simmi Jain,
       Encyclopaedia of Indian Women Through the Ages: Ancient India, New
       Delhi: Gyan Publishing House, 2003.

136   'through their faithlessness, cruelty, and violence killed all the
       European': Joyce Lebra-Chapman, *The Rani of Jhansi.*

136   'deal liberally' with her...'agrees with what I have heard': Ibid.

137   'not a paper incriminating the Ranee': Ibid.

137   'symbolically combined the elements of a warrior': Antonia Fraser,
       The Warrior Queens.

138   'bestiality, infanticide and murder': Niall Ferguson, *Empire: The
       Rise and Demise of the British World Order and the Lessons for Global
       Power*, Basic Books, 2004.

138   'their corpses hanging from branches and signposts': Bholanauth
       Chunder, *The Travels of a Hindoo to Various Parts of Bengal and
       Upper India*, London: N. Trubner & Co, 1869.

138   'smeared with the blood of the Englishmen': E. Jaiwant Paul, *The
       Greased Cartridge: The Heroes and Villains of 1857-58*, New Delhi:

Roli Books, 2011.

138 'I beg you will give me your support in the best way you can: Rainer Jerosch, *The Rani of Jhansi.*

139 '[I] have the honour to inform you Hindoo gentry that it is my intention': Extract from a letter by Charles Dickens to Emile de la Rue in October 1857.

139 'I have never witnessed such a spectacular celebration': Vishnu Bhatt Godshe, *1857: The Real Story.*

140 'If they stand at Jhansi,' he wrote dismissively: Joyce Lebra-Chapman, *The Rani of Jhansi.*

140 'The country about Jhansi was as bare as a desert': Ibid.

140 'The chief of the rebel artillery was a first rate artilleryman': Antonia Fraser, *The Warrior Queens.*

141 'The dauntless bravery of the Ranee': Joyce Lebra-Chapman, *The Rani of Jhansi.*

141 'a perfect Amazon in bravery': Ibid.

141 For a few hours...when news of the arrival of the guerilla leader: Tatya Tope, who had a reputation as a remarkable and elusive guerrilla leader, defeated the British garrison at Kanpur.

141 'Sometimes,' wrote Vishnu Bhatt Godshe succinctly: Vishnu Bhatt Godshe, *1857: The Real Story.*

142 'The Rani, dressed in male attire with a sword in her hand': Joyce Lebra-Chapman, *The Rani of Jhansi.*

142 'saw scenes of devastation...[the city] was still smouldering': Vishnu Bhatt Godshe, *1857: The Real Story.*

143 Although it is popularly believed that Laxmibai had her adopted son: Damodar Rao survived the Uprising of 1857-58 and surrendered to the British in 1860. He never won back the seven lakh rupees which the British government held in 'trust' for him though he was granted a pension. He died at the age of fifty-eight, a pauper. His descendants live in Indore to this day and call themselves 'Jhansiwale',

in memory of their illustrious ancestor Laxmibai.

143 **A British officer present at the battle noted that 'after the firing, down went':** Assistant Surgeon John Henry Sylvester, *Recollections of the Campaign in Malwa and Central India*, Bombay: Smith, Taylor & Co, 1860.

144 **'continually on horseback...':** Antonia Fraser, *The Warrior Queens.*

144 **Although the exact manner of her death is not known:** Joyce Lebra-Chapman, *The Rani of Jhansi.*

144 **There was no pretence of resistance any longer:** Antonia Fraser, *The Warrior Queens.*

145 **Killed by a trooper of the 8th Hussars:** Captain C. W. Heneage fought in the Crimean War and was present at the charge of the Light Brigade. He arrived in India in 1857 fought alongside Major General Sir Hugh Rose. Heneage commanded the 8th Hussars who surprised the rebels and caught them unawares. The 8th Hussars were awarded the Victoria Cross for their action at Gwalior. Charles Canning returned to England in 1862, but died a few months later.

146 **'In the Greek myths [the warrior women] Amazons always die':** Adrienne Mayor, *The Amazons: Lives and Legends of Warrior Women across the Ancient World*, Princeton: Princeton University Press, 2014.

146 **'embodiment of sacrifice, silent suffering humility, faith and knowledge':** Harleen Singh, *The Rani of Jhansi: Gender, History, and Fable in India*, Cambridge: Cambridge University Press, 2014.

147 **'on postage stamps, the names of streets and buildings':** Ibid.

147 **Though Lakshmi you are Durga:** Joyce Lebra-Chapman, *The Rani of Jhansi.*

Chapter 8. Hazrat Mahal: The Making of a Rebel Begum

150 **His mother is Begum Hazrat Mahal, one of the innumerable wives:** The exact number of the Nawab's wives is not known but he is believed to have married upward of three hundred women.

150 'This was no token ceremony by a group of rebels': Rosie Llewellyn-Jones, *The Great Uprising in India, 1857-58: Untold Stories, Indian and British*, Woodbridge: Boydell & Brewer, 2007.

150 'We affect to disbelieve his legitimacy': Rudrangshu Mukherjee, *Awadh in Revolt, 1857-1858: A Study of Popular Resistance*, Hyderabad: Orient Blackswan, 2002.

150 'but the zemindars, who ought to be better judges of the facts': Rosie Llewellyn-Jones, *The Great Uprising in India*.

150 'witnessed by the pomp and ceremony': L. E. Huutz Eees, Personal Narrative of the Siege of Lucknow From Its Commencement to its Relief by Sir Colin Campbell.

151 It was one moving mass of men: Landowners, often Rajputs, who collected land revenue from the peasants.

152 Three days later, watching the coronation: The fate of one of the key players of the Uprising, Nana Sahib, was never ascertained. He was either killed by the British, or made his way to Nepal and lived a recluse's life ever after.

152 He was appointed collector of revenue: Rudrangshu Mukherjee, *Awadh in Revolt*.

152 Muhammadi Khanum was born to a slave of African origin: Rosie Llewellyn-Jones has pointed to work done by an Indian scholar, Nusrat Naheed, who found through land revenue records that Hazrat Mahal's father was most likely an African slave. Umber, from ambergris, a complimentary term for dark-skinned people, was a name generally given to African males.

153 In another city or at another time: Taken from Zoya Sameen's 'Prostituting the Tawa'if: Nawabi Patronage and Colonial Regulation of Courtesans in Lucknow, 1847-1899'. Lakhnavi refers to the distinctive Indo-Islamic culture of Awadh centered in Lucknow.

153 'the seraglio singing and dancing girls called Kenchens': Writer and historian Abdul Halim Sharar wrote a first-hand account of life in Lucknow in the 19th century, published in 1913 as *Lucknow:*

153 **'Until a man had association with courtesans':** Also referred to as the East India Company, it was established with a Royal Charter from Elizabeth I on 31 December 1600. The Company was originally chartered as the Governor and Company of Merchants of London trading into the East Indies, with the intention of pursuing trade throughout the East Indies. As it turned out, however, the Company ended up trading primarily with the Indian subcontinent, Balochistan and the North-West Frontier Provinces.

154 **'There is a city more vast than Paris as it seems, and more brilliant':** Rudranghsu Mukherjee, 'A Study of a Dying Culture', *Seminar*, July 2007.

155 **'they had responsibility without power':** For a detailed analysis of Wajid Ali Shah's life, see Rosie Llewellyn-Jones' *Last King in India: Wajid Ali Shah,* London: Hurst & Company, 2014.

155 **'the nawabs one after the other increasingly abandoned the attempt to govern':** Ibid.

155 **Nawab Wajid Ali Shah, who ruled Awadh from 1847:** Rudrangshu Mukherjee, 'A Study of a Dying Culture'.

155 **'By all accounts his temper is capricious and fickle, his days':** Rosie Llewellyn-Jones, *The Last King in India.*

155 **forming cavalry regiments to which he gave poetic names:** Ibid.

155 **'The subjects of his Majesty of Oude are by no means desirous':** Ibid.

156 **'long, luxuriant hair flowing over his shoulders in ringlets':** A. H. Sharar, *Lucknow: The Last Phase of an Oriental Culture,* New Delhi: Oxford University Press, 1989.

156 **'a lover who was irresistible to women':** Ibid.

156 **'using a Shi'a variant of Islamic marriage :** A mu'tah marriage allowed a man to contract a limitless number of alliances with women, usually for a specified amount of time, which automatically ceased when the stipulated time elapsed.

156 **According to Sharar, the King 'fell in love with a large assortment':** Rosie Llewellyn-Jones, *The Last King in India.*

156 **'that not only did their style and clothing acquire':** Ibid.

157 **Nawab Wajid Ali Shah had 'all kinds of wives,' wrote Elihu Jan:** Elihu Jan was a servant girl in the Court of Lucknow from the age of seven. She was for many years hookah attendant to the queen of Awadh, and thus became acquainted with much that happened in the palace. After the Uprising, she was first an ayah in the household of Mr. Johannes, a wealthy merchant of Lucknow, and then joined the household of a Mr W. Knighton, who encouraged her to write down her recollections of life at the court of Wajid Ali Shah. For more, see William Knighton, *The Private Life of an Eastern King Together with Elihu Jan's Story or the Private Life of an Eastern Queen*, London: Forgotten Books, 2015.

157 **It can be gleaned from the paintings in the *Ishqnamah*:** Rudrangshu Mukherjee, *Awadh in Revolt*. The *Ishqnamah* was one of the few manuscripts that survived the sack of Kaiserbagh by the British. It was presented to Sir John Lawrence who in turn presented it to Queen Victoria. It has been at Windsor Castle ever since.

158 **The establishment with which a mother of a son was endowed:** Lisa Balabanlilar, *Imperial Identity in Mughal Empire: Memory and Dynastic Politics in Early Modern Central Asia*, London: I. B. Tauris, 2012.

159 **'She turned out to be very daring':** Rosie Llewellyn-Jones, *The Great Uprising in India.*

159 **They, too, presented themselves at the Begum's court at Kaiserbagh:** From James Anthony Froude's *Fraser's Magazine*.

159 **They 'called Birjis Qadr from the palace,' said an onlooker:** Rudrangshu Mukherjee, *Awadh in Revolt.*

159 **'The English like grass better than bazaars':** William Howard Russell was sent to India by *The Times* newspaper to report on the conflict of 1857-1859.

160 **'the warlike population of Oude':** Rudrangshu Mukherjee, *Awadh in Revolt.*

160 **'The sepoys, during the siege of the Residency':** Ibid.

160 **'... as God has given us back our hereditary dominions':** Ibid.

160 **'an advance to the walls of Lucknow involves the loss of this force':** Ibid.

161 **'it was then proclaimed in the city that the Europeans had abandoned the place':** Ibid.

161 **Great things were promised from the all-powerful Delhi:** Rosie Llewellyn-Jones, *The Great Uprising in India.*

162 **Fear not we shall fight, for if we do not we shall be hanged one by one:** Ibid.

162 **Once British fortunes began turning:** Ibid.

163 **Ahmadullah Shah preached as a fakir in Agra:** Rudrangshu Mukherjee, *Awadh in Revolt.*

164 **'a curious mixture, often remarked upon':** Rudrangshu Mukherjee, *Awadh in Revolt.*

164 **'Sir Colin takes long looks through his glass':** Rudranghsu Mukherjee, 'A Study of a Dying Culture'.

164 **The Kaiserbagh complex, the Moti Mahal Palace complex and the Khurshid Manzil:** Sam Fortescue, 'Rascally Pandies and Feringhi Dogs: a study of British attitudes to Indians during the 1857 uprising', Edinburgh Papers In South Asian Studies, School of History & Classics, University of Edinburgh, 2003.

164 **'It appears from the energetic character of these ranees and begums':** Veena Talwar Oldenburg, 'Lifestyle as Resistance: The Case of the Courtesans of Lucknow', *Feminist Studies*, Vol. 16, 1990.

164 **Suddenly, there came news of a far more deadly foe marching towards them:** Jung Bahadur, a man of great courage and ability, gained control over the government after killing a usurper, Gagan

Singh. Subsequently, he deposed and exiled both the king and the queen after they had attempted to have him assassinated. He was named prime minister for life and given the hereditary title of Rana. Jung Bahadur's diplomatic skill and conciliatory policy helped Nepal remain independent while the rest of the Indian subcontinent came under British rule. During the Uprising, he sent a contingent of Gurkha soldiers to aid the British, thus establishing a tradition of Gurkha military service in the British army. He remained a firm friend of the British for the rest of his life.

165 **The notion that India was won by a few, heroic men:** Jon Wilson, *India Conquered: Britain's Raj and the Chaos of Empire*, London: Simon and Schuster, 2016.

165 **'Penthesilea, the Begum is still undaunted':** Rudrangshu Mukherjee, *Awadh in Revolt.*

165 **'after an obstinate resistance by Pandy':** Ibid.

165 **'The begum alone stands undismayed':** W. H. Russell, *My Diary in India,* London: Routledge, Warne, and Routledge, 1860.

166 **'perhaps he was thinking that people at home would not be satisfied':** Ibid.

166 **[A] force is encamped on all sides of the Fort:** Rudrangshu Mukherjee, *Awadh in Revolt.*

167 **At present all Oudh may be regarded as an enemy's country:** Ibid.

167 **Do not attempt to meet the regular columns of the infidels:** Ibid.

168 **In the Proclamation it is written that the Christian religion is true:** Translation of a Proclamation by Begum Hazrat Mahal, December 1858.

169 **If our people were discontented with our Royal predecessor:** Rudrangshu Mukherjee, *Awadh in Revolt.*

169 **[T]he Begum's followers have been fighting against us and:** National Archives of India, Political Consultation, 19 August 1859, No. 183/4.

170 **The scene of plunder was indescribable:** W. H. Russell, *My Diary in India.*

172 **'Now there is not a shadow of a doubt:** Lisa Balabanlilar, *Imperial Identity in Mughal Empire.*

172 **'not with a line carved, not a stone raised, and left alone in her glory':** Article written for *The Commoner* by a staff reporter, 19 June 1959.

SELECTED BIBLIOGRAPHY

Anjum, Faraz, 'Strangers' Gaze: Mughal Harem and European Travelers of the Seventeenth Century', *Pakistan Vision*, Vol 12. No. 1, 2011.

Auboyer, Jeannine, *Daily Life in Ancient India: From 200 BC to 700 AD*, Simon Watson Taylor (trans.), London: Phoenix Press, 1965.

Balabanlilar, Lisa, *Imperial Identity in Mughal Empire: Memory and Dynastic Politics in Early Modern Central Asia*, London: I. B. Tauris, 2012.

Basham, Arthur Llewellyn, *The Wonder That Was India: A Survey of the Culture of the Indian Sub-Continent Before the Coming of the Muslims*, London: Sidgwick & Jackson, 1967.

Beck, Guy L. (ed.), *Alternative Krishnas: Regional and Vernacular Variations on a Hindu Deity*, Albany: State University of New York Press, 2005.

Bokhari, Afshan, 'Gendered Landscapes: Jahan Ara Begum's (1614-1681) Patronage, Piety and Self Representation in 17th century Mughal India', 2009.

———, *Imperial Women in Mughal India: The Piety and Patronage of Jahanara Begum*, London: I. B. Tauris, 2015.

Bose, Mandakranta (ed.), *Faces of the Feminine in Ancient, Medieval and Modern India*, New Delhi: Oxford University Press, 2000.

Brodbeck, Simon and Black, Brian (eds.), *Gender and Narrative in the Mahabharata*, Oxon: Routledge, 2007.

Brown, C. Mackenzie, *The Triumph of the Goddess: The Canonical Models and Theological Visions of the Devi-Bhagavata Purana*, Albany: State University of New York Press, 1990.

Buck, William, *Mahabharata*, New Delhi: Motilal Banarsidass, 2000.

Cabezon, Jos Ignacio, *Buddhism, Sexuality and Gender*, New York: State University of New York Press, 1992.

Chattopadhyay, B. D., 'Origin of the Rajputs: The Political, Economic and Social Process in Early Medieval India', *The Making of Early*

Medieval India, New Delhi: Oxford University Press, 2012.

Dalrymple, William, *The Last Mughal: The Fall of Delhi, 1857*, London: Bloomsbury Publishing, 2006.

Davids, Mrs Rhys, *Psalms of the Early Buddhists*, Vol. I, London: Psalms of the Sisters, 1909.

Dhar, Debotri, 'Radha's Revenge: Feminist Agency, Postcoloniality, and the Politics of Desire in Anita Nair's Mistress', *Postcolonial Text*, Vol 7, No 4, Rutgers University, 2012.

Debroy, Bibek (trans.), *The Mahabharata: Droupadi's Marriage and Other Selections*, New Delhi: Penguin Books, 2011.

Faruqui, Munis D., *The Princess of the Mughal Empire*, Cambridge: Cambridge University Press, 2012.

Dale, Stephen Frederic, 'The Legacy of the Timurids', *Journal of the Royal Asiatic Society*, 1998.

Futehally, Shama, *In the Dark of the Heart: Songs of Meera*, London: HarperCollins, 1994.

Hansen, Waldemar, *The Peacock Throne: The Drama of Mogul India*, London: Holt, Rinehart and Winston, 1972.

Harris, John, *The Indian Mutiny*, Hertfordshire: Wordsworth Editions, 2001.

Hawley, John Stratton (ed.), 'Morality Beyond Morality in the Lives of Three Hindu Saints', *Saints and Virtues*, Berkeley: University of California, 1987.

Hawley, John Stratton and Juergensmeyer, Mark (trans.), *Songs of the Saints of India*, Oxford: Oxford University Press, 2007.

Hawley, John Stratton and Wulff, Donna Marie (eds.), *Devi: Goddesses of India*, New Delhi: Motilal Banarsidass, 1998.

———, *The Divine Consort: Radha and the Goddesses of India*, New Delhi: Motilal Banarsidass, 1982.

Herbert, Christopher, *War of No Pity: The Indian Mutiny and Victorian Trauma*, New Jersey: Princeton University Press, 2008.

Hiltebeitel, Alf, *Rethinking the Mahabharata: A Reader's Guide to the Education of the Dharma King*, Chicago: University of Chicago Press, 2001.

————, *The Cult of Draupadi, Vols. I & II*, Chicago: University of Chicago Press, 1991.

Horner, I. B., 'Women in Early Buddhist Literature', in *The Wheel*.

Hossain, Purba, 'Of Kings, Courts and Saints: Legitimacy, Authority and the Sufi Shaykh in Mughal Political Culture', http://www.academia.edu/.

Jerosch, Rainer, *The Rani of Jhansi, Rebel Against Will: A Biography of the Legendary Indian Freedom Fighter in the Mutiny of 1857-1858*, New Delhi: Aakar Books, 2007.

Johri, Aarti, 'The Rani of Jhansi: Woman Warrior Queen of India', *Tangents*, Volume 9, Stanford: Stanford University, 2010.

Kapur, Ratna, *Erotic Justice: Law and the New Politics of Postcolonialism*, Hyderabad: Orient Blackswan, 2005.

Karve, Irawati, *Yuganta: The End of an Epoch*, Hyderabad: Orient Longman, 1991.

Keay, John, *India: A History*, New Delhi: HarperCollins, 2000.

Kinsley, David R., *Hindu Goddesses: Visions of the Divine Feminine in the Hindu Religious Tradition*, Berkeley: University of California Press, 1988.

Lal, Ruby, *Domesticity and Power in the Early Mughal World: Cambridge Studies in Islamic Civilization*, Cambridge: Cambridge University Press, 2005.

Lebra-Chapman, Joyce, *The Rani of Jhansi: A Study in Female Heroism in India*, University of Hawaii Press, 1986.

Llewellyn-Jones, Rosie, *The Great Uprising in India, 1857-58: Untold Stories, Indian and British*, Woodbridge: Boydell & Brewer, 2007.

————, *The Last King in India: Wajid Ali Shah (1822-87)*, London: Hurst & Company, 2014.

Mourad, Kenize and Naville, Marie-Louise (trans.), *In the City of Gold and Silver*, Europa Editions, Incorporated, 2014.

Mukherjee, Rudranghsu, *Awadh in Revolt, 1857-1858: A Study of Popular Resistance*, Hyderabad: Orient Blackswan, 2002.

Oldenburg, Veena Talwar, *The Making of Colonial Lucknow, 1856-1877*, Princeton: Princeton University Press, 2014.

Pattanaik, Devdutt, *Jaya: An Illustrated Retelling of the Mahabharata*, New Delhi: Penguin Books, 2010.

———, Myth=Mithya: Decoding Hindu Mythology, New Delhi: Penguin Books, 2006.

Pauwels, Heidi R.M., *The Goddess as Role Model: Sita and Radha in Scripture and on Screen*, Oxford: Oxford University Press, 2008.

Rag, Pankaj, *1857 The Oral Tradition*, New Delhi: Rupa Publications, 2010.

Rajagopalachari, C., *Mahabharata*, Bombay: Bharatiya Vidya Bhavan, 1958.

Roy, Tapti, *Raj of the Rani,* New Delhi: Penguin Books, 2006.

Russell, William Howard, *My Diary in India,* London: Routledge, Warne, and Routledge, 1860.

Sameen, Zoya, 'Prostituting the Tawa'if: Nawabi Patronage and Colonial Regulation of Courtesans in Lucknow, 1847-1899', http://www.academia.edu/.

Sangari, Kumkum and Vaid, Sudesh (eds.), *Recasting Women: Essays in Indian Colonial History*, New Delhi: Kali for Women, 1989.

Schelling, Andrew, *Love and the Turning Seasons: India's Poetry of Spiritual & Erotic Longing*, Berkeley: Counterpoint, 2014.

Schimmel, Annemarie, *The Empire of the Great Mughals: History, Art and Culture,* Waghmar, Burzine K. (ed.), London: Reaktion Books, 2004.

Schubert, Adrian, 'Women Warriors and National Heroes: Agustina de Aragón and Her Indian Sisters', *Journal of World History*, Vol. 23, No. 2, June 2012.

Sen, Indrani, 'Inscribing the Rani of Jhansi in Colonial "Mutiny" Fiction', *1857: Essays from Economic and Political Weekly*, Hyderabad: Orient Longman, 2008.

Shah, Shalini, *The Making of Womanhood: Gender Relations in the Mahābhārata*, New Delhi: Manohar Publishers, 2012.

Sharar, A. H., *Lucknow: The Last Phase of an Oriental Culture,* E. S. Harcourt and Fakhir Hussain (trans. and eds.), New Delhi: Oxford University Press, 2000.

Singh, Harleen, *The Rani of Jhansi: Gender, History, and Fable in India*, Cambridge: Cambridge University Press, 2014.

Spivak, Gayatri Chakravorty, *In Other Worlds: Essays in Cultural Politics*, Oxon: Routledge, 1998.

Sundararanjan, K. R. and Mukerji, Bithika (eds.), *Hindu Spirituality: Postclassical and Modern*, New Delhi: Motilal Banarsidass, 2003.

Sutherland, Sally J., 'Sita and Draupadi: Aggressive Behaviour and Female Role-Models in the Sanskrit Epics', *Journal of the American Oriental Society*, Vol. 109, No. 1, 1989.

Sylvester, John Henry, *Recollections of the Campaign in Malwa and Central India: Under Major General Sir Hugh Rose*, Smith, Taylor, 1860.

Tavernier, Jean-Baptiste, *Travels in India*, Valentine Ball (trans.), Cambridge: Cambridge University Press, 2012.

Thapar, Romila, *The Penguin History of Early India: From the Origins to AD 1300*, New Delhi: Penguin Books, 2003.

Various, *Collected Wheel Publications Volume II: Numbers 16-30*, Kandy: Buddhist Publication Society, 2008.

Varma, Pavan K, *The Book of Krishna*, New Delhi: Penguin Books, 2009.

Verma, Archana, *Performance and Culture: Narrative, Image and Enactment in India*, Newcastle: Cambridge Scholars Publishing, 2011.

Verma, Benu, 'Plenitude of the Singular: Draupadi in Literature and Life', *Society and Culture in South Asia*, Vol. 1, 56-57, January 2015.

Versaikar, Vishnu Bhatt Godshe, *1857: The Real Story of the Great Uprising*, Mrinal Pande (trans.), New Delhi: HarperCollins, 2011.

Warder, Anthony Kennedy, *Indian Buddhism*, New Delhi: Motilal Banarsidass, 1970.

Young, Serinity, *Courtesans and Tantric Consorts: Sexualities in Buddhist Narrative, Iconography, and Ritual*, New York and London: Routledge, 2004.